WINTER FROST

A Chris Matheson Cold Case Mystery

By

Lauren Carr

WINTER FROST

Published by Acorn Book Services

For information, call: 304-995-1295
or e-mail: writerlaurencarr@gmail.com.

Designed by Acorn Book Services

Publication Managed by Acorn Book Services
www.acornbookservices.com
acornbookservices@gmail.com
304-995-1295

Edited by Jennifer Checketts
oceanswave15052@yahoo.com

Cover designed by Acorn Book Services
www.mysterylady.net/acorn-book-services

ISBN: 9781791866235

Published in the United States of America

WINTER FROST

A Chris Matheson Cold Case Mystery

Cast of Characters

The Geezer Squad

Christopher Matheson (Chris): Single father of three girls. After his father's sudden death, he retires from FBI and moves to family farm in Harpers Ferry, West Virginia.

Francine Duncan: Retired investigative journalist from the Associated Press. Divorced children and grandchildren living with her.

Jacqui Guilfoyle: Retired medical examiner from Pennsylvania. Widowed with no children. Lives alone in elegant home on a mountaintop overlooking Shenandoah Valley.

Bruce Harris: Retired attorney general from Virginia. Owns a winery in Purcellville, Virginia. His wife is an architect with her own firm in Leesburg. Has son in college.

Ray Nolan: Established cyberwarfare task force after 9/11. Retired from Homeland Security after he took a bullet in the back from a home-grown terrorist. Lives with his daughter and her family.

Elliott Prescott: Founding member of the Geezer Squad. He could tell you what he did before he retired, but then he'd have to kill you.

Characters in Order of Appearance

Blair Matheson: Chris Matheson's wife. Communications officer with the state department. Left her family behind to take a position in Switzerland.

Anne Kidman: CIA operative. Helps Blair in Nice, France.

Emma (7 yrs old), Nikki (10 yrs old) and Katelyn (13 yrs old): Chris Matheson's daughters.

Helen Clarke: Lieutenant in charge of homicide with the West Virginia State Police. Chris's girlfriend. Divorced with one daughter, Sierra, sixteen years old.

Ripley Vaccaro: FBI agent. Chris's former partner. Her daughter Madison is close friends with Katelyn, who is spending the weekend at the Vaccaro home.

Leonardo Mancini: International hitman hired to assassinate Blair.

Murphy Thornton: FBI agent? Or he could be CIA? Whoever he works for, he's determined to get to the bottom of this case.

Stephens: Murder victim. Investigator working for Senator Graham Keaton. Killed before he can meet with Anonymous.

Hayes: Murphy's partner in this assignment.

Daniel Cross: Director of intelligence directorate at the CIA. Presidential nominee to lead the CIA.

Amabassdor John Brown: Ambasssador in Lithuania. Killed in car bombing.

Samuel Goldman: Chief of Station in Lithuania. Dies in car bombing with the ambassador.

Sterling: Eccentric German shepherd. Retired law enforcement canine. Instagram model for Katelyn's pet designer clothing line.

Thor: Female fifteen-pound tan and white rabbit with long floppy ears. Usually seen wearing frilly pink clothes.

Doris Matheson: Chris's widowed mother and grandmother to his daughters. Her late husband was Kirk Matheson, captain of the West Virginia State Police's local troop. Director of the Bolivar-Harpers Ferry Public Library.

Sadie (Doberman) and Mocha (golden Labrador): Sadie was a retired law enforcement canine. Mocha was a retired search and rescue dog. Doris Matheson's entourage.

Nigel: Super Smart Artificial Intelligence.

Tristan Farraday: Murphy's brother-in-law. Nigel's guardian.

Les Monroe: Blair's supervisor in Switzerland. Official reports say he committed suicide by shooting himself in the back three times.

Ivy Dunleavy: Blair's close friend. Married to high-profile attorney, who claims to be a fixer for billionaires.

Stu Dunleavy: Ivy's husband. High-profile attorney and fixer for billionaires.

CO: Lady in the back of the limousine. Murphy's commanding officer.

Bernie: CO's chauffeur and bodyguard.

Senator Graham Keaton: Judiciary Committee Chairman. He tasks Stephens to investigate letter from Anonymous.

Senator Kimberly Douglas: Minority leader for judiciary committee. Determined to get Daniel Cross confirmed no matter what.

Oliver Hansen: Senator Graham's assistant.

Leban Slade: Billionaire. Major government contractor. Rumored to own several politicians and lawmakers.

Jessica Faraday: Murphy's wife. Tristan's sister.

Spencer: Murphy and Jessica's blue merle sheltie. She's got a crush on Sterling.

Sierra: Helen's sixteen-year-old daughter. Chris gives her horseback riding lessons.

Paul Burnett: Officially, his company works in security. Unofficially, he's a cleanup man for the rich and powerful. He knows where all the bodies are buried--literally.

Sheriff Grant Bassett: Jefferson County Sheriff.

No man is above the law and no man is below it: nor do we ask any man's permission when we ask him to obey it.

Theodore Roosevelt

Prologue

Nice, France - Three Years Ago

Blair Matheson parted the curtains only enough to peer across the street to the shore of the French Mediterranean. The beach was packed with people, natives and tourists alike, celebrating Bastille Day. Many were staking claim to the best spots to enjoy the fireworks.

If it hadn't been for the fear consuming her, Blair would have enjoyed the party atmosphere.

"Get away from the window." Anne Kidman pulled her back and closed the curtains. She emptied the contents of a thick padded envelope onto the hotel room desk. She held out her hand to Blair. "Give me your passport."

Blair hesitated.

"They're going to be looking for you. They will be tracking everything that has your name attached to it. Passport, credit cards, cell phones, driver's license. The only way you can stay alive is to make Blair Matheson disappear."

Blair picked up her handbag from where she had dropped it onto the bed.

"I've got a new passport and a whole new identity for you."

Blair wrapped her fingers around her cell phone and closed her eyes. She remembered the sweet sound of her daughters' voices the day before. Their father was taking them to the mall in Washington to see the fireworks. Emma was so excited. Nikki had won a ribbon in barrel racing the weekend before at a horse show. Katelyn was mad because her father had said no to hair extensions. She prayed that one day she would hear their voices again.

"I'm willing to bet they're already tapping your family's phone back in the States—just waiting for you to call them to trace the call to your location." Anne grabbed the cell phone from her hand.

"So if I call my husband—"

"If you care about them, stay as far away as you can. These people wouldn't hesitate to abduct your daughters to get to you."

"But—"

"They've killed three people," Anne said. "Human lives mean nothing to them."

"I need my phone." Blair snatched it back. "We won't be able to bring them down without it."

The meaning behind her words struck home. A slow grin crossed Anne's lips. "Very well. Power it off." She gave her another phone. "Use this one when you need to make a call." She tapped the passport in Blair's hand. "Until we can expose these people, this will be your new identity. Our people will notify your family that you're away on assignment, so they won't worry. You'll get in touch with them when you can."

Blair examined the new passport and other identification. "This looks real."

"Because it is." Anne stuffed her original documentation into her bag. "Don't worry. All of this is only temporary. Once we expose and shut them down, then you can go back to being Blair Matheson." She handed her the room service menu. "In the meantime, take advantage of the mini bar and get some rest. You'll be able to see the fireworks from the balcony." She headed for the door.

"Where are you going?" Blair asked.

"To meet a colleague of mine down on the beach," Anne said. "He's my Australian counterpart. These slimebuckets have been working so hard to hide their dirty laundry from us that they haven't noticed what our allies have been able to uncover. He's going to fill me in with what they've got." She thrust a semi-automatic handgun into her hand. "Remember, trust no one."

Blair shuddered while recalling the close call from the night before. Never had she seen a man senselessly gunned down. A man trying to do the right thing—because she convinced him that it was their moral obligation.

That man was now dead.

If she had not run into Anne Kidman, a CIA operative on assignment in the area, Blair had no doubt that she would not have made it through the night. Twenty hours later, she was in another country regretting her decision to leave her family behind for what was supposed to have been a golden career opportunity.

She reached into her bra to extract the micro memory card on which she had copied the report and files and everything necessary to expose their sinister enterprise. How ironic that something so tiny contained the power to destroy so many lives.

"You should take this." She held it out to Anne.

The agent folded Blair's fingers over the disk. "You keep that. I'm more likely to get killed before you. If that happens, you need to get that to the Director of Central Intelligence in Washington. No one else. Her eyes only."

"But if—"

"You're going to make it, Blair." Anne flashed her a wide grin. "You were savvy enough to escape an assassination attempt by yourself yesterday." She hurried to the door. "Within twenty-four hours, you'll hand that report off to the Director of Central Intelligence. You'll be a hero. Then, you can start counting down the hours to when you can hug your family again." She put her hand on the door handle. "Guard that disc with your life. Your country is counting on you."

Blair dared to peer through the curtains to the street down below. The crowd was even thicker than it had been earlier. In spite of that, she could pick out Anne, with her blond hair and slender figure, jogging across the busy street. She rushed into the arms of a tall, hunky man with a dark tan.

Blair wondered if the kiss was part of their cover of being a romantic couple or if they were indeed more.

They wrapped their arms around each other's waists as they made their way down the street.

The thunder of the motor vehicles clogging the street grew louder—as did the crowd. The joyous sounds turned into a cry of terror that reached up to the wide-open blue sky above as a white truck jumped the curb and plowed through the partiers.

Blair's chest tightened while she helplessly watched the truck ram into Anne and the Australian agent and roll over them before moving on to more victims.

Dropping back from the window, Blair covered her mouth to hold back the high-pitched scream that exploded from inside her. She covered her ears. The wailing of the innocent people being murdered floated across the balcony and wrapped around her like a python squeezing every ounce of courage from her body.

Thanking Chris for the hundreds of times he had dragged her out to the shooting range to teach her how to shoot, Blair wrapped her hand around the grip of the gun and clutched it to her chest.

She could hear Anne's voice in her ear as if she were alive and there in the room with her. *Trust no one.*

Chapter One

Pentagon City Fashion Center – Present Day

"Dad, that's so not cool." With a frown, Katelyn Matheson shook her head.

It was bad enough that Chris Matheson had decided to turn a drop off in the city into a date night with Helen Clarke. What made it worse was that he had also insisted on hanging around to wait for Madison, her best friend from her old school and, heaven forbid! speak to her mother.

As if that wasn't bad enough, Katelyn discovered that it was a real possibility that they would eat dinner in the very same shopping center where Madison might see them.

"He's pulling your leg, Katelyn," Helen said when it looked as if the thirteen-year-old's head might explode from the trauma. "We're going to have dinner at an Italian bistro within walking distance of the Kennedy Center. Your father promised that it would be romantic." She grinned at how his gray eyes twinkled.

"You two can be so sickening sometimes." Katelyn fought the grin fighting to cross her lips at how Helen gazed up at her father.

Her dark eyes and hair gave Helen an exotic appearance. Also, she had a cool teenaged daughter, Sierra, who offered Katelyn fashion tips. Even though they lived in their own home, Helen and Sierra were almost like an extended family.

Chris checked the time on his phone. "We may have to find a romantic hot dog vendor if Ripley and Madison don't hurry up. The curtain goes up on the play in two hours."

Katelyn wrapped her arms around him. "Hug me now so we don't have to when Madison gets here."

"Katelyn!" A teenaged squeal erupted from the direction of the exit to the parking garage.

Katelyn pushed him away and the two girls embraced. In high pitched voices, they talked over each other while firing off compliments on hairstyles, clothes, and make-up. While the adults couldn't follow the simultaneous conversations, the teenagers could.

When they stopped to take a breath, Madison turned to her mother, a slender woman dressed in a dark trench coat over slacks. She wore her service weapon holstered on her hip next to her federal agent's shield. "I want to show Katelyn the shoes I'm saving up for. I suppose you want to talk business with her dad." She rolled her eyes.

Katelyn did likewise.

Her mother took out her cell phone and swiped her thumb across the screen. "We'll meet up here in one hour."

Katelyn shot Chris a warning glance when he moved in to hug her one last time. Adopting an exaggerated business-like expression, he shook her hand. "May the force be with you, Ms. Matheson."

Katelyn rolled her eyes again while Madison giggled. The two girls took off at a run toward the escalators leading to the upper levels of the fashion center. Quickly, they disappeared into the crowd of shoppers.

Chris introduced Helen to Ripley Vaccaro. "Helen is in charge of homicide with the West Virginia state police in the eastern panhandle."

"I hope Chris isn't using you to stick his nose into your cases?" Ripley said while shaking her hand.

With a toss of her head, Helen laughed. "Sometimes I wonder if he does." She shot him a grin. "Doesn't really matter. He's just so gosh darn cute when he gets nosy."

"I told him when he retired that he wouldn't be able to hang up his badge for good." With a wicked grin, Ripley admired his athletic build.

Taking care of his mother's horse farm kept Chris fit. He looked several years younger than his forty-seven years. A clue to his true age was his salt and pepper hair that reached the top of his collar. His gray double-breasted suit matched his eyes. The long red wool scarf added a dapper tone to his appearance for the evening out.

"I thought you'd turn into a hayseed when you told me that you were moving back to the farm. I must admit, you're looking good, Matheson."

"I clean up good."

"You cleanup so well that one would think you were civilized. I know the truth." Ripley turned serious. "How are things going?" She told Helen, "I was with Chris when he got the news about Blair."

With a shrug of his shoulders, Chris wrapped his arm around Helen and pulled her close. "Things are definitely looking up. Retirement is treating me good. You?"

"Since my divorce?" Ripley laughed. "I've devoted myself to my career, which was what basically led to my marriage breaking up. Occasionally, I've been loaned out to other agencies in the community to work on special investigations. That keeps things exciting."

"Well, don't let things get too exciting while you have my daughter."

"Of course not. I'm assuming you two are going to take advantage of his freedom this weekend, or did you fail to unload the other two?"

"We managed to unload all three of them," Helen said. "My daughter Sierra is spending the night at a slumber party."

"And both Emma and Nikki scored sleepovers tonight," Chris said.

"What about your mother?" Ripley asked.

"Which is why Helen invited me to her place for our own private party," Chris said with a grin.

"Leaving that helpless elderly woman all alone?" Ripley said.

"My mother is as helpless as a rattlesnake," Chris said. "She's invited a friend of hers over. The truth is, I got kicked out. I'm not allowed to go home until noon Sunday."

"Gives me hope that when I'm sixty-five I'll have a friend to invite over for sleepovers," Ripley said.

Before leaving for the Kennedy Center, Helen opted to visit the ladies' restroom. Since it was still the height of Friday night rush hour, Ripley decided to go as well to play it safe before getting into traffic.

Curious about the chit-chat the new acquaintances would share once he was out of earshot, Chris sat on a bench next to the escalators leading down to the Pentagon City metro stop. He imagined the secrets that they might be sharing in the mirror while washing their hands or checking their make-up.

Whatever. I just hope they don't decide to share too much. He checked the time on his cell phone. Time was getting short. He looked in the direction of the hallway in time to see a woman with blond hair pass him and stop at the newsstand next to him.

A Washington Redskins ball cap covered the top of her head. She wore a thick plaid jacket. A slender woman, her long blond hair was pulled back into a ponytail that spilled down her back.

He instantly recognized her face and her build, which was significantly leaner than the last time he had seen her. The tilt of her head. The way her hips swayed as she moved past him was unmistakable.

Upon reaching the newsstand, she picked up a newspaper and slipped it under her arm.

He was so certain it was her, that he almost dropped his cell phone to the floor. His knees felt numb when he stood.

Like prey sensing movement nearby, she jumped and spun around.

His eyes locked with her blue orbs. For an instant, the world seemed to stand still in silence.

No, it can't be. Blair? Blair.

Chris's mind raced to re-examine everything from the past—Blair's decision to leave him and their family to take advantage of the opportunity with the state department in Switzerland. Her departure. Their separation. His decision to not take their daughters to Switzerland that summer because Blair had said she would be too busy working on a project. She claimed she couldn't take any time off. Then, the worst day of his life—the day his supervisor had called him into his office to tell him about Blair's death on Bastille Day in Nice, France, while apparently traveling with an intelligence officer from Australia.

She had claimed she was too busy to take time off to visit with her family. Obviously, she had enough time to travel to France to meet another man.

Three years after receiving the cremated remains of his wife and the mother of his children, how could she be standing before him?

Should he feel happy to see that she was alive, saddened by her betrayal, or angry that she had put his daughters through such grief? Every one of those emotions swirled inside him like a cyclone.

"Blair." He took a step toward her only to have her spin around and run down the escalator.

He gave chase. He forgot about Helen and Ripley. All he could think about was that Blair was alive.

Why did they tell me that she was dead?

He weaved through people on the escalator—fighting to keep Blair in his sight.

Was it a mistake or a lie? Why didn't she tell us that she was alive? Where has she been all this time?

At the bottom of the escalator leading to the ticket area, he stopped. One needed a metro ticket to get through the turnstiles leading to the tracks below.

Peering into each dark corner, Chris turned around in a circle. A steady stream of commuters squirming around him to reach their individual destinations made it a difficult task.

Among the constant activity, one lone unmoving figure leaning against the ticket machines stood out. Clad in worn jeans and a hoodie pulled up over his head, he pretended to focus on his cell phone. While he held his cell phone in his hand, he was watching everyone.

Chris spotted him as being some part of law enforcement. Either a plainclothes security with the metro or a member of a federal agency keeping watch for a possible terrorist attack. Whichever it was didn't matter to Chris. All he cared about was which direction Blair had gone.

"Excuse me, did you see a blond woman in a plaid jacket, very pretty, go by?"

The man in the hoodie froze at his direct approach. He looked Chris up and down.

Up close, Chris saw that under the laid back, casual, even street-wise attire, he was an attractive, athletic man with striking blue eyes and dimples. *Yep, he's undercover. Vice maybe?*

"Sorry, bud, I've seen lots of pretty blond women go by." He glanced around Chris to continue his surveillance.

Dismissing him to return to whatever case he was working on, Chris rushed to the first ticket machine, stuck a five-dollar bill in, purchased a ticket, and hurried down the escalator. He spotted her on the train platform.

She was not alone.

A man wearing a red baseball cap was walking close to her—ushering her along the ramp toward the tunnel where the first car of the next train would stop.

Chris was so intent on catching her that he bumped into a man in a black coat at the bottom of the escalator—knocking him into the handrail. The man's black hat fell to the ground. Apologizing, Chris picked up the hat and stuffed it into his hands.

When the man responded in an Asian language, Chris turned to him to catch a fiery glare. While he didn't know exactly what the Asian man had said, Chris had no doubt but that it was a curse.

"I'm very sorry," he said before continuing his pursuit.

As he drew closer to Blair, he saw that her companion had his arm around her waist.

Blair stumbled—managing to pull away just a second—long enough for Chris to spot the muzzle of a gun aimed at her side.

With a glance over his shoulder, the man pulled her back to him. Under the ball cap, Chris saw the man's enormous Roman nose and weak chin.

Chris's heart sank to the pit of his stomach. He broke out in a cold sweat. He had seen that face before. It was hard to forget. Chris had seen it on more than one most-wanted poster issued by the FBI—one of their ten most wanted.

Leonardo Mancini was as evil as he was ugly. International assassin. Willing to kill anyone for the right amount of money.

The lights along the train ramp blinked to signal that the next train was arriving.

Passengers rushed to the ramp—jostling for easy access onto the train. Abruptly, there was a human barricade erected between Chris and Blair.

Minutes later, they would be gone. Blair would be really dead this time. Judging by the fear in her eyes, she knew it. Mancini would be on an airplane flying off to his next hit before they found her body.

Chris dropped to one knee and extracted the weapon he wore in an ankle holster. With the small handgun down at his side, he gently pushed his way through the passengers to get as close to Blair and Mancini as he could.

The train swooshed out of the tunnel toward them.

As he searched around for a possible solution, he noticed the man in the blue hoodie sliding down the escalator on the railing with his cell phone to his ear. Even if he was law enforcement, there was no way or time to let him know what was going on.

There was no time. Still, several people were crammed between him and Blair and Mancini.

Can't let them get on the train.

The train screeched to a halt.

He saw Blair's eyes filled with fright as she searched for help.

I have to save her.

With his eyes on Mancini's ugly face, Chris thrust the hand holding the gun up into the air and fired a shot into the ceiling. "Everybody down!"

Instantly, people hit the floor or dashed away—clearing a path for him to fire the next shot into Leonardo's head before he had time to realize what was happening.

Leonardo fell dead.

Once again, time seemed to freeze.

Released from Leonardo's hold on her, Blair stared at Chris with wide eyes.

Still not believing that she was standing before him, Chris stared back.

Almost with a swoosh, time resumed.

Blair was caught up into the stampede of commuters rushing onto the train.

Mancini's weapon was kicked around until it landed on the tracks by the hysterical mob trying to escape the shootout.

"Chris!" Blair reached out toward him.

His eyes never leaving her face, Chris tried to move toward her, but was pushed back by the mob who carried her onto the train.

"Chris," she shouted, "I wish we had more time!"

"What?" Chris dodged around people in a vain effort to reach the doors.

"I wish we had more time!" she yelled over the chimes signaling the shutting of the doors.

The doors closed, and the train pulled away with her on it.

She was gone.

Chapter Two

By the time federal law enforcement descended on the metro station, Chris was lying spread eagle on the subway ramp with his hands on top of his head. His gun rested next to him.

Feet away from him, Leonardo Mancini was bleeding out from the bullet in his brain.

As Chris was being escorted up the escalator in handcuffs, an officer pointed at the tracks. "I see a second weapon. Looks like he's telling the truth about the guy having a gun."

The cold November air hit Chris in the face when he was taken outside and placed in the back of an unmarked police cruiser. He recognized the make and model as the type assigned to the FBI. As the officers who had escorted him out of the metro station walked away, Chris noticed a man wearing a heavy jacket with "FBI" emblazoned on the back, take a position outside the rear door—presumably to keep the shooter from escaping—as if Chris would get far with his hands cuffed behind his back.

"Chris!" he heard Helen call his name.

Abruptly, the agent opened the door to allow Helen to reach in to hug him. Chris saw Ripley directly behind her.

"What happened?" Helen said with tears in her eyes. "We came out of the ladies' room and you were gone. Then we heard there was a shooting."

"They said you killed a man." Ripley eyed the agent guarding him.

If she was silently asking him to leave them alone, it wasn't happening. The agent remained with his arms folded across his chest. As it was, it was against protocol for him to allow anyone to talk to the suspect until the investigators questioned him. Chris assumed he was using the opportunity to gather information for the prosecution's case.

"It was Leonardo Mancini," Chris said.

Ripley's mouth dropped open. Her eyes grew wide. "Are you sure?" she asked in a hushed tone.

"Positive," Chris said.

"Who is Leonardo Mancini?" Helen asked.

"International assassin," Ripley said. "We know of at least six hits he's made—some of them contracted by foreign governments. Russia. China. Iran. North Korea. If he was on the scene, I guarantee something big was going down."

"He had Blair," Chris said. "He had a gun stuck in her ribs."

"Blair?" Helen withdrew her hand from where she had clutched his arm.

"As in the- wife- you- buried- three- years- ago- Blair?" Ripley's eyebrows furrowed.

"I know it sounds crazy," Chris said, "but I saw her."

"Maybe she just looked like Blair," Helen said.

"No." Chris shook his head. "She was two feet from me. Looked me right in the eyes. She recognized me, and I recognized her."

"Did she say—"

"She ran. She was scared out of her wits. By the time I caught up to her, Mancini had her by the arm and was forcing her to the train. I didn't have time to do anything except shoot him."

"If it was Blair, where is she now?" Ripley cast multiple glances at the agent.

"She escaped on the train."

"Why wouldn't she stick around to tell the police what happened?" Helen asked. "She had to have seen that it was you who saved her. Tell the police what was going on—whatever it is—and they could protect her. Where has she been for the last three years?"

Chris was shaking his head. "I'm asking the same questions. You two have to believe me. It was Blair. Leonardo Mancini was going to kill her."

"Which means she was mixed up in something horribly big, which is probably why she's been in hiding all this time," Ripley said.

"Like law enforcement is going to believe that I fired a weapon on a crowded subway platform to kill an international assassin zeroing in on my wife who has been dead for the last three years," Chris said. "If a shooting suspect told me that story, I'd think he was crazy."

"Don't worry," Ripley said. "We're going to do whatever it takes to get to the bottom of this. I'm going to get the girls and take them home."

"You're not going to tell Kate—"

"No," Helen said. "We'll try to keep this news from the girls until we get it sorted out. I'll go get your truck and drive back home and tell Doris what's happened. I'm sure between her and the Geezer Squad, we'll get this figured out."

"Geezer Squad?" Ripley asked with a laugh.

"Chris's book club," Helen said.

"I'm sorry about our date," Chris said.

"It's not your fault." Helen gave him a kiss on the cheek. "I'm just glad this assassin didn't take you out."

She rose to her feet. Chris's eyes locked with hers. He tried to will her to believe him until their connection was broken by the rear door of the cruiser slamming shut. He tried to reconnect with her through the side window while Ripley spoke to the agent standing guard. After a moment, Ripley ushered Helen toward the parking garage and they disappeared into the darkness.

Recalling the fear he had seen in Blair's eyes, Chris wondered what he had missed during their few conversations while she had been working at the embassy in Switzerland. Much of the work she had done was classified. That meant even if something terrifying was going on, she couldn't have told him.

But still—what could she have been involved in that necessitated her, a communications officer, to fake her death? *How could she do that? Allow our children to think their mother was dead? Or was it all a lie? Was she really a CIA operative and not a communications officer? Had she been lying to me all those years? If so, what else had she lied about?*

Chris was so absorbed in the questions swimming around in his mind that he jumped when the agent standing guard yanked open the door. "Okay, Mr. Matheson, time to go for a ride." He grasped his arm to help him out of the rear of the cruiser.

The flash of a cell phone camera from a few feet away blinded him. A split second before the spots exploded in front of his eyes, Chris noticed an Asian man wearing a black hat. *Wasn't he the guy I ran into on the escalator? The one who cussed me out? Must be happy to see karma in action.*

The agent stepped between Chris and the group of bystanders and journalists gathered behind the police barricades.

"We're not going in this car?" Chris asked.

"Too many windows." The agent's fingers dug into Chris's bicep as he hurried him through the law enforcement investigators questioning witnesses, gathering cell phones, and collecting evidence to put their case together. "I'm sure you'd feel much more secure riding in the back of a nice comfortable SUV."

They approached a full-zied vehicle with tinted rear windows. Another agent, clad in a dark jacket and wearing a ball cap with "FBI" across the top, stood next to the open door. Before placing Chris inside, the agent searched his pockets.

"I've already been searched. You've got my weapon."

"That's not what I'm looking for." The agent extracted Chris's cell phone from the inside breast pocket of his suit. "Have you got a passcode on this?"

"It's my fingerprint."

"Which one?" He stepped behind Chris and took turns pressing his fingertips to the phone's screen until he unlocked it.

"What are you doing with my phone? I do have rights."

"Just playing it safe and turning off your phone. Don't want any possible accomplices ambushing us on the way." He tucked the phone into the inside breast pocket of his jacket. "Watch your head." He helped Chris into the passenger seat and fastened the seat belt for him.

After the agent had closed the door, Chris heard what sounded like a tussle outside. When he looked, he saw a man in a black coat towering over the agent.

"Where are you taking him?" His voice was threatening, which struck Chris as odd.

If they're both on the same side, what's with the attitude? The man was so tall that Chris had to cock his head to see his face. The dim light prevented him from getting a clear look. His expression was intense.

The agent who had placed Chris in the SUV showed no intimidation. "Central processing for booking," he answered in a brisk tone while making his way around the vehicle.

The other agent climbed into the driver's seat and started the engine.

"We need to question him first." The tall man flashed a badge. "It's a matter of national security. I need to take him with me."

Chris held his breath. *National security? What did Blair get mixed up in?*

To his surprise, the agent chuckled. "Unless my CO tells me personally to hand him over, you're taking him over my dead body."

The tall man's legs were so long that he was able to reach him with one step. He grabbed his arm. "Now you listen to me."

The federal agent looked from the giant hand squeezing his bicep up into the man's face—contorted with menace. He then looked around at the mob of law enforcement and spectators around them—each one seemingly armed with a camera of some type. He was almost a head shorter, but he stared him down.

Chris could barely hear his response.

"Do you really want to go there? Here? Now? If you want to keep that hand, you'll let go of my arm."

The giant released his grip and stepped back. His eyes narrowed as he watched the agent continue around the vehicle to the passenger side and yank open the door. Like a statue, he remained fixed in the spot while the agent climbed into the rear seat.

"Let's get out of here, Hayes."

"That was close," the driver said.

"Too close."

The SUV eased its way through the horde of investigators and media milling around and turned out onto the street. As they drove past the journalists and cameras, Chris saw them darting and peering around for a glimpse of the shooter who had killed a man "innocently" waiting for a train at the metro. He could only imagine what type of monster they were painting him as being.

"Have your people released my name to the media?" Chris asked.

"I haven't," the agent sitting next to him said. "Vaccaro will talk to our CO. She'll pull in some favors to put a lid on it. Can't guarantee anything, but we'll do what we can to keep your children from finding out about this."

So he had been listening when I was talking to Ripley and Helen.

It struck Chris that the agent's low smooth voice sounded familiar.

"Are we clear, Hayes?"

The driver chuckled in response to his partner's question. "It'll be touchy. As soon as Mr. CIA talks to the lead investigator, they're gonna realize he's no longer in police custody." He turned onto the exit for Interstate 395 heading toward Springfield—away from FBI headquarters.

Not in police custody? Chris turned to the man sitting next to him.

The dimples in his cheeks had deepened. He winked at him with one of those blue eyes. "Mr. CIA isn't going to talk to anyone because he wasn't CIA. Real CIA operatives don't flash their identification like that."

Chris hadn't recognized him since he had changed out of the dark blue hoodie and into an FBI jacket and federal agent's badge.

What a newbie, I've become. I was seeing the uniform, not the man. How many times did I do that when I worked undercover? I'd slip on a uniform and walk in and out of a place and no one would see my face because they'd be focused on my clothes.

As charming as his smile was, Chris wanted to punch him. It was bad enough that his date with Helen had been ruined by him being forced to kill an international assassin threatening to kill the wife he had thought was dead. Now he had escaped from police custody without knowing it.

"Who are you?" Chris asked in a shaking voice. "Are you working for the people trying to kill Blair?" He struggled in vain to get out of the handcuffs.

"No, but I'm willing to bet Lurch back there was. Why else was he so anxious to get his hands on you? What's going on, Matheson?"

"I have no idea. I was minding my own business—going out on a date with my girlfriend and ran into my wife who's supposed to be dead."

"Maybe your dead wife didn't approve of you dating," the driver said.

The men in the back seat looked at the back of his head.

"Just saying," Hayes said.

"We had nothing to do with the attempt on your wife," the man next to Chris said. "I didn't even know her name until you told Vaccaro."

"You know Ripley. Are you FBI?"

"No, I work for someone else."

"Who?"

"I can't say."

"You're CIA." Chris laughed. "How do you know Ripley?"

"She and I have worked together on some cases that involved multiple federal agencies."

"Can you at least tell me your name?"

"You can call me Murphy. You're welcome, by the way."

"You're welcome?"

"Helping you escape."

"I didn't ask you guys to help me to escape," Chris said. "I didn't want to escape. I'd much rather be in jail now than on the run from the police—which never ends well. I've been on the other side of police dragnets. It never ends well for the guy on the run. If anything, you got me into deeper trouble than I was already in. So don't hold your breath for any thanks for getting me killed!"

"Do you want us to take you back?" Murphy asked in an ultra-polite tone. "Maybe we can catch up with Lurch."

"As big as he is, he should be easy to find," the driver said.

"You're damn lucky I'm cuffed." Chris narrowed his eyes. "You were there. Why didn't you stop Mancini?"

"I didn't see him until it was too late," Murphy said. "I was on the lookout for the investigator who was supposed to connect with an anonymous source. I believe Anonymous was your wife."

"But you screwed up and a hitman connected with her instead!"

"I did not screw up!" Murphy's blue eyes were flashing.

"Then why didn't you and your guy protect Blair? If I hadn't run into her and saw Mancini, she'd be really dead now! Where was your man?"

"Dead! That's where he was!"

Silence dropped over the inside of the SUV.

Chris stared at Murphy, whose face was filled with anguish.

"Stephens was a good man." Murphy swallowed. "I got the call *seconds* before you shot Mancini."

Chris tore his eyes away and sat back in his seat. He saw that the SUV was racing along the interstate out of the city.

Next to him, Murphy was rubbing his eyes. "I guess it had to be your wife …" his voice trailed off.

"Blair. Her name was Blair."

"Blair set up the meeting with Stephens. She was going to give him crucial evidence for him to get to the right people. She told him to wear a red ballcap and to carry a copy of the *Washington Times*. She had warned him that people had died because of this. I guess most of us thought she was being overly dramatic."

"Crucial evidence of what?"

"I have no idea," Murphy said. "All I was supposed to do was back them up during their meeting. Keep them safe."

"A lot of good that did."

"I had no idea what Blair looked like. Neither did Stephens. None of us even knew her name. *She* was going to find him. The last I spoke to him was ninety minutes before the meeting—that was right after your wife called and told him to wear the ballcap and carry the newspaper. Mancini must have killed him right after I spoke to him and taken his place."

"Which meant Mancini or whoever hired him knew about the meeting," Chris said. "How did Blair get Stephens's name and contact information?"

"I have no idea. She claimed to have crucial information that was important to national security. Whatever she told him must have convinced him that she was legit because he set up a meeting."

"You don't know much, do you?"

"I may not know much," Murphy said, "but I do know this. Someone had one of my teammates killed to keep whatever it is your wife knows from seeing the light of day. That tells me that she must know something important enough to kill to keep hidden. That means these people will stop at nothing—including abducting you or your children as leverage to bring her out into the open."

"That must be why she has been in hiding all these years."

"What was she doing in Europe when she was reported dead?"

"She was a communications officer at the embassy in Switzerland. What could she possibly have stumbled onto?"

"I was hoping you could tell me," Murphy said. "Why do you think we snatched you?"

"Because you're crazy."

Chapter Three

On the interstate, they traveled past Springfield, Virginia, before exiting the freeway and turning onto a side road that traveled deep into a dark rural area far away from the city. They rode in silence for much of the drive.

Murphy would often check messages on his phone and, occasionally, glance in Chris's direction.

Chris spent most of the drive remembering the conversation in which Blair had announced that she had been offered a promotion.

Was it really only five years ago?

Chris had arrived at their upper middle-class home tucked in the corner of a small lake after eighteen hours of working on a triple homicide. "I can't go to Switzerland."

Sensing a fight, Blair glanced upstairs to where their daughters were doing their homework. "Yes, you can."

"The FBI doesn't have field offices overseas." After returning a greeting from Winston, his German shepherd, Chris went into the kitchen to get a cold beer. He suspected he would be wanting something stronger.

She followed him. "You can take a leave of absence."

He stopped with the refrigerator door open. Slowly, he turned to her. "And live on what?"

"We have some savings. The state department will pay a cost of living allowance and we could get government housing. We'll rent this house out." The displeasure on his face made her rattle on. "The experience will be good for the girls."

"I'm not spending the next two years being a house husband." He grabbed the bottle of beer from the fridge and slammed the door shut.

"So I should flush my goals down the drain, huh? Because you're too important to stay home with the kids while I pursue my dreams."

Chris wrested the cap off the bottle. "I'm not important."

"Says the great Chris Matheson," she said with a roll of her eyes.

"What are you talking about?"

"Oh, you are so good at pretending you don't know."

"Don't know what?"

"Your reputation at the bureau," she said. "At the Christmas party, one agent after another, telling me how proud I had to be being married to one of the bureau's top investigators. Your undercover work brought down the Yurievich crime family and empire." Her tone grew mocking. "The department's most valuable agent. We can always count on Chris Matheson."

"They talk like that to all of the agents' spouses," he said. "If I was such a hot shot, Nikki would have her own horse instead of leasing one."

"This isn't about the money."

"Obviously it's not because you have to be aware that our income would be cut in half if I took a leave of absence. That would push my retirement out another two years."

Blair clenched her fists. "I want people at the state department to talk to you like that about me!"

Chris stared at her. Slowly, he shook his head. "Like what?"

"Someone everyone can always count on." Her eyes filled with tears. "At work, no one even knows who I am."

"You're valuable to us," he said. "That's where it counts."

"That's not enough. Not for me."

Chris felt a pang in his heart. It hurt like a bullet to the chest. "You've already made up your mind."

Her voice was soft. "You've done it, Chris. You don't know what it's like to be just another face in the crowd."

"Nothing I've done has been because I wanted people to notice me," he said. "I get up every morning and strap on my shield for the victims. The Yurievich family made a fortune conning vulnerable women to come to the States to force into prostitution. Families lost their homes because they were experts in identity theft. They were all lucky compared to the dozens of people who the Yuriviechs had killed on their way to the top. That's what I work for. Whether anyone knows my name or thinks I'm a hero means nothing to me."

"Easy for you to say," she said miserably.

"I can say that because I've seen the misery that surrounds those who put their own pride first."

"Is that what you think this is about?"

"Where have you been during this conversation?" he asked. "You want me to take a leave of absence. You want to uproot our daughters. What about Winston?" He pointed at his ten-year-old German shepherd who had been watching the conversation from his dog bed. "Do you think he's going to survive being shipped halfway around the world?"

"I was thinking we could ask some friends—"

"It'll be a cold day in hell before I abandon Winston to follow you just because your ego needs some stroking."

"Is that what you think this is all about?" Blair scoffed. "The little woman feels unappreciated."

Chris dropped into a chair next to the dog bed and stroked the top of Winston's head. Eying her, he took a long drink from the beer bottle. "More like a grown adult who's let her priorities get out of whack."

The cruiser hit a pothole hard. Chris woke up when he knocked his head against the SUV's passenger window.

"We're here," the driver of the SUV announced as he made a sharp turn onto a dirt road.

The road curved around a steep hill before leveling off at a single-story house that was so dark, it looked abandoned.

"How long are you going to keep me here?" Chris studied the rural area. He couldn't see lights from any other houses or buildings.

"Until we can locate Blair and figure out what she has that is important enough to kill for," Murphy said while checking a message on his phone. "Stephens's house was bugged. That's how they knew the details about the meeting."

"How did they know to bug *his* house?" Chris said. "What's to keep them from tracking your phone or this vehicle."

Murphy shook his head in response to his concern. "My phone has the most up-to-date encryption invented, and this SUV was swept for trackers before we picked you up. You're safe."

Hayes opened the rear door and unbuckled Chris's seat-belt. He removed the handcuffs after helping him out of the vehicle.

Murphy took a duffel bag from the back compartment. "We don't have much but it should be enough to keep you semi-comfortable until we can find a more secure place." He handed it to Chris. "It's my go-to bag. There's a change of clothes in there. I imagine that suit isn't too comfortable."

Together, they walked up the darkened sidewalk to the front door. Hayes went around to the back of the house to make sure the area was secure. In contrast to the rundown condition of the house, the door was secured with an up-to-date keycode lock worthy of a secure government facility. Murphy unlocked it with a code, opened the door, and ushered Chris into the foyer.

"Who's taking care of my family while you have me in protective custody?" Chris followed Murphy down a hallway to a master bedroom. They both turned on the lights and checked inside each room along the way.

"Vaccaro will keep your oldest daughter with her and arrange for a couple of people from our team to check on your family," Murphy said while closing the curtains. "I think you and I are about the same size. Those clothes should fit you. If not, I'll pick up some that will."

Chris tossed the duffel bag onto the bed and opened it. A cell phone and wallet rested on top of the clothes. It contained a toiletry bag and other items, including two handguns, four boxes of bullets, and an assault knife.

"That's a burner phone," Murphy said. "The number at the top of the contact list will take you to my boss. She can pass any messages on to me."

"I hope you don't take this the wrong way, but I don't feel very safe." Chris shrugged out of the the suitcoat and tossed it onto the bed. He picked up the assault knife and removed it from the sheath.

"I assume you know how to use a knife," Murphy said. "You did serve with the army rangers before going with the FBI."

Chris tucked the knife back into its sheath. "That's what you've been reading on your phone on the way here. You were running a background check."

"I'd be stupid to let you have those guns without doing one."

Chris checked the wallet, which was filled with a fistful of hundred-dollar bills. "How big of a file does the CIA have on me?"

"Big enough," Murphy said while checking out the window. "Your mother's file was more entertaining."

"The CIA has a file on my *mother*?"

"Don't ask."

Chris examined the clothes. The waist on the jeans was almost the same as his. The shirt was one size bigger. Murphy was more muscular than he was. The work boots were only one size too big. Even so, they were more comfortable than his dress shoes, which were starting to hurt his feet.

While Chris changed his clothes, Murphy sat on the foot of the bed and checked the news on the television to see what was being reported about the shooting in Pentagon City. He had tuned in at the start of a news segment about the recent presidential nomination for director of the Central Intelligence Agency.

As with everything else pertaining to the government, the nomination of Daniel Cross was fraught with controversy. Not quite forty years old, Dan had risen quickly through the ranks of the Central Intelligence Agency as an intelligence analyst to the director of the agency's intelligence directorate. Per usual, half of Washington, political and media, thought the President's nomination had all of the makings of brilliance. The other half saw it as a democratic crisis.

The news segment cut to a sound bite from Kimberly Douglas, the senator from the nominee's home state of California. The middle-aged woman's face was contorted with self-righteousness. "Senator Keaton needs to shut up and do what is right." She jabbed her finger in the air. "He and the members of the majority on this committee have no choice but to confirm Daniel Cross as director of the CIA. Daniel Cross proved that he is more than qualified ten years ago when he led the investigation into the car bombing that killed our ambassador to Lithuania and chief of station. He uncovered the evidence leading to the terrorist group responsible, which led to their arrests and justice for Ambassador John Brown and Samuel Goldman."

In the next sound clip, Senator Graham Keaton chuckled when a journalist recounted Senator Douglas's demand. "Once everyone gets a chance to fully examine all of the facts and talk to Mr. Cross, we will make our decision."

"Did Cross really uncover the group that planted the bomb killing Ambassador Brown?" Chris asked.

"All by his lonesome." Murphy regarded Chris out of the corner of his eye before saying. "From what I hear from those in the know, Cross is not shy about taking credit where credit *isn't* due. Those who do the real work in the intelligence community keep their mouths shut."

"So I've heard. I suspect the fact that Cross has claimed to play such a big role is a clue that he didn't."

"Exactly."

"What happened to the terrorist group that killed the ambassador and chief of station?" Chris asked.

"They were Islamic extremists bent on driving a wedge between the US and the Lithuanian president to create unrest. They kill our ambassador. We get mad at their president. He looks bad. In the next election, he loses, and their terrorist candidate wins. Next thing you know, Lithuania is under Sharia law."

"I imagine things didn't go well for the terrorist group after their plot was uncovered," Chris said. "When I worked undercover with the FBI, I had a couple of run-ins with crime organizations from that part of the world. They can be quite ruthless."

"Lithuania has a very low crime rate," Murphy said. "It's low for a reason. Let's just say that terrorist group is no more.

It was extracted from the country—all the way down to the roots."

As the news finally moved on to local coverage, a journalist stood in front of the metro sign for the Pentagon City station. The bright multi-colored lights flashed off to the side. "Details are still unclear," the reporter said, "but according to unidentified sources within the FBI, tonight's shooting victim was a dangerous felon known to authorities. He had been the target of an extensive investigation and was in the process of abducting a potential victim. An undercover federal agent was on the scene and had no choice but to use lethal force to save the woman."

The anchor responded, "So the shooter in this case was a hero ..."

A broad smile filling his face, displaying his dimples in his cheeks, Murphy turned around to Chris, whose mouth was hanging open. "You're welcome."

"We still have to find Blair," Chris reminded him as he finished getting dressed. He folded up the suit and stuffed it into the bottom of the duffel bag. "I assume you have contacts inside the state department." He slipped the wallet with the cash into his pants pocket.

"Some. But from the very little that I have been able to find out since we left the city, no one in the state department had any idea that Blair was alive, let alone what she could possibly have that would be worth killing over."

Chris strapped one of the guns to his ankle. "Then it must not be detrimental to the government, but rather to particular individuals. Whoever it is, we know one thing about this individual."

"What's that?"

"They have deep pockets. Leonardo Mancini doesn't come cheap and he's not someone you find on Angie's List." Chris examined the second handgun. "I just can't believe Blair would be savvy enough to fake her death so well that she could fool even the state department."

"We'll sort this out. Get some sleep. I'm leaving Hayes here to make sure you're safe." Murphy left the room and went into the foyer.

Tucking the second gun into his waistband, Chris followed him. "Are you leaving me here without a vehicle?"

"There's a car in the garage."

Chris clutched his stomach. "I've just remembered I haven't eaten since lunch. Have you got any food here?" He looked in the direction of the kitchen.

"Only frozen dinners and canned goods. This is a safe house. Sometimes no one is here for months. I'll bring you something to eat when I come back in the morning. Things will be clearer then. Get some sleep."

After Murphy left, Chris went into the country style kitchen to see what type of frozen dinners it had. The fridge turned out to be better equipped than Murphy had led him to believe. The freezer not only had well over a dozen frozen dinners of every type, but there was also a twelve pack of beer in the fridge. He helped himself to a can, opened it, and took a long drink before turning back to the freezer to decide what appealed to him.

When he saw that one was a frozen lasagna, he uttered a groan. If things had gone as planned, he would have enjoyed a plate of fresh linguini and red clam sauce with a robust bottle of Chianti. Not only that, but he would have been eating it with Helen, instead of alone in a dreary house in the middle of nowhere.

While examining the various dinners, he listened for Hayes to step through the front door. He had decided on a homestyle fettucine alfredo before realizing that quite some time had passed.

How long would it take Hayes to say all was clear and Murphy to leave?

Clutching the cold can of beer in his hand, Chris closed the freezer door and listened for the sound of the SUV driving away.

"Hey, Hayes, are we all clear to go?" Careful not to trip over a rock or stumble into a hole in the dark, Murphy jogged across the front yard to the SUV. The big guy was sitting motionless on a wooden bench between two trees next to a pond at the edge of the yard.

As Murphy drew closer, he noticed that Hayes made no move to acknowledge him. He seemed to be looking down at something in his lap.

Probably texting his girlfriend.

Upon reaching the bench, Murphy called his name again.

Still no response.

He squinted through the dark at where Hayes's head hung forward. That was when he noticed the blood seeping from his neck down the front of his jacket.

Jumping back, Murphy turned around to shout a warning to Chris as Hayes's killer jumped out of the shadows to throw the garrote over his head and around his throat.

Silence.

Chris strained to listen for Hayes to come inside and for Murphy to leave but heard nothing.

Abruptly, he noticed a red dot cross the front of the beer can making a path for his chest.

Chris plunged to the floor as the series of bullets shattered the kitchen window and ripped through the wall across the room. Beer foam spilled from the can as it rolled across the floor—drenching Chris's fresh clothes.

Chris grabbed the gun tucked in his waistband and reached up to slap the light switch off. The movement was all they needed to fire another barrage of bullets through the patio door.

Crouching behind the counter, he heard the hushed chatter of two men speaking to each other in a foreign language.

Where the hell are Murphy and Hayes?

Chapter Four

Murphy grabbed the garrote and yank it down from where it was pressed against his trachea. At the same time, he dropped back against his assailant and turned to deliver a fist to his groin. As his bald-headed attacker crumbled, Murphy kneed him in the face.

The killer dropped to one knee. The light from inside the house caught on the blade of a knife as he yanked it out from under his pantleg. The tip caught the front of Murphy's jacket before he could fall back.

Murphy saw the thrill of blood lust cross his opponent's face. His gaze fell on the image of a yellow claw reaching around from the back of his neck.

"I thought you Phantoms were supposed to be tough," the assassin said with a thick foreign accent while backing Murphy toward the pond filled with filthy dark water.

"I don't know what you're talking about."

Inches from his fingertips, Murphy's gun rested in its holster on his hip. Watching the knife threatening to slice him open, he thought of the adage, "Never bring a knife to a gun fight." The truth of the matter was that in the time it would take the average person to unholster his gun, a trained killer could plunge a knife through his heart—faster if he knew how to throw it. Murphy had no doubt that this guy could complete his mission in less time that it took him to reach for his gun.

"You probably don't know anything about the Yellow Dragons either." Murphy's opponent chuckled. "You notice my badge of honor. I saw the fear in your eyes. It'd almost be worth it to let you live to tell—too bad our orders are to leave no one to tell anything."

"Anything about what?" Murphy asked.

"Don't know." He raised the knife above his head. "Don't care. Only here to kill." With a gut-wrenching scream, he lunged forward. Murphy did the same. He grabbed the arm welding the knife, spun around, and brought his arm down on his attacker's elbow, breaking his arm.

Still, the paid killer refused to go down. He threw his other arm around Murphy and the two men fell into the pond together in a fight to the death.

Chris dared to look around the corner of the counter and through the shattered glass doors into the thick dark woods. He could sense rather than see them moving in. The front door was several feet away and in plain view of his assailants. He could make a run for it or remain trapped in the kitchen.

He didn't know who or what was waiting on the other side of the door. Obviously not Hayes and Murphy. If so, they would have come to help—unless they were in on it.

Take me out into the middle of nowhere, kill me, and get rid of my body where no one would find it.

He remembered Murphy mentioning a car in the garage. He swallowed when he realized he didn't have the keys. He'd have to hot wire it. His heart sank when he saw that the door to the garage was on the other side of the dining room—directly across the line of fire.

Go for the garage. I haven't been in the garage. I don't know what's in there. What if the car doesn't have any gas in it? I'll deal with that when I come to it. Right now, I've got to get out of this kill box called a kitchen.

Sucking in deep breaths, he extracted his second weapon from the ankle holster. Clutching both guns to his chest, he inched his way to the edge of the counter. As he peered around the corner, two men dressed in black charged through the broken patio doors with their assault rifles blazing. Bullets and drywalls flew everywhere.

At the same time, the living room wall exploded—sending glass and debris flying. The SUV didn't stop. It plowed through the living room into the dining room—picking up every piece of furniture along the way.

The explosion was enough to divert the two men's attention from Chris. They turned their automatic weapons on the vehicle. Bullets bounced off the hood and windshield as it sped straight toward them.

With a battle cry, one of the gunmen ran toward the vehicle, which gathered speed. It rammed the top of the dining table into him and crushed him against the wall like a bug. With nowhere else to go, Murphy threw open the driver's door and fired on the pinned man with two guns.

As soon as Murphy jumped out, the second gunman jumped up from where he had lunged out of the way and took aim on him.

Chris pulled the triggers on both guns in his hands. The assassin dropped onto the hood of the vehicle.

Ready to fire again, Murphy spun around in time to see the dead man slide off the hood.

"You're welcome!" Chris yelled.

"This safe house has been compromised!" Murphy reached across the front compartment to shove open the passenger door.

"Ya think?" Chris looked down at the man he had shot to make sure he was dead. When he saw his face, he realized he had seen him earlier. The metro. He was the irritated man Chris had collided with at the bottom of the escalator.

"Chris, get in the car! We need to get out of here! There may be more!"

Chris climbed into the passenger seat. "Where's Hayes?"

"Dead." Murphy put the SUV into reverse and backed out of the house. "By the time I realized things were going sideways, I got jumped. I found Hayes's body by the pond. He'd been garroted."

Chris noticed that Murphy was soaking wet. "You look like you went for a swim in the pond. You smell like it, too."

Upon reaching the driveway, Murphy spun the vehicle around and sped down the road. As they passed a street light, Chris saw that he was covered in more blood than pond water. His hands and knuckles were bruised. "Are you okay?"

Murphy wiped one hand after the other on his pants. "It's not my blood. How did they know where we were? Somehow they tracked us." He pressed a button on the steering wheel and the display screen on the console lit up. "Nigel!"

A deep, intimidating voice, not unlike Darth Vader erupted from the speakers. "Lieutenant Thornton, you sound agitated. Do you need backup?"

"The safe house has been compromised," Murphy said. "We got ambushed by hostiles. Hayes is dead."

Chris punched a button on the dashboard to disconnect the cell phone. "Did this Nigel guy you're talking to know where you were taking me?"

"Yes—"

"How do you know he isn't the one who leaked our location to whoever is behind this?"

The display lit up again. "Because my circuits are not capable of deception. Dishonesty is a human condition that has yet to be digitally created."

While Chris digested that information, Murphy said, "Still, Nigel, someone was able to track us. The only ones who knew we were going to that safehouse was me, Hayes, CO, and you. We need to find out how they got that information. Code EMCON."

"EMCON?" There was a note of indignation in Nigel's tone. "Lieutenant Thornton, you do realize that no one will be able to access the information in my databases during the scrubbing process if you call for Code EMCON. Are you sure you want to do this?"

"Two of my teammates are dead," Murphy said. "EMCON. Repeat EMCON."

"Very well, Lieutenant."

The dashboard screen went dark.

"Lieutenant?" Chris asked. "Is this Nigel CIA?"

Murphy glanced at him. "You never heard of Nigel. Understand?"

"Nigel who?"

Murphy was startled when he heard a familiar click. He looked to see that Chris was aiming one of his weapons at him.

"We did things your way and two members of your team are dead. Now, we're going to do things my way. *Pull* over."

"Are you serious? For all we know, some members of that death squad survived, and we're being followed."

"I'd rather deal with them here, out in the middle of nowhere, than lead them back to my family. Pull over. *Now!*"

Murphy lifted his foot from the accelerator and steered the vehicle off to the side of the road. He turned it off. Aware of Chris's law enforcement experience, he followed protocol and placed both hands flat on the dashboard.

Keeping one eye on the road behind them, Chris held out his hand. "Give me your cell phone."

"You can't have my cell phone."

"I recognized one of those men from the metro."

"That's probably where they followed us from," Murphy said. "The people behind this are very highly trained."

"Do you know who they are?"

"I don't want to say until I get more information."

"In the meantime, hand it over." Chris wiggled his fingers.

Grudgingly, Murphy took the cell phone from the case on his belt and handed it to him. Chris tossed it to the floor and crushed it with his heel. While Murphy cursed, he held out his hand again. "Now hand me the other one."

"What?"

"The real one. The one you keep in the inside breast pocket of your jacket. The one you just gave me was a decoy."

"You can't have it. If you smash it, we'll have no way to contact my home base. We'll be without a lifeline. I've turn it off."

"They can track us even if the phone is off," Chris said.

"I'll take out the battery." Murphy took the phone from his pocket.

Chris watched as he dismantled the phone and handed the battery and chip to him.

"I'm not going to let you disarm me," Murphy said. "There is no way I'm letting you leave me out here with no way to defend myself. You're going to have to kill me."

"I'm not going to disarm you." Chris pocketed the battery and chip.

Murphy let out a sigh of relief. "You trust me?"

"If you wanted me dead, you would have left me there for the death squad to finish off. What I don't trust is our technology. Whoever is behind this could be using any of it to track us."

"We're going to have to go completely off the grid," Murphy said. "Since you're holding the gun—you got any ideas?"

"First, we ditch this vehicle."

Chapter Five

Harpers Ferry, West Virginia

Normally, federal agents would seek and confiscate a shooter's vehicle for evidence. If that had happened, Helen would have been trapped in the city with no way to return home and help Chris. Without asking any questions, Ripley Vaccaro pretended not to notice when Helen ran into the parking garage where Chris had parked his truck and never returned.

After crossing the West Virginia state line, Helen's first stop was the Matheson family farm, which rested along the Shenandoah River.

At sixty-five, Doris Matheson exuded a timeless beauty. Wrinkles added character, not age. Her thick blond hair framed her lovely face. The widow of a West Virginia State Police captain, she volunteered much of her time to her church's mission work and animal welfare causes. As if having a full-time job as director at the library and volunteer work was not enough, Doris also taught yoga and swam three miles, four times a week.

Helen hoped she had as much energy and looked half as good when she was Doris's age.

After crossing the river, Helen turned right and traveled downstream until she came to the driveway. She punched the security code into the keypad to open the gate and drove up the hill to the farmhouse.

The time on the dashboard of Chris's truck read nine-seventeen. She could see that the main floor was illuminated, but the upper floors were dark. Aware that Doris had planned for a special weekend with Elliott Prescott, her first relationship since her husband's death, Helen felt a tinge of guilt.

She hated to interrupt Doris's date, but she'd want to know that Chris was in trouble—and that Blair was still alive.

Elliott would want to know as well. He was the leader of Chris's book club.

After parking Chris's truck in his spot next to the barn, Helen hurried across the barnyard to climb the steps to the wrap-around porch.

Recognizing the roar of his master's truck engine, Sterling, Chris's German shepherd met Helen in the mudroom. The hundred-pound dog repeatedly leapt, all four feet off the floor, to peep through the door. With an equal mixture of care to not hit the dog and eagerness to get out of the cold, she forced her way inside.

Sterling was not alone. Helen was also greeted by a Doberman pinscher, yellow lab, and a fifteen-pound French lop eared rabbit clad in a maroon lace wrap named Thor. The retired law enforcement K9, Sadie, and Mocha, a search and rescue dog, were Doris's constant companions. Chris called them her entourage.

"Christopher, did you do something to make Helen mad?" Doris called out from the living room.

"Chris is in trouble." Without bothering to take off her coat, Helen led the pack of critters through the country kitchen and into the living room where she found Doris perched on a stool in front of an easel.

Donning a painter's smock over her jeans and turtleneck sweater, she was putting the first coat of paint on a canvas. "What kind of trouble did Christopher get himself into now?"

Helen fought the tears returning to her eyes. "He killed a man in the subway."

Doris's gray eyes, the same hue as Chris's, tore away from the bananas she was painting. "Whatever for?"

"He was an international assassin. Chris said his name was Leonardo Mancini."

"Leonardo Mancini! He's one big gun," Elliott's voice came from the other side of the easel.

"That's not all—" Helen rounded the canvas and uttered a shriek when she found the elderly man posing on the sofa with an array of fruit positioned around his naked body. A clump of strategically placed bananas concealed his private parts. After getting over the initial shock, she had to admit that Elliott was in fairly good shape for his age. Still, she would have preferred not to have that information.

"Was this assassin working at the time that Christopher took him out or was he off duty?" Doris asked.

"Chris said he had a gun shoved into Blair's ribs."

"Blair who, dear?"

Tears spilled from Helen's eyes. "Blair."

"Blair?"

"His wife. Blair. Blair Matheson. Katelyn, Nikki, and Emma's mother."

Doris's face was blank. Blinking her eyes, she shook her head. "Blair's dead, Helen."

"Obviously not. Chris saw her."

It was not easy to shock Doris Matheson. The news that her daughter-in-law was alive did just that. She stared at Helen with her mouth hanging open. Sitting on either side of her, Mocha and Sadie gazed up at their master as if to ask what they could do to help.

Spotting an unguarded carrot, Thor climbed up onto the sofa at Elliott's bare feet. Sterling sniffed at the food arrangement in search of something he might like, with his snout zeroing in on what Elliott was hiding behind the bananas. Elliott tried to swat him away without moving. "Are you sure it was Chris's wife? Did Mancini shoot her before Chris took him out?"

"Chris said she jumped on the train and left. He never talked to her."

"Obviously, Christopher was mistaken." With a renewed sense of resolve, Doris turned back to the canvas. "Elliott, stop playing with Sterling and hold still."

"Doris, Chris doesn't make those types of mistakes."

"Helen's right about that, Doris." Elliott tried not to giggle at Thor chewing on the carrots near his toes. "Chris is not one to jump to conclusions." He grabbed the head of romaine lettuce that Sterling claimed as his.

"The state department told us that Blair was dead. She had taken leave to go to France with some intelligence agent from Australia. She'd told Christopher that she was too busy working to spend time with him and the girls. That's why he cancelled a trip to join her in Europe for the summer."

"Did Chris or you see Blair's body?" Helen asked.

"She was cremated there, and her ashes sent back," Doris said. "Elliott, why did you give the lettuce to Sterling? Now we're going to have to start over." She put the brush and palette on an end table.

Sensing that his modeling session was over, Elliott put on his bathrobe and joined them at the easel.

"That's strange that the state department cremated Blair's body overseas before her family had the opportunity to see her," Helen said. "Did Chris request that?"

"No," Doris said. "As a matter of fact, he was furious when he found out. He and Blair had agreed to be cremated, but he wanted to say goodbye before it was done. The state department claimed it was a clerical error. They mixed Blair up with someone else."

Elliott and Helen exchanged puzzled expressions.

"How did they identify Blair's body?" Elliott asked.

Doris put the tip of her paintbrush to her lips. Her gray eyes narrowed.

Seated on either side of her, Mocha and Sadie's eyes mirrored the question in their master's. Across the room, Sterling climbed up onto the sofa to take Elliott's spot. Thor was in bunny heaven chowing down on the lettuce and carrots.

After a long thought-filled silence, Doris removed the paintbrush from her lips and looked at Helen and Elliott. "To tell you the truth, I'm not really sure."

While most people were turning in for the night, things were just getting started in the club district of Georgetown. It was difficult for Murphy to not run over college students dancing in the streets to the music blasting from nightclubs or rushing across to meet friends.

Chris directed him to turn down a side street leading to the warehouse district.

The bright lights and party atmosphere quickly turned dark and ominous.

"Park over there." Chris gestured to a vacant area next to what looked like a deserted building.

Murphy took the gun out of his ankle holster and tucked it into his jacket pocket as he climbed out of the car.

Chris opened the glove compartment. "Take out anything that we need to keep."

Murphy opened the rear compartment and stuffed items into Hayes's go-to bag. "Are we just leaving it here?"

"It will be gone in an hour." Chris slammed the door shut and waited for Murphy to join him.

"Gone where?"

"Stripped."

Murphy stopped. "This is government property."

"Do you want to take it back to the motor pool? Possibly tip off whoever's trying to kill us? Based on what I've seen tonight, they don't care who or how many people they kill." When Murphy didn't answer, Chris turned around and trotted through a clump of bushes and a break in the wire fence to a jogging path.

Murphy slung the duffel bag over his shoulder and jogged to catch up. Chris led him along the river and back toward the street where they climbed through a break in another wire fence. They eventually came to the back of a brightly lit warehouse. The roar of power equipment filled the air.

"Moby Valente. Got out a few months ago." Chris chuckled in the dark. "I knew he'd be back in business in no time." He turned to Murphy. "We're on my turf now. You keep your mouth shut and let me do the talking." He crossed the back lot before stopping. "On second thought—when I saw you at the metro—do you remember that expression you had on your face?"

Murphy's eyes narrowed. "What expression?"

"That's the one. Go with that."

Chris yanked open the back door to the warehouse and strode inside. Keeping his hand on the gun in his pocket, Murphy followed him.

The warehouse was filled with one luxury car after another, each one being worked on, either stripped or rebuilt, by a crew of sweaty, tattooed, mostly menacing workers. Many stopped to regard the visitors with suspicion. More than one reached into tool boxes. Based on their expressions, Murphy surmised they were not reaching for screw drivers.

Seemingly undisturbed by the attention, Chris threw open his arms like the long-lost son returning home and rushed toward a glassed-in office in the corner of the warehouse. "Moby! It's good to see you back in business again! When did you get out?"

An enormous man spun around in his office chair and wheeled into the doorway.

Murphy quickly saw why Chris called him "Moby." The man had to be close to four-hundred pounds. The whale of a man was white, not albino, but pale as in he never went into the sun.

A broad grin crossed Moby's face when he saw Chris. "Georgie! My dear bud!" He remained in his seat while Chris bent over to give him a hug. "When did you get out?"

"I got out four months ago," Chris said.

"Four months? Why didn't you come look me up?" Moby told the other men milling about. "Georgie here was the best carjacker I ever had. He could boost a vehicle—any type, even the latest ones with all those anti-theft systems—in thirty seconds flat."

"If he's so good, how'd he end up in jail?" asked one of the younger men, who looked barely beyond his teenaged years.

"Trusted the wrong guy." Chris cocked his head at him. "You kind of remind me of him."

The young man slinked away under Chris's glare.

"So why didn't you look me up when you got out?" Moby asked.

"I didn't know you were out until just this evening," Chris said. "My bud, Wilder over there and I got ourselves in a jam. We need some wheels." He gestured over his shoulder to Murphy, who was eying the slick operation.

"If you're such a legend at boosting cars, why not steal one?" the kid asked with a note of disdain.

"Because we're in enough trouble without getting pulled over for driving a stolen vehicle."

"What kind of trouble you in, Georgie?" Moby asked.

"Wilder and I were cell mates in the joint." Chris tapped Murphy on the arm.

In keeping with his role, Murphy shot him a glare.

"We saved each other's butts more than once," Chris said. "We swore to keep our noses clean when we got out, and we were doing just that until tonight. We went to a club up in Georgetown and wouldn't you know it—Wilder's ex-wife's boyfriend was there. He recognized Wilder and next thing you know—"

"I take it that blood on his clothes is the ex's boyfriend's," Moby said. "Is he alive?"

Chris tossed his head in the direction of the river. "He's swimming with the fishes."

"Oh, man!"

"It wasn't Wilder's fault," Chris said. "We just need a set of wheels that isn't too hot to get out of the area before they find his body."

"I don't know, Georgie." Looking Murphy over, Moby rubbed his fat flabby face. He gestured for Chris to move in closer. "How well do you know this Wilder guy?"

"We were cell mates for close to a year."

Moby lowered his voice. "He looks like a cop to me."

Chris broke into a laugh so loud that it startled those around him—including Murphy. Chris's chortle had an insane sound to it. "Hey, Wilder, Moby thinks you're a cop!"

Murphy joined in the laughter.

Chris wiped tears of laughter from his eyes and turned to Moby with a serious expression. The shift in his demeanor was disconcerting. "You owe me, Moby. It was one of your crew who ratted me out." He picked up a crowbar and smashed a work bench with it. "Seven years! I spent seven years in a locked room because of you—"

"I didn't rat you out!" Moby said. "I lost a million-dollar business operation because that snitch turned on me, too!"

"I lost my woman!" Welding the crow bar over his shoulder as if he were ready to strike down Moby, Chris sneered. "She was gone faster than I could boost a bike." He pointed the end of the crowbar at Moby. "You hired that rat. He worked for you. That makes you responsible for me getting locked up."

Moby's jowls quivered. "Okay. Okay. Okay. I'll take care of ya. I promise. Right now, all we got here is hot. My crew is still working on them." He called over to one of his men. "Hey, Alex, is that Beemer ready to roll?"

"Just put the tags on it." Alex responded by tossing a set of keys to Moby, who caught them simply by raising his hand.

"How hot is it?" Chris asked.

"It's closer to lukewarm than hot." Moby tossed the keys to him.

"We'll turn it in to the police as soon as this case is over," Chris whispered to Murphy as they raced the red BMW out of the warehouse and onto the street.

Murphy waited until they were crossing the Potomac River, before saying, "You used to steal cars for that guy?"

"You'd be shocked and surprised at the skills I've developed during my career of working undercover." Chris flashed a wicked grin. "If I was on the other side of the law, I'd be a very successful criminal. That's what made me such a good agent."

"I take it the rat that got Moby arrested wasn't some kid on his crew, but you."

Chris shot a wicked grin across the front of the BMW. "If my cover wasn't still good, we would be dead right now instead of driving away in this nice luxury vehicle."

Murphy set his leather seat back into a reclining position. "Nice *hot* luxury vehicle."

"Not hot. Lukewarm."

Chapter Six

By the time they got on the road, both men were hungry. Luckily, Chris had thought to pocket the wallet from the duffel bag. They couldn't risk using debit or credit cards for fear of being tracked. It was at the fast food drive-thru that Chris discovered his partner on the run was a vegetarian.

"Do you know how much damage simple carbs do to your heart over time?" Murphy said between spoonfuls of a fruit yogurt parfait. "Simple carbs turns into cholesterol which turns into sticky gunk that clogs your arteries and gives you a stroke when you reach middle age."

"Isn't there sugar in those apple slices?" Chris asked around a bite of a double cheeseburger.

Murphy waved an apple slice in his direction. "These are complex carbs, which are packed with natural nutrients to provide energy."

"At my age, I want things simple." Chris waved a fry at him. "And you can't get much simpler than a fry."

"At your age, you should start watching what you eat."

Stuffing the last bite of the cheeseburger into his mouth, Chris took a sip of his soda. "Let's change the subject. Is your wife a health food freak, too?"

"No, she's a junk food junkie. Loves, I mean *loves*, chocolate." Murphy shot a glance in his direction. "How did you—"

Chris pointed at his left hand. "Ring finger."

"I'm not wearing a wedding ring and don't say anything about a tan line because there is none."

"But there is an indentation where you usually wear a wedding ring. I'm assuming you take it off when you go on assignment so that your targets can't go after your wife and family."

With a nod of his head, Murphy said, "I'm sure you did the same when you worked undercover."

"I quit undercover work when I got married. That's not the type of work for a family man. I'd be gone for months at a time and the type of people I would be investigating—" Chris allowed himself to shudder. "They were the type of people that if my cover got blown, no one would find my body."

"And yet your children lost their mother and still ended up being raised by a single parent," Murphy said.

"Is your wife with the agency?"

"She's in med school."

"Ah, a doctor, eh?"

"A psychiatrist."

"That should be helpful in your line of work," Chris said. "Kids?"

"No, there's lots of things she wants to do before we start a family." Murphy shrugged his shoulders. "Besides, I'm gone so much, it wouldn't be fair. My dad used to travel a lot and my mother had her hands full. She had five kids."

"Five?" Chris laughed.

"Dad used to say he traveled a lot and Mom got lonely," Murphy said. "It's hard to be lonely when you have five kids around."

"Did your father leave his family behind to go halfway around the globe for two years?" Chris asked.

"Dad was active military. He didn't have a choice. He'd done a couple of deployments, but generally—"

"Blair was not in the military," Chris said through clenched teeth. "She had a choice. When it came down to it, she chose her career over our family."

"Maybe—"

"I know it sounds sexist, but it's not," Chris said. "I left a good career path in undercover work for my family—my wife—before we had kids. Family comes first. That's how I was raised."

"I was raised the exact same way," Murphy said. "But when I chose to join the military, I made the conscious decision to put my country first. When Jessie and I got married, I told her up front that I would put my country before her. She went into our marriage with her eyes wide open."

"You chose to serve your country because of patriotism. Blair didn't. Her decision was because of—" Lost for words, Chris pounded the steering wheel.

In silence, Murphy wrapped his empty yogurt cup on a napkin and placed it in the fast food bag, which he crumbled up. "I don't know Blair or what your family life was like—but, based on what I saw my mom go through—it's hard being a wife and mother. You spend so much time taking care of other people's needs. You do that day in and day out. Sometimes, you can feel like you spend so much time taking care of other people, that you feel—" He searched for the right word.

Chris recalled his conversation that night five years earlier. "Under appreciated."

"When she got that offer to go to Switzerland, she felt like it was a chance for her to do something for herself."

Chris slowly shook his head. His voice was soft when he said, "Blair could be so self-absorbed sometimes. It was like …" His voice trailed off. "Like she wouldn't know what was going on around her."

"Ditzy?"

"No, she was smart," Chris said. "Like … a little over a week after I got word that she had been killed in Nice, I got a watch from her."

"That must have been awful," Murphy said.

"I was stunned. It was a Rolex watch—engraved with my name. 'Darling Chris, Fly Away With Me. Your Angel, Blair.'"

"She did love you," Murphy said.

"She loved watches and clocks. She had a dozen of them. All different kinds and watchbands. But you know what." Chris held up his arm. "I don't. Never wore watches and never will. She sends me this expensive watch that she had to know I would never wear. I can't sell it because she had it engraved with both our names. It's been sitting in my jewelry box ever since." There was a growl in his voice when he said, "And now, just as Helen and I get back together, Blair decides to come back from the dead and drag me into Lord knows what."

"Look on the bright side."

"What bright side? People are trying to kill me."

"You met me and because of that you're not sitting in a federal holding jail for firing a weapon at a crowded subway stop and killing an international assassin." Murphy flashed him a broad toothy grin. "You're welcome again."

An hour later, the BMW came to a stop at Route 340. They were on the Virginia side of the Shenandoah River. The tiny town of Harpers Ferry rested on the other side of the river, which marked where the Shenandoah River flowed into the Potomac.

With a snort, Murphy woke up, righted his seat, and looked around.

"We're almost there." Chris pressed his foot on the accelerator and turned left to drive along the river.

"There where? Where are we going?" Murphy looked out the window at the dark murky river as Chris drove across the bridge and up a hill.

At the top of the hill, the road widened at an intersection marking the national park of Harpers Ferry. Instead of turning into the park, Chris turned right and drove past the visitor's center. He made another left turn to travel down a small side road next to a middle school.

"One of my daughters goes to that school," Chris told Murphy.

The next building was a single-story building with a sign out front reading, "Harpers Ferry-Bolivar Public Library." Chris made a sharp left turn into a small parking lot and around to the back of the building.

Surprisingly, the lot contained several vehicles. Chris wasn't surprised to see his truck parked next to the door.

There were lights on inside the library. Murphy checked the time on the BMW's dashboard. It was one o'clock. "Kind of late for the library to be open, don't you think?" He reached into his pocket for his weapon.

"Book club meeting." Chris slid out of the driver's seat.

"Book club?" Murphy threw open the door. "What kind of book club meets at one o'clock in the morning?"

"The Geezer Squad, that's who."

The library was divided into two sections. The children's wing had a wide, round house effect to make for an airy, forest atmosphere.

The older wing was a traditional library with stacks and bookcases between the library's check out station and the side entrance. Four conference tables had been joined together in the common area. An assortment of snacks, including three pizza boxes, filled the center of the tables.

A white board filled with notes was stationed at the head of the table. Armed with a black marker, an attractive older woman with long blond hair wrote notes and drew diagrams.

In a wheelchair, a man with thick eyeglasses and gray beard and a short woman in a thick sweater scrolled through articles on their respective laptops and compared notes.

Donning a tweed deerstalker hat not unlike the type Sherlock Holmes wore, Sterling the German shepherd studied an array of playing cards. He placed a paw on a pile of chips and pushed them toward a bigger pile resting between him and a tall, slender man.

The other card player had the sophisticated bearing of an executive, but the weathered face of a man who spent much time outside. He set down his wine glass and shook his head. "You're bluffing."

"Sterling doesn't bluff," the man in the wheelchair said. "Bruce is never going to learn, huh, Francine?"

"Nope," the woman in the sweater said.

Sterling took his paw off the pile of chips and nudged a pile of cards in his direction with his nose.

Bruce turned over Sterling's cards. After seeing them, he tossed his cards down.

At the other end of the table, the blonde paused in her writing and turned to him. "Beat you again, huh, Bruce?"

Bruce got up from the table. "I know you're cheating," he whispered into Sterling's tall ears on his way to a side table filled with wine bottles, soft drinks, and an ice bucket. "I just can't prove it."

Sterling stuck his snout into a bowl of popcorn and proceeded to chow down.

"Have you checked to see if he has any cards hidden in his dog collar?" Francine laughed at him without looking up from where she was reading an article on her laptop.

"How does it feel to get cleaned out by a dog at every meeting?" the man in the wheelchair asked.

"He's not a dog, Ray," Bruce said while refilling his wine glass. "He's a shark in a dog suit. What have we got, Jacqui?"

The woman at the whiteboard stepped back to study her findings. "We have a lot of nothing."

"Where's Helen?" Bruce asked.

Jacqui pointed in the direction of the library director's office. "She's in Doris's office. Chris's old partner called. Maybe she can make heads or tails out of this."

Chris and Murphy threw open the side door and walked in. "Well," Chris called out, "I see Helen called out the troops."

Ray rolled back from the table and spun his chair around to face them. "It's about time." He rubbed his hands together. "Now we can get this party started." He frowned when he saw Murphy. "Who's the kid?"

"This is Murphy." Chris jabbed a thumb over his shoulder in Murphy's direction. "He's with me."

Ray scoffed. "I have underwear older than he is."

"But not nearly as fine." The woman in the sweater jumped out of her chair and hurried over to Murphy with her hand held out. "I'm Francine Duncan. Did you work undercover with Chris in the FBI?"

"Actually, his former partner and I worked together on a few assignments," Murphy said.

"So you're with the FBI," Bruce said.

"Not exactly."

"He's CIA," Chris said.

When Murphy shot a glare in his direction, Chris said, "You might as well just cop to it. They'll figure it out eventually."

"We're very good at what we do." Francine wet her lips while looking Murphy up and down.

"Chris, if you keep bringing young people into the club, then we're not going to be able to call ourselves the Geezer Squad," Bruce said. "We're just going to be the 'Squad.'"

"I had to bring him along," Chris said. "He saved my life tonight."

"We had each other's backs," Murphy said.

"We've had a very rough evening. It didn't go at all the way I expected. Speaking of which, where's Helen? I saw my truck outside." Chris passed the table and food to go into his mother's office.

Francine gestured at the pizza boxes and food. "You look hungry," she told Murphy. "Why don't you eat and tell us all about yourself? You can start with your marital status."

"He can tell us about himself later," Bruce said. "We want to know why our state department declared Chris's wife dead when she wasn't. We also want to know why an international assassin was trying to kill her."

Chris found Helen sitting in the corner with her head in her hands. The bright cocktail dress and wool coat that she had put on earlier for a glamorous evening out with her guy had lost its glitz hours earlier.

"Helen?" When he entered the office, Chris couldn't help but smile at seeing her. Just the sight of her brought a smile to his lips.

With a quick motion, she wiped her cheeks and rose to let him take her into his arms. He kissed her on the mouth and then held her in a tight hug. "Ripley told me that they let you go," she said into his neck.

"Well, not exactly."

She pulled away. "We all saw it on the news. The FBI released a bunch of bull about you being undercover and that Mancini was a serial killer that you'd been tracking …" She let out a shuddering breath. "They're covering it up. I'm glad you're not in jail, but why the cover up and how were they able to do it so quickly? Obviously, the FBI knows a lot more than they're telling." She looked up into his eyes. As her hand brushed across his shoulder, she noticed that he had changed his clothes. "Whose clothes are those? Where did they take you? What happened tonight?"

"It's a long story." Chris took her hands. "In a nutshell, they know about as little as I do."

"They who?"

"The FBI. CIA."

"CIA?"

"That's who Murphy's with," Chris said. "I think. Someone called him 'Lieutenant,' and he told me that he was active military. He must be military intelligence on loan to the CIA."

"If you don't even know who he is, and they're covering up assassinations, then why did you bring him here? He could be working for the same people who hired that hitman to kill Blair."

Chris shook his head with determination. "No. I may not know exactly who Murphy works for, but I do know that whoever it is, he's on our side."

"And you know this because—"

"My instinct. My instinct has never failed me. It told me who I could trust when I was undercover. If Murphy wanted me dead, he could have killed me hours ago. We were hit by a death squad who killed one of his men. He could have escaped. Instead, he risked his life to come back and save me." He kissed the palm of her hand.

Helen let out a sigh. "He knows you're Blair's husband. Could he … maybe he's using you to lure Blair out into the open so that he could kill her."

"He didn't even know who she was until I told you and Ripley."

Helen shook her head. "None of this makes sense. If no one even knew she was alive, then she must have been safe. Why now, has she suddenly shown up out of nowhere with hired guns trying to kill her?"

"Good question."

Chapter Seven

"Finally, someone who appreciates the value of healthy eating." Jacqui cast a grin at her fellow Geezer Squad teammates as they watched Murphy eating a second slice of vegetarian pizza, something Jacqui had insisted on ordering to go with the other two pies.

Murphy had changed out of his bloody and damp clothes into a spare set that Bruce kept in his truck for emergencies when working in his vineyard. They were just a bit loose, but wearable. The shoes were much too big, so Murphy opted to take off his work boots and dry them by the heater.

"If you're so health conscious, why don't you drink wine?" Bruce asked. "They say everyone should have one glass of red wine every day to prevent heart disease."

"I need to keep my mental faculties at their best at all times," Murphy said.

"Because you're a spy with the CIA?" Francine asked.

Murphy flashed a grin at each of them while they waited anxiously for his response. "Tell me about the Geezer Squad."

"We're a book club," Ray said.

"That meets in the middle of the night?"

"We're retired," Bruce said. "It isn't like we have to get up to go to work in the morning." He puffed out his chest. "I was the Virginia state attorney general. Bruce Harris."

"I heard of you," Murphy said. "You were an officer in the navy before you went to law school. Naval intelligence."

"How did you know?"

"I've studied some of your past investigations."

"All of my work with the navy was classified," Bruce said with a furrowed brow.

"What do you do now that you've retired?"

"I own a winery over in Purcellville—just across the state line in Virginia."

Murphy turned to Francine who was grinning. "What role do you play on the Geezer Squad, Francine?"

She held out her hand. "Investigative journalist. I was with the Associated Press."

Ray clasped Murphy's hand. "Ray Nolan. Retired from Homeland Security. Got transferred over there when they were established after 9/11. I set up their cyberwarfare system."

"Ray here was shot in the back by a home-grown terrorist after he ended up on Al Qaeda's hit list," Jacqui said.

"I hope they got the shooter," Murphy said.

"My daughter blew the guy away right there in the parking lot at Chuck E. Cheese." Ray shook his head. "Mess with my daughter's family and you mess with her—and it's never a good idea to mess with my daughter."

Murphy turned to Jacqui. "What do you do besides watch all of their diets?"

"I was the state medical examiner in Pennsylvania," Jacqui said. "I retired with my husband. We'd built a big house up on Eagle's Nest."

"Eagle's Nest?"

"Top of the mountain," Francine said. "Jacqui's house has a bird's eye view of the whole valley."

Murphy saw a shadow of sadness cross Jacqui's face.

"Eight months after we had finished building our dream house, my husband died," Jacqui said. "He was my whole world. I became a recluse—only coming into town once a week to get groceries and visit the library. One day, I saw a notice on the wall for a book club for law enforcement retirees. They read only crime fiction. I came to the very next meeting and—"

The members around the table grinned at each other.

"The Geezer Squad gave me a new purpose. They're my family."

With a chuckle, Murphy sat up. "I don't see any books on this table."

Perched on the other side of the table, Sterling was staring at him.

"I do see a German shepherd wearing a hat, though."

"Sterling's retired, too," Francine said. "He was a police K9. He and his handler got caught in an ambush. Sterling survived but failed the psyche exam for returning back to duty."

"He's eccentric," Ray said. "That's why he fits right in with us."

"I see that," Murphy said while taking note of the tweed hat on Sterling's head. "Must be a German shepherd thing. My father-in-law's German shepherd has psyche issues, too. He's a kleptomaniac."

"Sterling's a card shark," Bruce said.

Narrowing his eyes, Sterling let out a low bark.

"What does the Geezer Squad do, if you don't read books?" Murphy asked.

Bruce made a shushing sound. "What's our number one rule?"

"Never talk about the Geezer Squad," they said in unison. Sterling let out a bark and a low growl to punctuate their statement.

"We investigate cold cases," Bruce said. "We each have proficiency and connections in our areas of expertise. When we put our talents together, we're able to come at a cold case from a totally different direction in order to heat it up again."

"Why the secrecy?"

"Because our families scare the hell out of us," Ray said.

"That's why Elliott isn't here," Bruce said.

"Elliott?"

"Elliott Prescott," Jacqui said. "We aren't sure who he's retired from."

"He could tell you," Ray said, "but then he'd have to kill you."

Francine leaned into Murphy to whisper, "He's dating Chris's mother."

"That's one church lady who knows how to scare the hell out of you," Ray said. "Elliott couldn't come up with a lie good enough to get out. He's interrogating Doris to see if she may know something to help us."

"Chris's late father was a founding member of the Geezer Squad," Bruce said. "Kirk Matheson was a captain with the state police. He got shot in the line of duty and Doris insisted that he retire. He was going stir-crazy, so she got him to join a book club here at the library."

"That's where he met Elliott," Jacqui said. "They became best buds."

"Then, they got kicked out of the book club," Bruce said.

"How do you get kicked out of a book club?" Murphy asked.

"They'd only read the crime fiction books and then they'd go off on tangents about how much the writers got wrong," Francine said. "Doris expelled them from the group, and so they started their own club. Retired law enforcement only, and they'd read nothing but crime fiction."

"But I don't see any of you reading books," Murphy said.

"Well," Bruce said with a coy grin, "we've been busy."

Murphy laughed.

"But we can't let our families know about it. Doris can be one tough cookie on the outside, but on the inside." Jacqui shook her head. "She was devastated when Kirk had that heart attack. Christopher is her only child. If she knew some of the stuff he's done for the club—"

"She'd castrate him," Ray said.

"Our families would be worried sick about us," Jacqui said.

"I know exactly what you're talking about," Murphy said. "Better for your families to think you were going off to a nice safe library to meet with your book club than to know that you were digging into real life murder and mayhem."

The library director's office door opened. Chris and Helen emerged.

"Is everything okay?" Francine asked upon seeing the red in Helen's eyes.

"Considering." Chris pulled out a chair for Helen to sit at the table. He sat next to her with Sterling on the other side of him. After introducing Murphy to her, he asked the other members of the book club, "I take it you've been spending the night trying to find out if the state department made a mistake, or did they conspire to fake Blair's death?"

"I think they conspired to fake her death," Helen said. "Your mother told us that Blair's body had accidentally been cremated."

"That's true." Chris let out a breath. "I forgot about that. They explained it as a clerical error. Since the body had been cremated, there was no way for me to identify her."

"Which means you wouldn't have noticed that it wasn't her body," Jacqui said.

"If the state department helped your wife fake her death," Murphy said, "why?"

"A cover up, of course," Francine said.

"To what end?" Chris said. "Blair was a simple communications officer. She wasn't a spy or—"

"Maybe she was a killer," Ray said. "From what little bit Francine and I have been able to uncover, something rotten was going on in Switzerland."

"Denmark," Jacqui said.

"No, Switzerland," Ray said.

"But the saying is, 'There's something rotten in Denmark.'"

"The *murder* happened in *Switzerland*," Ray said.

"Which is where Blair was assigned," Chris said. "What murder are we talking about, Ray?"

Ray tossed a photograph that he had printed up from the internet along with a story to the middle of the table. Jacqui picked up the papers and taped them to the whiteboard. The man in the photograph was a middle-aged, heavyset man. He had a thin patch of hair around the sides and back of his head with a shiny bald spot on top.

"According to records, Blair Matheson was killed in Nice on Bastille Day three years ago," Ray said. "She was a communications officer with the state department stationed in Switzerland."

"Now tell me something I don't know," Chris said.

"Did you know Les Monroe, chief of communications in Switzerland, died just the day before?" Ray said.

Speechless, Chris stared across the table at him.

"Les Monroe was Blair's boss," Ray said. "His body was found in his home on the same day she was supposedly killed in a terrorist attack. No one noticed the dead guy in Switzerland because the terrorist attack in Nice sucked up all the oxygen in the airwaves."

"What was the cause of death?" Jacqui asked.

"Officially," Ray said, "the cause of death was suicide."

"What was not made public was that the poor guy somehow got rid of the gun after shooting himself in the back three times," Francine said. "I found that out from one of my old sources."

"How reliable is that source?" Chris asked.

"Very." Francine slapped a sheet of paper down on the table. "He got a copy of the medical examiner's original report."

"Will this medical examiner—" Murphy asked.

"Medical examiner's dead," Francine said. "Killed in a house invasion less than three weeks after Monroe's suicide." She made air quotes when saying the word "suicide."

"This isn't sounding good," Murphy said. "This isn't sounding good *at all*."

"Would Blair have been capable of—" Bruce started to ask Chris, only to find him vigorously shaking his head.

"No," Chris said. "Never. Blair would never have killed anyone for any reason."

"No offense, Chris," Bruce said, "but during my career, I'd seen a lot of nice looking, wife and mother types in my courtroom who ended up being cold-blooded killers when they felt it suited them."

"I know," Chris said. "I've ended up on the wrong end of a gun against those very types, but Blair was not like that. I know enough to be able to spot someone who, when backed into a corner could pull the trigger to kill someone. Blair is not one of them. My mother? Yes. Blair? No."

The members of the squad quickly nodded their heads to the reference. Sterling placed his front paws on the table and howled in agreement.

"My point is, I don't believe Blair would have killed anyone, let alone her boss and then go on the run," Chris said. "If she got into trouble, she would have come to me."

"With all due respect, Chris, from what I've seen tonight, she has been in trouble and never came to you," Murphy said.

"Are you sure, Chris?" Jacqui asked. "Is there any doubt in your mind? Could the woman you saw in the metro be someone else?"

"No!" Chris slammed his palm down on the table. "She's the mother of my children. We were married over twelve years. I know my wife."

In silence, Helen shifted in her seat to move away from Chris. She dropped her eyes to her hands in her lap. Noticing, Jacqui and Francine exchanged solemn expressions.

"If the woman you saw was your wife, then she couldn't have been killed in that terrorist attack," Bruce said. "That's what you're saying, Chris."

"That's exactly what I'm saying."

"Which means she's been alive for the last three years," Jacqui said.

Chris nodded his head in agreement.

"But she never notified you that she was alive," Jacqui said.

"Never."

"Why would she do that? Why would she let those little girls think their mother was dead?"

Chris stared at Jacqui.

"Lesser of two evils," Murphy said in a strong voice while reaching for a slice of pizza. "It was safer for them to believe she was dead than to know she was alive and become vulnerable to whoever was after her."

"But why?" Chris asked. "I keep coming back to the same question. Blair was just a communications officer. She was a techno geek—one step up from a clerk—and she hated that. She worked with office equipment. She managed communication transmissions and data."

"She *archived* communications data." Ray jabbed a finger into the air.

"She did that. Yes."

Ray shook his finger. A chuckle grew from deep in his chest while he used his other hand to bring up information on his laptop.

"Ray's onto something," Francine said.

"How long ago did Blair go to Switzerland?" Ray asked Chris.

"Four years ago. She left in August and was killed—well, she wasn't killed—"

"The next July," Ray said. "She was there eleven months. Did she tell you what she was going to Switzerland for?"

"It was classified," Chris said. "Everything she did was classified."

Ray looked at Chris from under his thick gray eyebrows. "But she was going to Switzerland to work on one specific project for the state department."

With a sigh, Chris nodded his head.

"What are you on to, Ray?" Bruce asked.

"I think she was archiving old communications data," Ray said. "Remember Eric Snowden? The traitor who dumped a bunch of classified NSA records across the globe."

"Some people think he was a hero," Francine said.

"Whether he was or not is irrelevant to this case," Ray said. "Point is, when Eric Snowden dumped all that classified information and took off with who knows what else he had, our intelligence system took a serious hit. We had to scramble to come up with bigger and badder encryptions to protect our communications systems because Snowden had showed everyone our cards."

"And Blair worked in communications," Murphy said.

"Based on the timing, she went to Switzerland to work on a project about the same time our intelligence systems were undergoing a major encryption upgrade," Ray said. "I'll bet money that's what she was working on."

"Blair wasn't a cybersecurity engineer," Chris said.

"I'm talking about the major headache that all of our embassies and bases had to go through afterwards. Let me explain it this way." Ray lay his hand on Francine's laptop. "Suppose you've always worked with one type of laptop—an android type. You have everything on it." He reached over to his state-of-the-art laptop. "Then, you upgrade to a more sophisticated system. But not everything on your old computer is compatible with the new system. Now what do you have to do?"

"You need to clean out and organize your data," Francine said. "Archive what you don't need to transfer to the new system, so that you don't bog it down."

Ray jabbed his finger up into the air. "And that is what was going on in the intelligence community at the same time that your wife went to Switzerland to work on this classified project! There was so much data that had to be sifted through. American bases and embassies were divided into regions. Switzerland was the home base for Central Europe. Countries in that area were sending their data to Switzerland to be compiled onto a database mainframe. How long was she going to be gone?"

"Two years. Probably three," Chris said.

Ray clapped his hands together and pointed at Chris with both fingers. "That's what she was working on! We're not exactly talking about backing up a laptop onto an external drive and tossing it into a drawer. There was a ton of data—historical information that needed to be examined and converted to the new system and archived. She would have been working with a couple of other officers under the chief of communications."

"The same chief of communications who ended up committing suicide by shooting himself in the back three times?" Murphy said.

"The very same," Francine said. "Les Monroe."

"I think you're on to something, Ray."

"Right now, this is all speculation," Bruce said. "We need confirmation that Blair was working on that project before we can move forward in that direction."

"How much communications data would she have been going through?" Murphy asked. "How far back are we talking about?"

Ray shrugged his shoulders. "There's no telling. There was a total overhaul of the intelligence community's communications systems. Some of those smaller countries were probably still working with carrier pigeons."

Chris and Murphy exchanged long glances.

"Like you were saying, Jacqui," Chris said, "Blair allowed us to think she was dead. She went underground and was safe. But then something happened to make her come out of hiding."

"I guess," Murphy said with a heavy sigh, "based on what you've been able to dig up, I should come clean with what I know." His eyes met with each of theirs before landing on Chris's. "Nothing that I say can leave this room until our investigation is over."

Each member of the squad exchanged silent glances before Chris asked, "What have you been holding back?"

"This case does involve national security," Murphy said. "I need everyone's word that there will be no leaks."

They nodded their heads in agreement, except Francine. Finally, under the group's stern glare, she sighed and shrugged her shoulders. "I agree." She shook her pen at Murphy. "But Blue-Eyes here is giving me an in-depth interview for my blog after we break this case wide open."

Every head at the table jerked around to face Murphy. "I guess I can agree to that."

"Now that's out of the way," Chris said, "spill it, Blue-Eyes."

"I wasn't exactly truthful earlier when I said I knew nothing about this case going into it tonight," Murphy said. "A couple of weeks ago, the judiciary majority chair, Senator Graham Keaton received an anonymous letter. The sender stated that she had information critical to national security. There was a burner phone in the envelope. When she called, she verified her credibility by giving the investigator the name of a missing CIA operative and the date she had gone missing. That was the same date that Les Monroe died." He sighed. "Our team knew about Monroe's murder. That case has been cold from the very beginning. When Senator Keaton's investigator verified Anonymous's information about the operative, my team was brought in. We thought Anonymous was the agent—that maybe she'd gone rogue or had been captured by a hostile government and had managed to escape. I was assigned to be at the meeting to back up the investigator and tail the operative afterwards to ascertain the situation." He glanced at Chris. "Instead of a missing CIA agent, we ended up with a communications officer who was supposed to be dead and a dead international assassin who can't tell us who'd hired him."

"There was a leak somewhere between Senator Graham Keaton and the meeting." Bruce chuckled. "It's been a long time since I've been to Washington, I think it's time I meet up with one of my old pals on Capitol Hill."

"These people play for keeps," Murphy said with a shake of his head.

"No offense, Murphy," Bruce said, "but we've all had experience with people who play for keeps."

"Not the type of muscle these players have."

"I think you should elaborate, Murphy," Chris said.

"It's class—"

"We're not active duty soldiers who have to blindly take orders and ask no questions," Chris said. "Everyone around this table came here tonight because they care about me and my family. But they also have loved ones. You owe it to them to give them all the facts so that they can make informed decisions about whether they want to stay in or back out while they still can."

"We already gave our word to be discrete," Francine said. "There's no way we're going to get to the truth with only half of the facts. Cough it up, Sweet Cheeks."

"Don't make us bring out the big dog." Ray jerked his chin in Sterling's direction.

Sensing their attention, Sterling lifted his head from where he had slipped it into a pizza box. Caught red handed in the act of sneaking a slice of cold pepperoni pizza, he flipped the lid the concealed his snout and sent the box sliding across the table. His hat fell to the floor. His eyes bulged as he looked around the table. If he sat very still, maybe none of them would notice the crusty goodie spilling out of both sides of his mouth.

"He can be quite scary when he's on his meds," Bruce said.

Murphy took his time looking around the table.

Yellow Dragons sounded like the name of a wannabe street gang in some big city borough. But they weren't any made up street gang in some fictional movie. They were real—enough to be listed in the Pentagon's classified listing of highly skilled death squads. Murphy had the bruises to prove it.

"Murphy, I can assure you that what you tell us won't leave this room," Bruce said.

"Have any of you heard about the Yellow Dragons?" Murphy asked in a quiet tone.

"The yellow dragon is the zoomorphic incarnation of the Yellow Emperor, who is the center of the universe in Chinese religion and mythology," Jacqui said in a matter-of-fact tone. "The Yellow Deity was conceived by a virgin mother, Fubao."

"Do you mean in the way Mary conceived Jesus by the holy spirit?" Chris asked.

"Not exactly. Fubao became pregnant after seeing a yellow ray of light turning around the Northern Dipper." Seeing their puzzled expressions, Jacqui said, "Don't any of you read anything besides crime books?"

"Are you saying this Chinese virgin got pregnant from star gazing?" Francine said.

"There was a little more to it than that."

"The Yellow Dragons, an ultra-secret, highly trained group of assassins, mercenaries, whatever you want to call it, have named themselves after this powerful deity," Murphy said. "They believe they are blessed with their exceptional fighting skills. They go into each mission believing that they are destined to succeed. Sources say their training is more like torture. If you survive, you've been blessed. If you don't …" He shrugged his shoulders. "The Yellow Dragon has deemed you unworthy, therefore, you die. They mark their soldiers with a tattoo of a yellow dragon on the back of their neck with its claws around your throat—kind of like the dragon having your back."

"What is this group?" Francine asked. "A religious sect or a death squad?"

"From what I have read about them, they are a highly skilled special forces team originally established by Chinese leaders for special missions that they don't want traced back to the Chinese government. They're so classified—they aren't even supposed to exist. There aren't even any former members you can talk to because once you're in, you're in for life. The only way to quit is death."

"Murphy said the assassin who attacked him had a yellow dragon tattooed on the back of his neck," Chris said.

"But he wasn't Asian," Murphy said, "which is very strange because what I read about the Yellow Dragons was that they did not accept anyone who was not of Chinese birth."

"Anyone can get a tattoo," Ray said.

"Ray has a point," Chris said. "If the Yellow Dragons are as highly trained as you're claiming, then you wouldn't have come out on top in that ambush. Maybe he learned about the Yellow Dragons, got one of their tattoos, and convinced whoever put this death squad together that he was one." He added, "The important thing for you all to know is this, whoever is behind this has a team of highly skilled special force type enforcers to keep their dirty secret under wraps. They are trying to kill anyone who they even suspect of knowing what they're up to. They found out I was Blair's husband and without even waiting around to find out what I knew, if anything, they followed us and set out to kill everyone."

"They're not taking any chances," Helen said.

"But we're not going to be able to stop 'them' until we find out who 'they' are," Chris said.

"That starts with finding out what Blair uncovered in Switzerland," Ray said.

"Someone has to know," Francine said. "Chris, do you know who Blair worked with in Switzerland? Some of them must be back in the States now. They may know something without being aware of it."

"There was an office manager who Blair seemed to be pretty friendly with," Chris said. "I have to think to remember her name. She was planning to retire after finishing her tour in Switzerland."

"Is there any possibility of us seeing that anonymous letter she'd sent to Senator Keaton?" Francine asked.

"I suggest that you not contact anyone until we get a better idea of who we are actually going up against," Murphy said.

"How can we do that without talking to anyone?" Francine asked.

Murphy looked around the table. "Can I borrow someone's cell phone?" He flashed a bright toothy smile at Francine.

"You. Francine, you're a journalist, your phone will work fine."

Francine unlocked her phone and slid it across the table-top to him. "Just keeping smiling that smile and you can have anything you want, sweetheart."

With a wink, Murphy picked up the phone and slid his thumb across the screen.

"I thought we were going off the grid," Chris said.

"Nigel should be fully scanned and clean by morning," Murphy said.

"Who's Nigel?" Jacqui asked.

"My version of Ray," Murphy said while texting. *"Source in Annapolis said contact U for feature about Ingle. Visiting city tomorrow. Meet @ Panera Dupont Circle 9am after butler cleans cupboards?"*

"That message doesn't make any sense," Bruce said.

"Not supposed to," Murphy said. "Tristan will understand."

"Who's Tristan?" Chris asked.

"Tristan is Nigel's guardian," Murphy said.

The phone dinged and Murphy smiled as he read the text. "The butler has finished. The cupboards are clean." He slid the phone back to Francine. "Nigel wasn't the leak. That means the leak happened somewhere between Senator Keaton's office and his investigator."

"How certain are you that the report about Nigel being free from hacking is right?" Chris asked. "Be careful in answering because, as you said so yourself, lives are at stake."

"One hundred percent," Murphy answered as the phone in Francine's hand dinged. "I'd trust Nigel with my life."

"Tristan says Nigel is just a little bit offended that you didn't trust him enough to ward off an attack from a foreign body," Francine read.

"Better to be safe than sorry," Murphy said before turning back to Chris. "I have connections who will be able to confirm or deny if Blair was actually involved in that project archiving old communications data."

Francine's phone dinged again, prompting her to read the message.

"Do you have any idea where Blair could have been hiding the last three years?" Helen asked Chris.

"Tristan wants to know when you're coming home." Francine held up for the phone for Murphy to read the message. "He says it's important."

"I'm working," Murphy said in a low voice.

Francine tapped out the reply.

"Blair has to have been hiding out somewhere," Helen said. "If we can figure out where she's been, we might find someone she trusted enough to tell what she'd uncovered."

Chris shook his head. "That's something I'm having a hard time wrapping my head around. Blair was a techno geek. She had no law enforcement training. She had a gun and only knew how to shoot because I dragged her to the range. My worst nightmare was my family being targeted because of my past. That makes this whole thing totally ironic. What I'm saying is, Blair did not know the fine details of going off the grid. How did she do it? How did she fake her death and stay off the radar all these years?"

"She had to have had help," Helen said.

"Who would Blair have trusted enough to help her?" Murphy asked. "What friends would have known how to help her?"

"How about that office manager you mentioned earlier?" Jacqui said.

In silence, Chris stared across the room. Slowly, he began to nod his head. "Ivy Dunleavy. She was Blair's best friend. They'd met when they both moved into the area to work for the state department. Ivy was maid of honor at our wedding and Blair was matron of honor at hers when she married Stu, the jerk."

"Tell us how you really feel about him," Ray said with a laugh.

"Blair was disappointed that I never became buds with Stu. She envisioned the four of us double dating and hanging out together."

"My wife has a close friend that she wished we could be couple friends with." Murphy shuddered. "The guy is a total leech. Lives off his wife's money. I have no respect for him."

"I've never been that crazy about Ivy either. It always seemed like Blair and I would have problems after they'd get together." With a shake of his head, Chris sighed. "Once a month, Blair and Ivy would have a girls' night out. They'd drink martinis and bitch about their awful lives. Rather, Ivy would complain about how hard it is being a rich man's wife. The pressure of keeping up appearances. Energy drinks in the morning, laser surgery for lunch, network cocktail parties at five, and sleeping pills at ten. Blair would come home drunk and depressed about our boring lives."

"What did her husband do?" Bruce asked.

"Corporate attorney," Chris said. "Partner with this huge firm that deals with international conglomerates. He brags about being a fixer for billionaires. They're both all about the status. They have a huge house in Chantilly. The luxury SUVs. Last I heard, they even have a live-in nanny for their daughter. Hannah is seven years old—the same age as Emma, our youngest daughter. They used to be friends, but since we moved out here to West Virginia, Ivy won't even return my phone calls. I had promised the girls that we'd stay in touch with their friends. Now Ivy looks down her nose at us. Her precious private school girl can't be seen hanging out with us hillbillies."

"Hey," Murphy said, "my roots are from West Virginia."

Chris cocked his head at him. "Really?"

Murphy nodded his head.

"Did you say Ivy's jerky husband was a fixer?" Bruce frowned. "Fixer as in covering up the rich and powerfuls' crimes."

"He'd know what to do to help Blair stay under the radar," Chris said. "The problem is that she doesn't answer my phone calls."

"I hate to be the wet blanket, but it is my job to be the squad's devil's advocate," Bruce said as the phone in Francine's hand dinged a response. "Maybe Blair faked her death to get away from Chris."

"Excuse me?" Chris replied.

"How are we to know what kind of husband you were," Bruce said.

"She did leave the country to get away from you," Ray said.

"Not to—"

"Tristan says Jessica told him that you two were going to Paris for New Year's Eve," Francine swooned. "How romantic? Who's Jessica?"

"My wife," Murphy replied.

"You're such a good husband."

"I try."

"But Tristan said he promised Sarah he'd take her rock climbing in the Grand Canyon for the break between Christmas and New Year, so he can't house-sit; and he's out of beer and just drank the last Red Bull. Can you pick some up on the way home?" Francine joined the others in looking at him questioning.

"Nigel's guardian is having a meltdown," Murphy said.

The Geezer Squad ended the meeting in the early morning hours with each one taking on a task in the investigation.

Ray was going to continue digging into the communications overhaul. While the project was classified, he hoped he could find some chatter about any strange happenings in Switzerland about the time that the chief of communications had "committed suicide" and Blair was supposedly killed.

Following the same angle but from a different direction, Murphy and Francine were going to meet up with Tristan to find out what Nigel uncovered through his classified connections via government databases. Someone had to know what had gone down in Switzerland.

Bruce believed he'd have no trouble setting up a meeting with some of his old cohorts to identify the leak responsible for getting two of Murphy's people killed.

Jacqui was going to join Bruce in his trip into the city. The scientist was an expert in the human psyche. She had the ability to analyze movements and other slight clues that could point them to who was lying and more.

Chris hoped to be able to relax enough to spend some time alone with Helen while figuring out his next move. The thought of Blair's unidentified enemy coming after his family to get to Blair had crossed his mind.

Those hopes of being with Helen were dashed when she told him that Jacqui was driving her home after the meeting broke up. "She drives right past my place on the way up the mountain."

While Jacqui and Helen lived on the same mountain, that was not exactly true. Helen lived on a different part of the mountain.

"I don't mind driving you home," Chris said. "I was hoping we could have some time alone to talk."

"About what's going to become of us now that Blair has come back from the dead?" Helen said.

"Not exactly."

"Chris." She pressed her hand on his arm. "There isn't really anything to discuss."

He held her eyes with his. "I love you, Helen. Blair being alive changes nothing."

"Yes, it does." She blinked the tears from her eyes. "Twenty-four hours ago, your wife was dead. Now she's not. That means you're married."

"We'll get a divorce."

Helen let out a slow deep breath. "Chris, are you seriously going to tell me that you can tell your daughters that the mother they had loved and mourned is really alive, and oh, by the way, after being on the run from international assassins trying to kill her, now that we've got her back, I'm divorcing her."

Chris clenched his teeth. "I don't want to lose you, Helen."

She swallowed. "Chris, one of the things that made me fall in love with you was your compassion. If you were able to do that to those sweet girls, then you wouldn't be the man I fell in love with." She kissed him quickly on the cheek before running out into the cold night air.

At Chris's side, Sterling gazed up at him as if to tell him that he still had him, his best friend. "This weekend just keeps getting better and better."

Chapter Eight

The sun was flirting with the notion of rising. The pastures leading up to the Matheson farm were coated with a thick layer of crusty frost. Winter was on the way.

Chris parked his truck next to the barn and turned off the engine.

Across from him, Sterling perked up when he saw a cat scurry into the brush in pursuit of some possible prey. His nose twitched while he wondered if the barn cat needed backup.

Frustration bubbled up from the pit of Chris's stomach. With a groan, he punched the steering wheel with both fists.

Helen was right.

There was no way he could tell his daughters that their mother was alive and in the next breath announce he was divorcing her. Marriage was not to be taken lightly. *You vow 'til death do you part and you do everything in your power to keep that promise.*

He dropped his head down over the steering wheel.

But Blair was the one who left me. I gave her a choice. Our family or her career and she chose to leave. Why am I the bad guy?

He banged his head against the steering wheel.

The knock on the truck window startled him. He grasped the gun in his pocket and looked up to see his mother, clad in her bathrobe, her arms folded across her bosom, on the other side of the window.

"Christopher, why are you beating up that steering wheel?" She peered around him at Sterling in the passenger seat as if to see if the dog was concealing someone. "Where's Helen?"

"She went home." With a heavy sigh, Chris opened the truck door. Sterling practically climbed across him to offer his assistance to the barn cat.

"I am so sorry to hear that, Christopher." She took him into a hug, when she pulled away, she looked him up and down. "Weren't you wearing your gray suit when you left last night?"

Chris looked down at his clothes. He had been through so much that he had forgotten about the change of clothes Murphy had given to him.

Doris tugged on the sleeve to his jacket. "Whose clothes are these?"

"I got them from a spy."

"A spy?"

"One of the good guys." His voice trailed off into a mutter. "At least, I think he's one of the good guys."

"What's the spy wearing now?" With a frown, she fingered the jacket. "He's not wearing your suit is he?"

"No, Mother."

"Where is it?"

"What does it matter? Blair's out there and someone, we don't know who, wants her dead."

"I know, Helen told us last night." She looked down at the athletic shoes he was wearing. "You gave him your shoes, too."

"I'm sure I'll get them back. Mom, did you hear what I told you? Blair has been in hiding all these years."

"Those were nice dress shoes. And that suit was tailored." With a sigh, she gazed up at him. "That suit was the perfect shade of gray. It brought out your pretty eyes."

"Forget the suit already!"

"Christopher, you don't have to yell."

"I'm sorry. Mom, in the last fifteen hours, I've gone from a widower to married, shot an international assassin, got arrested, escaped federal custody without knowing it, got ambushed, killed a second hitman, and got dumped by the love of my life."

Doris wanted to give him another hug, but sensed he preferred to be left alone in his misery. "Are you hungry?"

"All I've had to eat was a greasy fast food burger and fries."

"You didn't even buy Helen dinner?"

"Why do you think she dumped me?" he said with heavy sarcasm.

"Well, Elliott is fixing breakfast. Come in and eat a nice hot meal. It'll make you feel better and think more clearly."

"Elliott's still here?" Chris noticed the SUV was parked behind his mother's sedan. "I'm glad to see your date worked out."

"Well," she demurred, "at least no one tried to kill us. Come in and eat."

Chris checked the time on the phone in his pocket—the burner phone Murphy had given him at the safe house. Soon, it would be time to feed the horses, barn cats, and clean the stalls. "I'm going to get started on my chores. I'll be inside in a little bit."

"Okay, I'll go tell Elliott to put on his pants."

Chris turned away with a groan.

"All right, but don't blame me if breakfast seems a little awkward," she said to his back while he walked over to the barn door.

"TMI, Mom. TMI."

Her heart aching for him, Doris covered her mouth with her hand as she watched her son shuffle into the barn. His shoulders slumped, he had the posture of a man who had taken an emotional beating. Sterling galloped into the barn behind him.

A brisk morning breeze swept across the barnyard and up her robe to send a shiver up her spine. Hugging her robe around her, she trotted back into the house to start the coffee brewing to have it ready when Chris finished with his farm chores.

Sadie and Mocha sat side by side inside the mudroom. Their eyes were focused on the plastic bin where their food was kept to remind her that it was time for their breakfast, too, just in case she might forget.

In the kitchen, Elliott was dressed and preparing the coffee to brew. "Well, if you aren't a sweetheart." She wrapped her arms around him and gave him a tender kiss on the lips.

Perturbed to see her master leave the room without feeding them, Sadie, the Doberman, uttered a noise that was an equal mixture of a whine and a bark while looking back and forth between Doris and the mudroom.

"Don't be so bossy, Sadie," Doris said with a shake of her finger.

Elliott took a carton of eggs out of the refrigerator. "How many will we have for breakfast?"

Excited about the prospect of raw eggs on their food, Sadie and Mocha sat at attention. More focused on the birds gathering around the feeders in the backyard, Thor remained curled up in her bed next to the patio doors.

"Just Christopher," Doris answered Elliott while scooping food into the dog bowls. "Helen went home."

"Did they have a fight?"

"I suspect it was more of a discussion," she said. "I'm not surprised. Helen is a woman of principle. If Blair is alive, that means Christopher is still married to her, and Helen will not date a married man—no matter how much she loves him."

"At this point, I would say Chris and Blair's marriage is only a technicality," Elliott said with a scoff.

"Married nonetheless. Helen has a daughter to think about. Sierra's father was a cheat. He didn't take his wedding vows seriously, and that's why they got divorced. If Helen got involved with a married man, then that will send the message to Sierra that marriage is only as valuable as the sheet of paper the certificate is printed on."

Elliott looked worried. "Then what will become of Helen and Chris?"

"I'm sure the two of them will work that out."

Doris set the dog bowls on the floor. Sadie and Mocha remained seated until she told them that they could eat, at which point they dove in as if they hadn't eaten in days. She set Sterling's bowl on the counter for Chris to give him later.

Clutching Thor's bowl, she stepped into the kitchen and set the bowl next to the rabbit's bed. Her snout picking up the scent of the pellets, Thor leisurely stretched across her bed to inspect that morning's meal. Fully aware of Sadie and Mocha watching, she took her time relishing every bite while watching the sun rise. She had no fear of the big dogs making a move on her food. Their fear of Doris's chastising finger wagging at them was greater than their hunger.

Behind the kitchen counter, Doris poured coffee into two mugs—one for her and the other for Elliott, who was preparing a pan of home fries from leftover boiled potatoes from their dinner the night before. She set a third mug next to the coffeemaker for Chris.

"Christopher and Helen always belonged together," she said with a sad shake of her head. "I was almost as upset as he was when they broke up after high school." She looked up at the ceiling. "I knew Christopher had a thing for her before he did. It was such a blessing when they got together." She looked at Elliott. "I admit it. I even had names picked out for their children. They were going to have two boys and two girls."

"Sounds like Blair never stood a chance of getting into your good graces after Helen." Elliott swept chopped onions into the home fries.

"Blair wasn't good enough for Christopher. She was incapable of appreciating what a prince she had." Seeing Elliott's lips curl, she let out a huff. "Face it. Christopher is the total package. Handsome—especially when he cleans himself up. Courageous. Intelligent. He gets it all from his father. Did I mention handsome?"

"Spoken like a doting mother. I suspect Blair's biggest fault was that she wasn't Helen." He looked at her out of the corner of his eye. "She had to have had some good qualities. I can't see Chris marrying a woman he didn't love."

"Oh, yes, he did love her," Doris said with a heavy sigh. "But not the way he loves Helen."

"Of course not. Helen was his first love. No one ever gets over their first love. Not really."

"Frankly," she said, "I've always suspected the real reason Christopher married Blair was because she asked—"

Elliott spun around. "*She* asked him?"

"Of course. Christopher is a catch," she said. "And I think he agreed because he was over thirty, tired of working undercover, and ready to settle down and have a family. Problem is—"

"Obviously, Blair wasn't ready for all of that," Elliott said. "If she was, she wouldn't have taken off to Switzerland."

"Blair threw Christopher and those three beautiful little girls away and traveled halfway across the globe. Now, just when I was thinking that finally Helen was going to be my daughter-in-law, she shows back up—"

"Careful." Elliott shook a paring knife in her direction. "You're getting dangerously close to becoming a suspect."

When Chris opened the door, the wind caught it to blow it wide open. Sterling rose up onto his hind legs and planted his front paws on the counter. He looked from Chris to his bowl to request breakfast.

"I guess you feel like it's your turn, huh, big guy?" Chris put the bowl down on the floor on his way into the kitchen. Sterling plunged in.

"Looks like everyone's fed except the humans," Doris said. "What do you want with your scrambled eggs, Christopher? Bacon or Sausage?"

With a shrug of his shoulders, Chris poured coffee into his mug. "Doesn't matter. I'm not really hungry."

She frowned. "Christopher ditched Helen to whack an international assassin instead of buying her dinner."

"Assassins are known for their notoriously bad timing," Elliott said with a chuckle.

Doris directed Chris to sit at the table to drink his coffee while she cooked the bacon and made toast. "Tell us about the spy who gave you the clothes off his back." She went on to point out the change in Chris's clothes.

"Spy?" Elliott's eyebrow arched. He caught Chris's eye behind Doris's back.

"I think he's military on loan to the CIA," Chris said as he took his seat. "Name's Murphy. I'm not completely clear on his connection to all this. He was there at the metro when the assassin intercepted Blair while she was trying to make contact with the investigator from the senator's office. He says his orders were to back up the investigator and tail Blair, who they had thought was a CIA operative who had gone missing about the same time Blair was supposed to have been killed."

"That answers my question then," Doris said as she buttered the toast that popped out of the toaster.

"What question?" Chris asked.

Doris carried two slices of toast to his place at the table. "Whose ashes did you scatter off the hillside in Shenandoah National Park? They must have been the missing CIA operative."

Chris let out a groan. "I actually didn't think about that." He took a bite from the end of the toast. "You're right. If the CIA is missing an operative, who disappeared the night before Blair was supposed to have been killed, then it only makes sense that she was the one killed at the terrorist attack and Blair escaped."

"Blair took over her identity," Elliott said.

"Was Blair smart enough to assume the identity of a CIA agent and fly under the radar?" Doris looked down at Chris. "Why would she do that?"

"Blair happened onto something." Chris took the cell phone from his pocket. "She had sent a letter to Senator Keaton claiming there is a threat to our national security." He went to the contacts, which contained only one number. "The CIA agent must have been working on that case and pulled Blair in on it. I'm going to find out what this operative was working on when she disappeared." He pressed the number and put the phone to his ear.

"Then it was the CIA agent who was with the Australian when she got killed." Doris sighed. "Maybe Blair wasn't cheating on you after all."

The phone rang once before connecting with a woman on the other end. "Good morning, Mr. Matheson." Her voice was so low and sensuous that Chris wondered if there had been a mistake. A quick glance at the clock revealed that it was not yet eight o'clock in the morning.

Maybe it was Murphy's wife. Jessie. But then, how did she know his name?

"I'm looking for Murphy," Chris said.

"I'm his commanding officer," she said. "I will take a message and have him contact you. What do you need, Mr. Matheson?"

She sounded more like a sensuous seductress than a military commanding officer. Chris fought the urge to visualize a face and body to go with her voice. "Ma'am, what do you know about—"

"Lieutenant Thornton has been keeping me informed," she said. "Have there been any developments? Has your wife been in contact with you?"

"No," Chris said. "I've realized that if she is alive, then the state department cremated and sent someone else's ashes back to me after the attack in France. I'm wondering if that someone was the missing CIA operative that Murphy—uh, Lieutenant Thornton—was supposed to tail last night."

There was silence on the other end of the line.

"Where are those ashes now?" she asked.

Chris rubbed his face with his hand. "I scattered them off the top of a mountain. It was a favorite place we liked to go hiking."

"That is unfortunate," she said. "If there was a tooth or something that had remained, we'd be able to identify her with DNA."

"I was told at the time that my wife was with another man, an Australian, at the time of the attack," Chris said. "If it was not my wife, then that means the agent was with him."

"If it was indeed the operative who was killed," she said. "Since the ashes are gone, now we may never know."

"The Australian—"

"He was also killed," she said. "To answer your next question, I wish I could tell you that he was a member of the Australian Secret Intelligence Service, but I can't because that information is classified."

Chris was still deciphering her message when she told him that she would have Lieutenant Thornton return his call.

"Did you find out anything?" Elliott asked as he set a plate filled with scrambled eggs, home fries, and bacon in front of Chris.

"Since the ashes are gone, we can't prove it was the CIA operative killed in the attack," Chris said. "Apparently, it's a good bet because the man she was with was an agent with the Australian Secret Intelligence Service."

"They told you that?" Elliott sat at the table next to Doris.

"They told me that they wished they could tell me that, but they couldn't."

Elliott nodded his head. "He was."

Deep in thought, Chris poked at the food on his plate. "The night before Blair was supposedly killed, her boss was murdered."

"After which, Blair goes on the run," Doris said.

"Was she running with the CIA agent or running from the CIA agent?" Elliott asked.

"That is the question," Chris said. "According to Murphy, they don't know if the agent went rogue or why she disappeared. Most likely, though now it can't be proven, she died while meeting with this Australian agent."

"How did the state department identify Blair's body?" Doris asked. "Was it on purpose or an accident?"

"They found Blair's passport in a handbag. The bag was with a badly mangled body that the truck had run over."

"Surely they went by more than passports," Doris said. "How were they to know that the passport hadn't been stolen?"

"Or switched," Chris said. "How did Blair get back into the country without her passport? She had to have been living under a different identity these last few years."

"A CIA agent would know how to get everything she needed to create a whole new identity and get back into the country," Elliott said. "My bet is on the agent getting Blair another passport."

"And she has been living under this new identity for the last three years," Chris said. "But then, something happened, and she resurfaced. Why?"

His mind swimming, Chris looked down at Sterling, who was sitting next to his chair with a look of expectation on his face. After eating his breakfast, the German shepherd had gone into his basket and traded in his deerstalker hat for a black one with a gold buckle, which he had clutched in his teeth.

Thor was perched between Sterling's front paws. The rabbit was dressed in a black and white Pilgrim's costume in anticipation of the upcoming Thanksgiving holiday.

Emma loved to dress the pair up in costumes. Thor seemed to love it. Sterling, not so much. However, they discovered, he did take to wearing hats, when he could keep them on. His tall ears were a challenge.

One day, when Emma was struggling to get a Western hat to stay on him, Katelyn used her sewing skills to cut out holes for the ears and added a Velcro strap for the chin. A picture of her creation modeled by Sterling became an Internet sensation. The next thing they knew, Katelyn had a growing business in designing dog hats and vests. Katelyn's top model, Sterling had his own Instagram account where she posted pictures and videos of him in her designs.

Sterling had a basket in the mudroom for his hats. He would pick out what he felt like wearing that day. This day, he felt like a Pilgrim.

Across from him, the dignified Doberman peered at Sterling with wide eyes as if to say, "Seriously? That dog—the card-playing, hat-wearing German is the alpha of our pack?" Licking her chops, she backed away and went to her bed next to the windows.

"You two are no help," Chris told Sterling and Thor while placing the hat onto the German shepherd's head.

"Eat, dear." Doris tapped the edge of Chris's plate. "It will help you think."

"I'm not hungry." Chris tossed his napkin onto the table and went to his bedroom on the top floor of the farm house.

Chapter Nine

After leaving the library, Murphy drove the BMW to a brownstone on Capitol Hill to freshen up and change his clothes. While Murphy was confident that he and Chris had managed to shake off the death squad, he wasn't taking any chances by returning to the home he shared with his wife.

Jessica was too precious to him.

On the outside, the brownstone looked like an average residence. Those who lived on the upscale block would never have guessed that the quiet looking townhome was a safe house for an ultra-secret team of agents to gather, rest, or use as need be while on assignments. Equipped with a multimillion-dollar security system and computer equipment, not only was Murphy able to freshen up, but he could also check his emails for messages. In addition, the safe house kept a complete inventory of weaponry and ammunition for him to replenish his weapons.

He jogged around the Capitol Building.

The blue sky was so clear that it seemed to go on forever. The morning sun cast a golden glow across the mall. The sunlight reflected off the remaining crystals from the thick frost that had blanketed the landscape that morning.

First frost of the season.

With a shiver against the cold, Murphy blew out a gentle breath. Grinning, he watched the cloud of condensation float away. That was always fun to watch.

A white stretch limousine was parked at the bottom of the Capitol's steps. Murphy trotted down the steps to the huge chauffeur slash security guard waiting motionless next to the rear door. Behind the sunglasses, his eyes bounced around the mall in search of possible threats. Murphy recognized the unmistakable bulge of a weapon under his black jacket.

Even when Murphy walked up to him, the mountain of a man did not move. "Good morning, Lieutenant. You're right on time." He opened the door. Murphy climbed into the back seat and Bernie closed the door.

Her long slender legs seemed to stretch the length of the limousine's rear compartment. They appeared even longer with her black stilettos. Her hair was pulled up into a twist covered by a black hat with netting pulled down over the top half of her face. The black matched the trim on her white fitted dress and jacket.

Murphy heard the driver's door shut and felt the limousine engine turn on.

"I heard things went sideways last night, Lieutenant," she said after Murphy sat across from her. "You were given a very simple assignment. Back up Keaton's investigator while he met with a missing agent. Tail the agent to find out if she'd defected to a hostile government or, worse, has joined parties within our own government working to undermine our democracy."

He couldn't see her eyes behind the netting, but he could feel her glare demanding an explanation.

"Stephens is dead," she said. "He didn't even make it out of his house."

"Hayes is dead, too," he said in a soft voice.

"So our cleanup team reported after finding several bodies at the Springfield safehouse. What happened?"

"Death squad. Did the cleanup team tell you that one of the assassins had a yellow dragon on his neck?"

"The body they pulled out of the pond." She did not appear surprised—at least, as far as Murphy could tell. Nothing fazed CO.

"Was he a Yellow Dragon?"

"No," she said. "He was a Yellow Dragon wannabe. There's no ex-Yellow Dragons, only dead ones. This guy was a psychopath. He had his fingerprints removed with acid. His body was shaved all over. There wasn't a hair on him. He had no identification. Nigel ran a facial recognition and got a match. A security camera in Germany had captured his image in the vicinity of a murder. This wannabe Yellow Dragon had been lurking around the home of a medical examiner working for the state department."

"Did this medical examiner do an autopsy on the chief of communications in Switzerland?"

"I'd have to check on that. Do you believe there's a connection between her murder and what happened last night?"

"Most definitely," Murphy said. "He was a paid assassin."

"Every man in that death squad was a killer for hire."

"Leonardo Mancini is a very heavy hitter," Murphy said. "That means whoever is behind this has a lot of juice. If I knew what we were going up against, then I would have escorted Stephens to his home and he'd still be alive."

"Or you would both be dead," she said. "Someone killed Stephens after collecting what information Mancini needed to intercept the target, who apparently was not Anne Kidman, but the wife of Vaccaro's former partner—FBI."

"Someone? Not Mancini?"

"Couldn't have been Mancini. Too short," she said. "A neighbor saw an extremely tall man wearing a cable utility company uniform working on the box outside Stephens's house shortly before the murder. A van was parked in front of his house. The company confirms they had no trucks in the area yesterday afternoon."

"The tall man must have been working for Mancini."

"Well, our cleanup team found no extremely tall men among the bodies at the safe house. That means he's still out there. Watch your back."

"I always watch my back." He shot her a charming grin. "Their target was obviously Matheson's wife, a communications officer with the state department—"

He stopped when she raised her hand for him to stop. "Vaccaro briefed me on that part." She pressed a button on the console next to her. "You have no idea how deep our people had to dig to get Blair Matheson's paperwork and background check. I just sent her information to your phone. I also sent Chris Matheson's information from the FBI. Is he on board with us?"

"He assumed I was CIA. Then Nigel called me 'Lieutenant.' Now he thinks I'm active military on loan to the CIA."

"Then you haven't totally blown your cover. Don't do anything to contradict his assumption," she said with a shrug of her shoulders. "It's imperative that he, or anyone else for that matter, doesn't find out about the Phantoms. Vaccaro says he can be trusted and believes he can be quite helpful in tracking down his wife. He's brilliant, especially when it comes to thinking fast on his feet." She gestured at Murphy's encrypted phone. "You'll see in his record that the FBI considered him one of their top agents—especially when working undercover."

"I saw that last night," Murphy said. "Oh, speaking of that, there's a red BMW parked in front of the safehouse. Matheson and I had to use it last night after we got ambushed. It's stolen."

She held up her hand. "I don't want to hear anymore."

While Murphy scanned the background information on Chris Matheson, she pressed a button on the console. "Bernie, please contact the police to pick up a red BMW from in front of our Capitol Hill safehouse. Make sure it gets back to its owner."

"The CIA operative who went missing in Switzerland," Murphy said, "what was her assignment?"

"That's classified."

Murphy glanced up from the report. "Maybe if I had more information about what I was going up against last night Hayes and Stephens would still be alive."

"We now believe that Kidman's assignment is irrelevant to her disappearance," she said. "She went missing on the same day that Blair Matheson was reported killed. Of course, the two events were never connected because Kidman was CIA and Matheson was state department. No one in this town talks to each other. The state department found Matheson's passport in a woman's bag. She was supposedly on leave. The body had been hit by a truck. They assumed the victim was Blair Matheson."

"And they cremated the body so Chris Matheson had no idea that it wasn't his wife," Murphy said. "The woman killed in the terrorist attack was Anne Kidman."

"Unfortunately, we'll never know for certain," she said. "Chris Matheson called."

"Has he heard from Blair?"

"I wish."

"What did he say?"

"He had come to the same conclusion and wanted to confirm it," she said. "However, he no longer has her ashes. He threw them off a mountain. Something about a place they used to hike."

"Bummer," he said. "What else did he say?"

"He was told that his wife was in Nice with an Australian," she said. "Witnesses claimed she looked pretty tight with him. Our information says a member of the Australian Secret Intelligence Service had been murdered in the attack. Kidman was romantically involved with that agent. I believe we are safe to assume Kidman had given Matheson a new identity to escape the same people who had killed her boss. My guess is that she had Blair Matheson's identification in her purse to destroy."

"And I think the Yellow Dragon had been hired to murder the medical examiner after she refused to cover up the communication chief's murder," Murphy said. "Everything's connected."

"Blair Matheson must have used the passport that Kidman had obtained for her to return to the United States," she said.

"She stayed away from her family to protect them," Murphy said. "What did she uncover?"

"At this point, we can only guess. Blair Matheson was archiving old communications from bases and embassies. NSA had installed an updated system after that whole Snowden mess. Matheson was assigned to catalog and archive old communications records for the entire Central Europe region."

Murphy grinned. Ray Nolan had been right on target.

"According to the communications chief's administrative assistant, Marianne Landon," she said, "Blair Matheson had a number of closed-door meetings with the communications chief in the days leading up to his death. At one point, they had a meeting with the chief of station, Ned Schiff. It became extremely loud. She heard them mention Lithuania and the car bombing several times."

"Matheson must have discovered additional information about the bombing that killed Ambassador Brown," he said. "Did Schiff act on it?"

"That twerp?" She scoffed. "Ned Schiff only became deputy director of the CIA's intelligence directorate by kissing Daniel Cross's butt."

"The same Daniel Cross who had been stationed in Lithuania when that car bomb killed Ambassador Brown and the chief of station," Murphy said. "That attack put Cross on the fast track after he uncovered the extremist terrorist group responsible for the bombing."

"After Les Monroe, the communications chief, committed suicide and Matheson died in a terrorist attack, Ned Schiff came home to become deputy chief of the intelligence directorate, directly under Daniel Cross," she said. "Do you think maybe that promotion was a nice reward for playing ball?"

"Schiff must have ordered Matheson and her boss to cover up whatever it was they'd found," Murphy said. "When they didn't go along, he killed the communications chief and hired a hitman to take out the medical examiner who refused to cover it up. Matheson escaped and assumed a new identity. The big question is, what did they uncover?"

A slow grin crossed her lips. "That's where it gets interesting. The last communication that Agent Kidman's handler had received from her was on the morning that Blair Matheson had supposedly died. Kidman reported that they had uncovered a possible spy working out of the American embassy in *Lithuania*."

"Inside the embassy?" Murphy noticed that Bernie had pulled the limousine up in front of the Panera Bread in Dupont Circle where he was meeting Francine and Tristan.

"Keep in mind that was three years ago," she said. "The CIA did a security sweep through that embassy and conducted a complete investigation of all personnel after Kidman's handler forwarded that message up the line. They found nothing. Either the handler misunderstood Kidman, or it was false information."

"Or the bad guys got wind of it and covered everything up before the security team could get there," Murphy said.

"That's what makes you such a good Phantom, Lieutenant." She allowed herself to smile. "You're a cynic."

Chris Matheson's bedroom suite occupied the top floor of the three-story farmhouse. It was the same room he had slept in when he had been a teenager demanding privacy from his parents. Thirty years later, when he returned with his family, his mother understood that her grown son needed a place to escape the overpopulation of females.

Spacious, the attic had everything he needed, including a full bathroom. It was removed from the bedrooms on the second floor. His mother's suite was on the other end of the house.

Also, a lone male among a pack of female critters, Sterling could often be found stretched out across Chris's bed. Preferring Doris's company, Sadie and Mocha rarely went up to Chris's room. However, Thor, who had grown quite fond of the German shepherd, could often be found tucked against Sterling.

After abandoning his breakfast, Chris stopped on the second floor upon hearing the anniversary clock's chimes in the dining room marking the eight o'clock hour.

The farmhouse had been in the Matheson family for several generations—over which time furniture and antiques had been passed down as well. Among those possessions were two grandfather clocks and two anniversary clocks. The big grandfather clock in the living room and the other in the study. The gold anniversary clock was on the fireplace mantle in the dining room and another in the sunroom. Each clock announced the hour with various tunes, chimes, and bongs. As hard as Doris tried, she could not get them in sync. Every hour was announced with a clock works version of "Row Row Row Your Boat" played over the course of two to three minutes.

The family had become so used to the hourly symphony that they had tuned it out.

That morning, Chris found the musical broadcast annoying. He stopped at the top of the stairs to count the bongs from the grandfather clock in the study.

BONG! BONG! BONG! BONG! BONG! BONG! BONG! BONG!

Eight o'clock.

In the next beat, one of the anniversary clocks started its tune. While it's notes were higher, they were louder since the clock was located at the bottom of the stairs.

The last chime ended and the clock in the sunroom took up the next round. Then, like the grand star of a major production, the big grandfather clock in the living room seemed to rock the house with its deep bongs.

The last bong echoed throughout the house until it died away.

With a sigh, Chris made his way down the hallway to the stairs to take him up to his room—taking him past each of his daughter's bedrooms. Every door was closed except for Emma's. She kept her door open for Thor, who liked to sleep among the stuffed animals that filled her bed.

The light notes of a song floated from her room.

Thinking he was imagining it, he paused to listen.

The faint notes continued.

Am I hearing what I think I'm hearing? That couldn't possibly be Emma's angel clock. He charged into the bedroom to determine what had prompted the music box in his daughter's clock to start playing on its own.

Emma Matheson's bedroom reflected her personality. Her room was decorated in pink with stuffed bunnies, kittens, puppies, horses, unicorns, and angels were everywhere. Like her mother, Emma had developed a fascination with angels. The centerpiece of her collection was an ornate gold pendulum table clock that rested on the top shelf of her bookcase. A gold angel watched over her from the tip top point.

Ivy Dunleavy had delivered the clock to them on Emma's birthday, ten days after they had learned of Blair's death. Blair had shipped the clock and the Rolex watch to Ivy along with an order they had made from an exclusive clockmaker in Switzerland.

Blair had asked Ivy to deliver the clock, which was also a music box, to Emma on her birthday. The clock with the angel on top had become Emma's most prized possession. She would twist the turnkey to play the song last thing before climbing into bed at night.

Chris followed the song across the room to the clock and put his ear to it. It was "Fly" by Celine Dion, a song about an angel flying up to heaven. He picked it up.

As soon as he touched it, the song ended. The room fell silent.

He turned the clock over to examine the turnkey in the back. Everything appeared normal.

Puzzled about the music box going off in an empty room, Chris placed the clock back on the shelf and backed away. He took one last look around the room before closing the door

Having ditched the Pilgrim hat, Sterling lay at the foot of the bed with Thor stretched out between his front paws. The bunny had a pleased expression on her face as the dog licked her back.

What an odd couple. In any other world, the bunny would be prey for the predator. In this world, they're best friends.

Chris dropped down sideways across the middle of his bed and stared up at the ceiling fan above him.

Sensing his master's melancholy mood, Sterling stretched over to lick Chris's cheek. Displeased about being abandoned, Thor thumped the bed with her hind legs. When that didn't work, she crawled over to wedge her body between them until Sterling had no choice but to resume licking her.

Chris remembered the expression on Blair's face when she had seen him. Surprise. He was also surprised. More so. Afterall, he'd thought she was dead.

He wondered if she knew that he had sold their home and moved in with his mother. Did she know his father had passed away a little more than a year after she had—no. She didn't die. After she … faked her death.

That had to be it. She was alive. She had to know that the state department had reported her dead. She didn't correct them. She'd made no attempt to contact him or their children.

Chris felt anger brewing inside him. His teeth clenched. With a groan, he sat up and buried his face in his hands.

Blair was ambitious. She wanted to be more than a wife and mother. She aspired to move up the ladder in the state department—but always, it seemed, just when she was on the brink of a great position or a promotion, someone else always seemed to swoop in ahead of her to snag it.

Either that or she blew it somehow. During one job interview, she was well on her way to the position until the last interview when the manager pushed the wrong buttons. Blair was usually a calm person. She would keep everything bottled up inside until someone pushed the wrong button. Then, she'd explode.

Since Blair had been so unhappy with her professional life, Chris and the children tried to make her home life stress free. The endeavor was fruitless. A failed homework assignment, a forgotten chore, an abrupt out of town case that meant juggling of schedules—any of those was enough to fuel an explosion of Blair's pent-up frustration.

As much as Chris hated to admit it, the Matheson home became much calmer after Blair had gone to Switzerland. It was difficult being a single dad, but even that was easier than walking on eggshells.

Still, he loved her, not just because she was the mother of his children, but because he knew the woman underneath it all. She did love her family—in her own way.

He got up from the bed and went to the dresser. He opened the jewelry box and dug through the few items inside until he found the Rolex. It was plain as far as designer watches go. The gold watch was as shiny as it had been on the day Ivy had given it to him at Emma's birthday party.

What a waste of money? She had to know I'd never wear it.

He turned it over to read the inscription.

Darling Chris,
Fly Away with me.
Your Angel, Blair.

Weird.

Chris had called Blair by the usual pet names. Dear. Sweetheart. Darling. Never "Angel." *Where did she come up with that? It must have been on her mind. Most likely the Rolex was an impulse buy when she'd bought the clock for Emma. At least she was thinking about me.*

Narrowing his eyes, he studied the engraving. Below the last line there were tiny numbers. They were about half the size as the letters in the message. He had noticed them when he first received the watch:

06-28-04

Their wedding date. Another slap in the face because their wedding date was the twenty-sixth, not the twenty-eighth.

Maybe it was the jeweler's mistake. Maybe not.

He tossed the watch back into the jewelery box and slammed the lid shut.

Even so, she was his wife and he had grieved her death. So did their children.

They grieved over their loss and then moved on with their lives. He had reconnected with the love of his life and things were going well. He gave horseback riding lessons to Helen's daughter Sierra every Saturday. It was something the two of them shared—a love for horses. They had been conspiring to convince Helen to allow Sierra to have her own horse. He could see making plans with Helen to join their two families together.

Out of the blue, Blair is back and there goes all of my plans.

Chris lifted his head and looked at his reflection in the mirror.

Blair's back and running from some very dangerous people. Who?

There was one thing he did know. He had to protect her—no matter what it took.

Chris reached for the burner phone that Murphy had given to him. Murphy still had his phone after confiscating it the night before. *He'd better give that back to me—along with my suit.* That meant he didn't have his contacts.

He went to his laptop to search his contact list. It was questionable if he still had Ivy Dunleavy's information. Even if he had it, he couldn't be sure it hadn't changed since he had last spoken to her.

Ivy and her husband had been friendly and comforting at Blair's funeral. Then, something changed.

The Dunleavys had dropped out of their lives. It wasn't a huge surprise. Ivy had been Blair's friend. Apparently, with Blair gone, there was no reason for the Dunleavys to remain in the Mathesons' lives.

The hectic life of being a single father did not give Chris time or concern to worry about it—until he had run into Ivy at the shopping mall the Christmas season following Blair's death. It took him a moment to recognize the brunette donning a leather coat with fur trim, laden down with shopping bags, as she ran out of the department store and slammed into Chris, causing her to drop one of her bags.

Chris found his voice first after the initial shock of the collision. "Ivy?" He was surprised to see the color drain from her face.

She gazed at him with wide eyes.

Must be guilt for dropping out of our lives. Chris knelt to collect the items that had scattered from the fallen bag before they got kicked into traffic—a pair of earrings, a scarf, and a bottle of perfume. "How are things going?"

"Fine," he heard her say with a meek tone. "And you?"

"Okay. Busy. I'm trying to make Christmas merry without Blair, which is going to be hard for the girls." With everything collected, he rose to his feet and dropped each item into the bag—pausing when he noticed the bottle of perfume. "White Shoulders. That was Blair's favorite perfume. I bought her a bottle every Christmas."

"I'm sure you did." Ivy snatched the bottle and dropped it into the bag. She closed the top and held it tight in her grasp.

Chris was startled by the spark of anger in her eyes. "How are things in your neck of the woods, Ivy?"

"Fine."

"Emma says you've hired a live-in nanny for Hannah."

The anger in her eyes turned to fear. "When was Emma talking to Hannah?"

"Sheerah's birthday party last month," Chris said. "They spent the whole party catching up. Emma really misses Hannah. I know we're both busy, but we should try to arrange for the two of them to get together more often. It's bad enough that Emma lost her mother. She shouldn't lose one of her best friends, too."

Ivy backed away from him. "I know, but things are really busy—"

"After the holidays." He stepped toward her. "How about if I give you a call. Hannah can come for a sleep over?"

"Sure, give me a call." Ivy spun on her high heels. "I'm late. Call me and we'll do lunch." She trotted away as fast as her heels could carry her.

As she had instructed, he called several times after the holidays, but never did she return his call. He didn't expect her to.

Chris sensed that she was afraid of him but couldn't understand why. He didn't see that fear before Blair had gone away to Switzerland. Nor did he see it at the funeral.

What happened between the funeral and Christmas—a matter of five months—to make you so afraid of me, Ivy?

As Chris pressed the phone number he found on his laptop into the burner phone, he was determined to ask her just that.

One advantage of the burner phone was that there was no caller ID. For that reason, Ivy Dunleavy picked up on the third ring. "This is Ivy Dunleavy."

"Hello, Ivy Dunleavy. This is Chris Matheson."

There was an audible gasp from the other end of the phone.

"Judging by that, I guess you remember me," he said in a pleasant tone.

Her tone was sharp—accusing—when she replied, "Where's Blair? What have you done to her?"

Chapter Ten

"Nice to have good friends in high places," Jacqui said to Bruce after they breezed past the security checkpoint at the Russell Senate Office Building on Constitution Avenue. Familiar with the building's layout, Bruce led her to the stairs.

"Keaton's office is on the second floor."

Bruce usually donned slacks and sweaters or button-down shirts over oxfords. While always stylish, Jacqui also leaned toward a casual style in clean jeans or slacks or a loose skirt.

For their trip to the city, they had dressed to impress. Bruce traded in his sweater for a sportscoat and tie. Jacqui opted for a steel blue fitted women's suit with pencil skirt and heels under a matching wool cape coat.

Senator Keaton's office was at the end of the corridor. Bruce held open the door for Jacqui. As they entered, a woman's shrill voice blared into the reception area from the corner office.

"Don't underestimate my power, Graham! If you don't get your senators in line to approve Cross, I'll do everything in my power to ruin all of you!"

Behind the reception desk, the administrative assistant rolled her eyes.

Senator Graham Keaton's calm voice was a direct contrast to his visitor's hysteria. "I never said we weren't going to confirm Cross. I simply said we needed to wait and see. That's what we do with every nominee."

"You told the *Times* that you were concerned that he was too young to head up the Central Intelligence Agency! Of course, you and I both know your real objection."

"Which is?"

"You're racist!"

"Racist? He's a white male. I thought *you* considered all white males the enemy."

"He's Chinese-American," the senator said.

"Give me a break!"

"His great-grandmother on his mother's side was from China," Senator Douglas said.

There was a silence from the office. Jacqui and Bruce exchanged questioning glances before Senator Keaton asked the same question they had. "So? Why would any of the senators on my side of the aisle object to his nomination because of who his great-grandfather slept with a hundred years ago?"

"Precisely! Why would they?"

"You must see it as an issue since you brought it up. I'm more interested in knowing what terrorist groups he's been friendly with than what Ancestry.com has found in his DNA—unless he's an alien from outer space." He gasped. "You don't think …"

Senator Douglas uttered a long string of profanity.

"Don't get your panties in a knot over it, Kimberly." Senator Keaton laughed.

With a fury-filled shriek, Senator Douglas flew out of the office. Bruce barely escaped being body slammed during her exit.

Senator Keaton's laughter floated out of his office. "Like I really care if his ancestors are space aliens—unless they weren't properly documented."

"She's mad as hell." A fresh-faced young man in a sweater and slacks followed the gray-haired man into the reception area.

"Of course, she is. Kimberly has been mad since the day she was born. I don't know why she's so upset—just because I'm not jumping up and down praising the virtues of Daniel Cross. I'm doing my job—waiting to see what his qualifications are before making my decision. But Kimberly—she sees a candidate with a drop of non-white blood—therefore, he's more than qualified for the job!"

"Isn't that racism, too?" Jacqui asked. "Looking down on a whole class of people because their skin is white is just as bad as looking down on a class because their skin isn't."

"It's only racism or sexism if you're opposing Douglas." Senator Keaton flashed Bruce a broad grin and held out his hand. "Bruce Harris. You son of a gun. What are you doing here?" He shot a sly grin in Jacqui's direction. "Don't tell me you left your wife."

"Oh, no," Bruce said. "I'm much smarter than that. This is Jacqui Guilfoyle. She's a friend of mine. We belong to the same book club."

Senator Keaton introduced them to the young man. "This is my assistant, Oliver Hansen." He added as Oliver and Bruce shook hands. "Oliver, Bruce Harris is someone that you'd like to get to know. Not only was he Virginia's greatest state attorney general, but he also graduated top of his class from the University of Virginia's law school." He told Bruce, "Oliver graduated this past year."

"And he's already on Capitol Hill. Are you eying the Oval Office, son?"

"I'll be happy with attorney general." Oliver shook his head with a humble smile.

Jacqui shot a glance in Bruce's direction. His eyes met hers. While Oliver's words stated modest ambitions, his body language revealed loftier goals.

"Do you have a few minutes for an old friend?" When the senator paused to check his watch in response to Bruce's question, he added in a low tone. "It's about a certain letter you received."

The senator squinted at him.

"Stephens is dead," Bruce said in a soft whisper.

The color drained from Oliver's face.

Senator Keaton asked, "How—"

"We believe we know the anonymous source who'd sent the letter, but we need to be sure," Jacqui said.

Senator Keaton led them into his office and closed the door. To Jacqui's surprise, Oliver followed them. Aware that the senator's assistant's duty was to be Keaton's right hand, Bruce was not surprised.

After shutting the door, Oliver dropped into the first chair he came to. He swallowed. "Is—is Anonymous—"

"We hope not," Jacqui said. "We're trying to locate her."

Oliver was breathing hard. "How did Stephens—"

"It's an open investigation," Bruce said. "I can tell you that Stephens never made it to the meeting with Anonymous. Whoever killed him knew that you had assigned Stephens to investigate the matter and meet with her. They bugged his house. Once they knew the details of the meeting, a hit man murdered him and took his place to intercept her."

"That means whoever is behind the risk to national security got wind of her letter and found out about Stephens investigating the matter," Jacqui said. "Who knew about it?"

From behind his oversized oak desk, Senator Keaton looked around the office. "Only me, Oliver who read the letter first, and Stephens."

"We were told that there was a cell phone in the envelope along with the letter," Jacqui said.

"She would call that phone to verify her credibility," Oliver said.

"Who had access to it?" Bruce asked. "The phone could have been cloned or tapped."

"I gave everything, envelope and all, to the senator," Oliver said. "He handed everything to Stephens."

"Can we see the letter?" Bruce asked.

"What role are you playing in this investigation?" Senator Keaton asked. "With all due respect, Harris, Stephens was a good man. Obviously, there was a leak somewhere here in my office. I never even told any of the other senators on my side of the aisle about the matter because I wanted to know if Anonymous was the real deal. Now that I find out people are being killed—"

"Which is why I want to examine the letter." Bruce held his hand out, palm up, and crooked his fingers.

With a snort, Senator Keaton unlocked the bottom drawer of his desk and yanked it open. He extracted a folder, plopped it onto the center of his desk and opened it. He handed the letter, which had a padded envelope stapled to it, to Bruce. "The original. Including the envelope with the post mark. I gave Stephens a copy and the phone."

Both Bruce and Jacqui put on their reading glasses.

Bruce took the letter while Jacqui examined the envelope. "Where did Christopher say Blair's best friend lived?" she asked. "You know, the one who married the pompous business attorney?"

"Chantilly, Virginia."

Holding out the envelope to him, she pointed a manicured fingernail tipped in white at the postmark, which read, "Chantilly, VA."

Together, they read the letter printed on a single sheet of paper.

Dear Senator Keaton,

I am writing to you in regard to the nomination of Daniel Cross for Director of the Central Intelligence Agency. This nomination to a most sensitive post, putting him in charge of a major intelligence gathering agency, has me extremely distressed because I know for a fact that Daniel Cross is a traitor to the United States.

To accuse someone of treason against their country is not something that someone should do lightly. I also know that making such an accusation against someone with such powerful people behind him would be a dangerous endeavor.

Everyone else who has tried to expose Cross for his crimes against our country has died.

However, as an American citizen, I cannot continue to hide in the shadows and do nothing now that it is apparent that the job of protecting our nation's intelligence information is being placed in the hands of a traitor. I am duty bound to come forward, even as I know that doing so will put my life in jeopardy.

Of course, you will not act on this information without verifying that I am not a crackpot. For that purpose, I have enclosed a phone. I will be calling.

Sincerely,
Anonymous

Everyone else who has tried to expose Cross for his crimes against our country has died," Jacqui read.

"Considering that all Stephens did was talk to her on the phone," Senator Keaton said, "I guess it's safe to say Anonymous wasn't exaggerating."

"Nice ride." The last thing Francine expected to see when she turned the corner in Dupont Circle after exiting the metro was Murphy climbing out of the back of a white stretch limousine. "I thought secret agents had to keep low profiles."

With a toothy grin, Murphy waved farewell to the limousine easing into traffic. "You can't get any lower of a profile than hitching a ride."

"In a limo?"

Murphy slid his arm across Francine's shoulders. "Admit it, Francine, if you saw this face—" He gestured at his attractive, pretty boy face. "—on the side of the road with a thumb sticking out, you'd stop to give me a ride, wouldn't you?"

She looked him up and down. "I'd take you as far as you'd be willing to go and then some, Blue Eyes."

With a laugh, Murphy opened and held the door to the busy café for her. As she stepped past him, she added with a grin, "You remind me of my ex-husband."

"Was he a charmer, too?" Murphy followed her inside.

"He was a pathological liar," Francine said. "But damn, if he didn't look good doing it."

Murphy scanned the faces of the patrons who filled the restaurant. They were an equal mixture of professionals and students from in and around the capital area.

"Is your friend here?" Francine peered around for their contact, even though she had no idea what he looked like.

Murphy waded into the sea of the customers and turned the corner around the service counter to a small sitting area where Tristan frequently hung out. The area consisted of two loveseats facing each other with a coffee table between them. Murphy spotted him as soon as he broke through the throng of customers.

The lanky young man wearing dark framed eyeglasses had reclined across one of the loveseats with a laptop. There was a travel mug, the remnants of a consumed expresso and two plates showing evidence of a recent meal, plus a tablet and a cell phone scattered across the table.

"Hey, Trist." Tapping him on the shoulder, Murphy rounded the edge of the sofa and came to an abrupt halt.

Tristan looked up from the screen. "What's up?"

Murphy turned his back. "I can't believe you brought *her* here to a public place."

"She's allowed. Monique is my emotional support animal." With a sly grin, Tristan stroked the huge tarantula resting on his chest.

Even though he was familiar with Tristan's pet, Murphy could not bear to look at the black hairy spider that, at eight inches in diameter, was the size of a dinner plate. "Are you kidding me?" He shot a glance at the plastic case on the coffee table which Tristan used to transport Monique. Sure enough, there was numerous stickers announcing "support animal" on them.

"Certified and everything." Tristan extracted a plastic card from his cell phone case and held it out in Murphy's direction. "Here's her card."

Murphy refused to examine the card. To do so would mean laying his eyes on the huge spider.

"Monique gets bored sitting in her tank all day." Tristan returned the card to its case. "She likes to get out and explore."

"Does she have to explore a coffee shop?" Murphy looked around at the other patrons in the shop, none of whom seemed to mind the spider.

"Everyone here knows me," Tristan said. "I practically live here. And they all know Monique. As a matter of fact, she has a calming effect on them, too."

"She doesn't have that effect on me." Murphy was feeling anything but calm as he saw the creature making her way from Tristan's chest up to his shoulder.

"Sounds like a personal problem to me. Have you talked to someone about that?"

"Yes, your sister, and Jessie insists that it's a stage you'll outgrow."

"Oh, Murphy, if I didn't have Monique with me, I wouldn't be able to talk to you right now." Tristan's tone dripped with sincerity.

"Bull!"

"That's my story and I'm sticking to it." Tristan looked over his shoulder. "I thought you were bringing someone else to help us with the case."

Reminded of Francine, Murphy craned his neck to search for her. "Yes. She's an older woman. Francine. Can you put Monique in the box, so you don't freak her out?"

Before Tristan could object, Murphy dove back into the crowd.

Taking in the restaurant's atmosphere, Francine didn't notice that she was alone. A people watcher, she enjoyed the diversity of the patrons—young college students kicking back with their games to stressed out mothers with young children taking advantage of the free wi-fi to busy professionals dressed in athletic togs taking advantage of the brisk but sunny Saturday morning to get some exercise.

Francine spotted one professional in particular.

Clad in biking pants with matching jacket, he had blue-black hair and dark eyes. Despite the build of a much younger man, Francine knew him to be in his early forties. With a brisk motion, he stepped away from the service counter with his travel mug in hand and swung around to the condiment station. There, he peeled the lid off the mug.

His attractive features had been splashed all over the the television and Internet ever since the President had nominated Daniel Cross to lead the Central Intelligence Agency.

The media portrayed Daniel Cross as Tom Clancy's Jack Ryan character brought to life. After his boss had been murdered in a car bomb with the ambassador in Lithuania, Cross had made it his mission to use his skills as an intelligence analyst to track down the terrorist group responsible.

A young man picked up his backpack and magazine and got up from a table next to the condiment station. He stepped over to the counter and pried the lid off his mug, which was identical to Cross's. He then tore the corner off a packet of sugar, dumped it into the cup, and replaced the lid. Leaving the mug on the counter, he turned to toss the magazine back onto the table.

In the instant his back was turned, Daniel Cross scooped up the other man's mug and headed for the main exit behind Francine. Without a second glance, the younger man picked up the other mug and left through the side door.

Francine was still in shock with what she had witnessed when Daniel Cross breezed past her and out the door where he extracted his bike from the rack, slipped the mug into the cup holder, put on his riding helmet, and sped away.

Did I really just see that?

A hand grasped her arm in a firm grip which caused her to cry out.

"It's me!" Murphy hushed her. He smiled at the patrons looking their way.

She clutched his arm. "You totally aren't going to believe what I just saw."

"Tell me over here." He jerked a thumb over his shoulder. "I need to warn you, don't freak out."

"Why would I freak out?"

"Tristan's eccentric." He led her by the hand to the sitting area. "He's brought a friend with him."

As they rounded the loveseat, Francine let out a gasp upon seeing the tarantula on Tristan's shoulder. "Is that—"

"A tarantula," Murphy said. "Tristan's emotional support animal."

"Her name is Monique," Tristan said.

Francine was surprised to see how young he appeared. He was younger than Murphy, who she gauged to be barely out of his mid-twenties. Tristan was in his early twenties. She concluded that he appeared that much younger due to his lean build clad in khaki slacks and a baggy striped shirt. Then, she told herself that everyone looked youthful to her.

Francine dropped onto the sofa next to him. "Can I pet her?"

"She loves attention." Tristan smiled up at Murphy, whose eyes grew wide at the older woman's fascination with the huge spider.

Francine gingerly placed her hand on Tristan's shoulder and urged Monique to crawl up her arm. "My grandson named his Thanos. He's a male. Just a little bit bigger than Monique." She peered closely at the spider. "She is a beautiful girl. Much calmer than Thanos. If you brought Thanos here, he'd jump into someone's drink." She stuck her other hand out to him. "I'm Francine by the way."

"Tristan Faraday."

Their hands remained clasped as Francine smiled. "Are you any relation to Mac Faraday? He was a homicide detective here in Washington before he came into an inheritance and became filthy rich."

Tristan gave her the standard eye roll. "That would be my dad."

"I worked with him," she said. "Well, he wouldn't say we exactly worked *together*. He'd probably tell you that I hounded him into looking into a murder case. A couple of young men had been convicted of murdering a college girl. The police had a confession. The mother of one of the suspects contacted me for her last hope because her son told her the confession had been coerced. I talked to the young man in prison and I believed him. Mac Faraday was the best detective in D.C., so I went to him. It took some persuading to get him to look into the case. He'd call it nagging. But I convinced him that we were right and then the two of us found the real killer and those young men were let go."

"Dad doesn't work with the media," Tristan said.

"That's what he told me, too, but I didn't give him a choice." She scrunched up her nose while petting Monique. "He pretends to be a mean old dog, but inside he's really a pussy cat."

"Funny, I've never seen any sign of a pussy cat in him," Murphy said.

Tristan leaned in to tell her, "Murphy makes it a point to sleep with one eye open when he visits Dad."

Sensing she was missing something, Francine cocked her head at him.

"Dad is the last person anyone would want for a father-in-law," Tristan said.

"Father-in-law?" Francine looked over at Murphy. "You're Jessica's husband?"

"That would be me."

"What a small world." Monique tickled her neck as Francine turned back to Tristan. "So you're Monique's dad and Nigel's guardian?"

"Someone has to keep a leash on Nigel," Tristan said. "Sometimes, he does have a mind of his own." He gestured at Murphy, who had taken a seat on the sofa across from them. "How do you know, Murph?"

"We met at my book club meeting last night."

Tristan's eyebrows rose. He adjusted his eye glasses while looking at Murphy. "You *read*?"

"Stop being a smartass."

"Did I just see Daniel Cross?" Francine pointed in the direction of the condiment station.

"Most likely," Tristan said. "He comes in every Saturday morning at nine o'clock like clockwork." He glanced at his watch. "Yep, right on schedule. I don't know if he lives around here. He comes on his bike."

"Every Saturday morning?"

"This is Dupont Circle," Tristan said. "Sit here all day and you'll see half of the faces on any news cable station."

"I'm talking about the director of the intelligence directorate at the CIA," Francine said in a hushed tone, "passing Lord knows what to Lord knows who."

Tristan and Murphy exchanged long silent glances.

Wordlessly, Tristan left it up to Murphy to respond. "Are you—"

"Hey, I was an investigative journalist back before you two were being potty trained," she said. "I know all about how to covertly hand off information, pay offs, whatever, and

I just saw him either handing off information or collecting it from some guy."

"Maybe he was collecting information about an adversary from an informant," Tristan said.

"Isn't he kind of high up the ladder in the agency to be collecting information?" Murphy asked.

"You should know, being with the CIA and all." Francine put her hand under Monique for her to climb onto.

Tristan opened his mouth to ask what she was talking about but stopped when he caught Murphy's eye and a toss of his head for him to remain silent. Instead, Tristan picked up his tablet and opened an application. "What did this guy that Cross supposedly passed government secrets to look like?"

"I didn't say they were government secrets," Francine said.

"What else would Cross have been slipping to him?" Murphy asked.

"His phone number?" Tristan arched an eyebrow at them. "He's not married. I hear he's a womanizer."

"Why would he have given his phone number in such a clandestine manner?" Francine asked. "The guy he gave it to was medium build. Khaki slacks. Blue button-down shirt. Untucked. Loafers."

"You just described half of the people in the room." With a grin, Tristan handed his tablet to Murphy and Francine.

A video was displayed on the screen. The paused image was a downward angle from the corner of the café. Daniel Cross was at the condiment counter. The man with the magazine was seated at the table next to it.

"How?" Francine looked up to the ceiling and spotted the hidden security camera. Her voice dropped to a whisper. "You hacked into their security system?"

"*Hacked* is such a dirty word."

Murphy pressed the screen to play the security video. It happened exactly as Francine had recalled. Leaving his mug behind, Daniel Cross took the other man's. There was no moment of distraction, eliminating any possibility of him taking the other mug by mistake.

"Most likely he's a journalist," Tristan said. "Cross has been on the news a lot lately."

"He's on the brink of becoming a member of the President's cabinet. He didn't get where he is by being stupid. To suddenly leak information to the media now would be idiocy." Murphy handed the tablet back to him. "Can Nigel run facial recognition to identify the other guy?"

"Facial recognition?" Francine's eyes widened before narrowing as she turned to Murphy. "What exactly do you—"

Murphy shushed her. "Write anything about what you see and hear, and I'll tell your children what you've been doing at the library after dark."

Her lip pursed together. "You *wouldn't*."

His eyes locked on hers. "*Try* me."

"That must be *some* library." Tristan's fingers flew across the screen of the tablet while eying them from over the top of it. "The other guy is a regular here. I see him practically every day. This facial recognition will take some time. I'll probably have better luck identifying him the old-fashioned way." He peered at them over the top of his glasses. "Asking one of the servers. Even so, we can't just assume Cross was doing anything illegal."

"If it was on the up and up, then he would have just handed whatever it was to him." Francine slipped Monique onto his shoulder and stroked her back.

"True." Tristan stroked the spider who returned to her favorite spot against his neck.

"In the meantime," Murphy said, "what have you and Nigel been able to figure out about Blair Matheson and the state department? Did they help her fake her death or make a mistake?"

Tristan cast a tentative glance in Francine's direction. He didn't feel comfortable revealing Nigel's capability to extract highly sensitive information from the most secure government systems to outsiders.

"I'll take responsibility for her discretion," Murphy said.

Hesitant, Tristan remained silent.

"Seriously, Tristan," Murphy said. "I'm not going to let you get into trouble. A death squad came after Blair Matheson's husband and me last night. I lost two teammates."

"I know," Tristan said with a sigh.

"You didn't tell Jessie, did you?"

Tristan shook his head. "The last thing she needs right now is to worry about you." He sat up. "Here's what Nigel and I figured out. Based on what we were able to find out in the Office of Personnel Management records, Blair Matheson was killed in a terrorist attack in France and declared dead. They paid out death benefits, the whole nine yards. Her records were sealed and closed. The federal government doesn't do that if you're not dead."

"But if they faked her death," Murphy asked, "wouldn't they still do that to make it look like she was dead?"

"If they knew she was still alive, they'd have her on some sort of payroll, wouldn't they?" Tristan asked.

"Years ago, I did an expose on the federal witness protection program," Francine said. "The government pays out an average of $60,000 a year to witnesses in the program until they are able to get jobs and support themselves. So, if Chris's wife, who was not a criminal, was still working for the federal government, she'd have to collect a paycheck and there'd have to be a record of it somewhere."

"As we were saying," Murphy said, "if the federal government knew Blair was still alive and she faked her death for a mission—"

"Somewhere in the federal records, there would be a cross-reference connecting Blair's new identity to the one who had passed away," Tristan said. "For retirement records—whatever. Nigel found no cross-reference. We think it was an honest mistake. Blair was identified based on her identification being found in a bag among the debris from the terrorist attack. The bag was in the possession of a woman generally matching Blair's description. Unfortunately, this woman was hit head on by the truck that plowed through the crowd. Her body was badly mangled, and the bag's strap was in her hand."

"Why didn't they run a DNA test?" Francine asked.

"DNA tests are expensive. They only run them if they have to," Tristan said. "Blair Matheson was on annual leave. Granted, she took it at the last minute, but she was. It was Bastille Day. A holiday. Blair wasn't home. Her passport was found in a bag with a woman matching her description. Circumstantial evidence suggested the woman was Blair Matheson."

Francine crossed her arms. "If the state department is so innocent, why did they cremate her body so that Chris couldn't see that it wasn't her?"

"Mistakes do happen," Tristan said. "I found news report of a family here in the States complaining that the state department *did not* cremate their grandmother who had been killed in the same attack. Their last name was Mahadev. They were Hindu and they had requested immediate cremation on religious grounds."

"Matheson," Murphy said. "Mahadev. The names aren't exactly the same, but close enough that it could have been an honest mix-up."

"Not everything is always a grand conspiracy," Tristan said.

"Okay," Murphy said. "The state department made a mistake. They thought Blair was dead."

"But Blair had to know she was still alive," Francine said, "but she told no one."

"And she was overseas," Murphy said. "She needed money and a passport to enter back into the United States."

"Didn't you say you were missing an operative about that same time period?" Tristan asked with a cryptic tone.

Murphy's eyes met his.

"The missing agent was close to an Australian agent, who was killed in the same terrorist attack that Blair Matheson was supposed to have died in," Tristan said. "Now, Nigel's access to Australian intelligence records is very limited. However, less than a week after the terrorist attack, a woman flew into Dulles International Airport from France with an Australian diplomatic passport." He handed the tablet to Murphy. "Her name was Charlotte Nesbitt. According to immigration records, she's still in the country."

"How did this woman come to your attention?" Francine asked while studying the state department data on Charlotte Nesbitt, which included a picture of a pretty woman with blond hair. Francine wished she knew what Blair looked like.

Tristan took the tablet and swept his finger across the screen. He handed it back to them. "Her picture is the same one that was on Blair's passport."

Indeed, the image on both passports was the same.

"Once Nigel and I concluded that the Australian agent was connected to our missing operative, we jump to the conclusion that the American agent went through her Australian friend to get Blair a new identity."

"Via a new ID to come home," Murphy said. "Blair survived the terrorist attack, went off the grid, and came home under the radar. Whatever got her boss killed was so dangerous that she's stayed off the grid." He extracted his vibrating phone from its case.

"But recently she decided to come back on the grid," Francine said. "What happened to make her take such a risk?"

"We'll have to ask her." Tristan peeled Monique off his shoulder, set her on his chest, and stroked her fur. "There's no address for Charlotte Nesbitt in the database, which is suspicious. Not uncommon, but suspicious. We put a flag on her passport. If she so much as gets pulled over for a speeding ticket, we'll find her."

Murphy answered the phone. "Lieutenant Thornton here."

The sultry voice of his commanding officer said, "Lieutenant Thornton, there's been a development."

At first, Chris was uncertain if he had heard Ivy correctly. "Where's Blair? What did you do to her?"

He looked at the phone in his hand and shook his head. He'd been right. Blair went to Ivy after being declared dead. Ivy knew all along. That's why she had never returned his calls or attempts to get their daughters together for playdates. She couldn't risk him finding out.

He wanted to reach through the phone and throttle Ivy for the deception. Deciding it was best to walk off his mad, he paced the length of his bedroom. He placed the phone to his ear.

"You tell me where she is, Ivy. You wouldn't be asking me that if you thought Blair was dead—like the girls and I have. Why didn't you tell us?"

"Like you don't know."

"No, I don't know. Tell me."

"Oh, your devoted husband and father act won't work with me, Chris. Blair told me—*everything.*"

"Told you everything about what?"

"She had to fake her death to stay alive! Yes, she'd been staying here because she was scared to death of you. She'd been afraid to leave the house. But yesterday, she sucked up enough courage to go out to spend the day downtown—only to run into you. She was terrified when she called me. I tried to tell her to call the police—as much good as it would have done since you have half of the cops in your pocket."

"What are you talking about?"

She hissed through the phone at him. "So help me—if you tracked her down and killed her—Stu will do everything in his power to have you locked up for good."

Click.

Chris went numb. Ivy sounded sincere in her fury. He pieced together her accusations. Blair was afraid of him. More than afraid of him. She thought he was going to kill her. He was the one she had been hiding from.

Where was that coming from? I've never touched her or any woman in anything other than a loving manner. Well, there had been a couple of women during my career in law enforcement who I have had to slap around—but that was only when they tried to kill me first. And there were a couple who I killed—but none of that counts. Does it?

The burner phone in his hand vibrated. Hoping it would be Murphy with some answers, Chris answered on the first ring.

"Murphy?"

"Chris, it's me." His tone was more serious than usual. He paused. "Chris, I'm sorry."

Chris dropped his head. He rubbed his face with his hand.

"They've found Blair's body," Murphy said.

Chapter Eleven

As soon as she learned about the discovery of Blair's body, Doris jumped up from the table where she and Elliott had been talking and followed Chris into the mudroom. Before she could shrug into her coat, he took it from her.

"You can't go." He returned it to the hook.

"I'm not going to let you go through this alone." She snatched her coat from where he had hung it. "I wasn't there for you the first time Blair died—"

"Yes, you were." Chris grabbed the tunic.

"Not physically." She seized one of the sleeves. "I should have driven out to Reston to be with you the second you called," she said while attempting to yank it out of his grasp. "I don't know what I was thinking that I had to be here because of that open house at the animal shelter. You needed me!"

Chris released his hold on the coat, which caused her to tumble back into Elliott. "Mom, I'm a grown man." He wrapped both arms around her and held her tight. "I can handle anything that anyone throws at me. You came out after the open house, and the girls and I didn't doubt for a second that you weren't with us emotionally." He pulled away and looked into her eyes. "You have always been there for me and the girls." He took the coat from her. "Now, the girls need you more than ever." He returned it to the hook. "Emma and Nikki are coming home at noon. You need to be here for them."

"What are you going to tell them?" Elliott asked while putting on his coat.

"Nothing for now," Chris said. "I have no idea how I'm going to explain it. I need more answers. How can I expect them to understand it if I don't?"

"She was dead before, and now she's dead again," Elliott said. "Maybe you can get away with not saying anything."

Chris shook his head. "I promised all of them a long time ago that I will never keep any secrets from them. If they ever want the truth, the good, the bad, the ugly, they can come to me and I will give it to them straight. I'm not breaking that promise."

The thought of her granddaughters discovering that their mother had allowed them to believe she had died caused Doris to be overcome with a wave of emotion. Her lips trembled. "How did she die this time?"

"They found her body dumped in Lake Audubon," Chris said while slipping on his coat. "A runner found her. That's all I know."

"You used to live on Lake Audubon." Doris's brow furrowed.

"They found her at the end of the same block where we used to live."

"Could she have gone there looking for you after seeing you on the metro?"

"Anything's possible."

"I'm coming with you." Elliott gave Doris a quick kiss on the lips. "I'll keep you in the loop about what's happening, my love." He winked at her.

"Hi, Tristan."

Tristan almost dropped his tablet when Chloe, the server behind the counter, approached his sofa from behind. That was one thing he didn't like about Chloe. He could never hear her coming. Always, she would be watching him with her big glassy eyes. Her tone oozed of so much sweetness that he felt like he was going to go into insulin overload.

She had even startled Monique, who hopped from his shoulder down onto his chest.

Hoping she didn't see the café's security recordings on his computer screen, Tristan snapped down the lid.

She pointed at his empty mug. "Would you like another expresso?"

He considered her offer deciding a seventh expresso would be overdoing it. He turned around to decline her offer when he spotted a familiar face behind her.

He's back! Tristan looked at the time on his phone. Two hours after leaving the restaurant with Daniel Cross's travel mug, the young man was back. Tristan rose from his seat to watch as he moved through the café, which had thinned out since the morning rush. Their suspect took a seat at the same bistro table he had been sitting at previously.

"Sorry, Chloe, but I just remembered that I have to be somewhere."

Quickly, Tristan placed Monique in her plastic box, fitted with airholes, and packed his backpack. With a quick glance over his shoulder, he saw that the young man was reading the same magazine he had left before.

Wait for it. If he keeps to his routine, then the switch off will happen in a few minutes—just enough time for me to get into position.

He placed Monique's box on top of his belongings in the backpack and zipped it only enough to hold everything inside. Checking over his shoulder, he stacked the used cups and dishes onto his serving tray and carried it to the trash, where he took his time clearing them.

Out of the corner of his eye, he saw a red-headed woman with a black travel mug in her hand step from the service counter to the condiment station. She removed its lid.

On cue, the young man went to the condiment station. He set his mug next to hers and removed the lid. He turned to toss the magazine onto the table, and then picked up her mug and lid. He placed the lid onto the mug and made for the side door.

Reaching the door at the same time, Tristan held it open for him. The young man gave him a polite nod.

Several inches shorter and slightly built, Tristan thought he didn't appear to be much older than himself. He may not have even been twenty years old.

Once he was outside, the young man turned right to continue down P Street toward Dupont Circle. Tristan paused on the street to adjust his backpack in order to not appear too obvious while following the man with the travel mug.

From his position behind him, Tristan saw that he carried the mug in his hand, which was interesting because his backpack had a sleeve made specifically for holding mugs. Tristan's own pack had such a sleeve.

He could be carrying it because he wants to drink it.

After two blocks, Tristan saw that he was not drinking it.

He's delivering it to someone. Who?

At the corner of 20th Street NW, the young man stopped at the newsstand and picked up a newspaper. He set the mug on the counter to pay the vendor. Then, he walked away without the cup.

For a second, Tristan was torn. Should he follow the young man from the restaurant or stay with the mug?

Stay with the mug! Tristan swore he heard his father's voice scream inside his head.

Trying to appear as casual as possible, Tristan stepped up to the newsstand to read the headlines.

"Can I help you?" The grossly overweight, stubble-faced owner of the newsstand picked up the mug and set it behind the counter.

"Just looking."

After several minutes of the man glaring at him, Tristan bought a paleontology magazine and sat on a bench nearby where he pretended to read it. With one eye on the newsstand, he hoped the travel mug would start travelling again soon.

It was close to an hour later before the newsstand owner placed the mug back on the counter. Moments later, a woman on a bike rode by. As she past the stand, she reached out, snatched the mug, and peddled away.

Damn!

Tristan took out his phone and snapped her picture while trying to follow her as best he could. His fingers flew across the screen as he opened up Nigel and ordered him to tap into traffic security cameras to track her.

"Where is she, Nigel?" Tristan gasped into the phone while chasing the bike.

"She is going into Dupont Circle Metro."

"Swee-eet!" He slowed to a comfortable pace. "It's the weekend. The trains are running twenty minutes apart. Which direction is she going, Nigel?"

"Red Line heading to Glenmont."

At the metro station, Tristan used his monthly fare card and descended the stairs on the side for the trains heading deeper into the city. He hoped she was not planning to get off at the Metro Center, the subway hub of the city. Four subway lines converged at the center to take travelers in every direction. If she got off there, Tristan knew it would be a challenge to follow her.

Late Saturday morning, the subway stop was sparsely populated. Tristan easily spotted the girl with the bike standing on the platform.

The travel mug was in a mount on the handlebars of the bike. *If* it was the same mug. Aware that he had lost sight of it, Tristan had to accept the fact that she could have already made the hand off.

Then, Tristan recalled that she simply took the mug from the newsstand. There wasn't a switch. She didn't give the newsstand operator a mug to replace that one. Therefore, odds were, it was the same mug.

It has to be the same mug.

The train arrived, and she climbed aboard. She took the first seat next to the doors with her bike propped up in front of her.

Trying not to appear too obvious, Tristan waited for everyone else to board before sauntering on. The train was moderately filled—mostly with tourists. Tristan stood at the pole directly next to her bike, which was practically resting against his leg.

"Red Line to Glenmont Station." Chimes signaled the doors closing.

The train rolled out of the station.

"Next station. Farragut North," the automated announcer said.

If she was planning to get off at the Metro Center, which Tristan was willing to bet money she was, he only had minutes to act. He adjusted his backpack and opened the back to check on Monique, who was curled up inside her box. Reaching deep into the bag, he extracted a small black case and quickly unzipped it.

The train slowed.

Tristan glanced up to see if the girl showed any indication that she was getting off. There was none. He reached into the case of technical goodies that he had collected through the years. The case contained a hodgepodge of stuff. Tiny micro computer chips that acted as spyware, spy cameras, bugs, and stickers that contained almost invisible GPS chips that he had pre-programmed to transmit to Nigel.

"Farragut North."

The doors slid open.

People bumped and cursed while making their way around him to board the train. Tristan clung to the pole to stay close to the bike and the travel mug.

He peeled the black GPS sticker off the waxed paper. He had only a split second to note the number on the chip.

"13"

Seriously? Thirteen? Why did I mark a chip with that unlucky number? I must have been in a weird mood that night.

With the chip stuck to his fingertip, he closed the case and slipped it back into his backpack. He slung the backpack onto his shoulder.

Just then, a big man slammed into him while rushing to board the train before the doors shut.

Tristan fell into the bike and the girl. "Oh, I'm sorry!"

"No, that's okay!" She helped him back up onto his feet.

"Is your bike okay?" Tristan examined the bike. "I think I knocked your cupholder loose." He took the travel mug out of the mount and slipped the sticker onto the bottom while checking the mount.

With one quick move, she grabbed the mug from him. "It's fine." Clutching the cup, she righted the bike.

Looking down at her, Tristan saw that like the young man who had collected the mug at the café, she was young—barely out of her teens if that. She had a slender—almost boyish figure—not unlike his girlfriend—a midshipman at the naval academy in Annapolis.

Seeing that, he felt a tinge of guilt about tagging the mug. Depending on what type of mess she was involved in, she could get into a lot of trouble if they discovered it.

The guy at the café had definitely collected something from Daniel Cross. Any information Cross had was not small potatoes. It was the type of stuff that could get people killed.

Would they hesitate to kill this girl for bringing them a marked travel mug?

Clinging to the pole, Tristan vacillated between warning the girl and not doing anything. He was on the side of warning her that she could be in danger when the train rolled to a stop again.

"Metro Center."

The doors swung open and Tristan was swept into a tidal wave of tourists rushing off the train. By the time he broke free, the girl was in the elevator going to the lower level.

Tristan stuck a wireless bud into his ear. "Nigel, activate GPS chip number thirteen."

"GPS chip thirteen activated."

While he was confident that Nigel could follow the travel cup, Tristan felt there was nothing like a human pair of eyes. He took the escalator to the lower level where trains from three lines rolled through.

"Silver Line to Wiehle-Reston East."

The train rolled into the station.

Standing back against the far wall, the girl held the cup in one hand and the bike with the other. She made no move to board the train when the doors opened.

Since the train was heading into the suburbs, only a few passengers boarded. Most remained on the platform. Tristan moved down the platform to get as far from her as possible since she was suspicious of him.

Mentally, he made a bet of which train she was waiting for—the Orange or Blue Line. Both crossed the Potomac

River. The Orange Line went beyond Rosslyn and Arlington to go out into Falls Church. The suburbs that in recent years had become more urban than suburb. The Blue Line turned right after crossing the river to go to the Pentagon, Pentagon City, and Crystal City, which was home to a host of government contracting companies.

I bet a thousand bucks it's the Blue Line. That's the biggest market to sell information.

The Blue Train rolled into the station.

She stood up from where she had been leaning against the wall and moved to the door.

Tristan smiled. He had won the bet against himself. On second thought, he also lost the bet since it was against himself. *When am I going to learn to stop betting against myself?* With a shake of his head, he boarded the train.

She guided her bike onto the train, which was not as full as the train on the Red Line had been. Tristan noticed that she had placed the travel mug back into the mount. To not make her any more suspicious, he got onto the same car but sat against the wall far in the back.

The doors closed, and the train eased out of the station. Tristan could feel the train descending into the tunnel to race under the Potomac River before rising to the surface again on the Virginia side.

"Arlington Cemetery," the automated voice announced.

Tristan was surprised when the girl moved her bike to the door. He had expected her to get off at Pentagon or Crystal City. He was so anxious to follow her that he almost tripped over his own big feet to make it to the platform.

She carried her bike to the street before climbing on and riding off into the cemetery. At that point, Tristan decided she would definitely become suspicious if he ran after her. So, he went into the cemetery and took a seat on a bench.

"Nigel, do you still have the GPS signal?" he asked while taking Monique out of his backpack to give her fresh air.

"It's on the move," Nigel said.

Tristan brought up the map on his phone. He could see the GPS signal moving at a steady pace through the cemetery.

After several minutes, it came to a halt on the other end of the cemetery. Seconds later, the GPS chip was moving again, in the opposite direction and at a much faster pace.

"It's coming back to you, Tristan," Nigel said.

His finger on the blinking light on the tablet, Tristan followed the signal moving through the cemetery. Not only was it moving fast, but it was moving with no regard for the roads or bike trail. As the signal moved toward him, he looked up to the sky.

As the drone flew overhead, Tristan saw the signal sweep across the screen on his phone.

Ah, you clever spy.

Tristan watched it fly toward the river and out of sight.

Patting himself on the back for thinking of the GPS chip, he turned his attention to the map with the blinking light travelling across the freeway.

Don't tell me it's going back across the river.

It didn't. At the river, the drone turned right and flew a half mile before coming to a stop.

"Nigel, where is it now?"

"According to the address, our target is now at Slade industries."

Chapter Twelve

"There he goes." Bruce pointed across the street to where Oliver Hansen had trotted out the door and made his way toward Union Station.

"Maybe he's just going to get some lunch." Jacqui tossed her empty bottle of water into a trash bin and fell in step with Bruce.

"Maybe," Bruce replied. "What I'm interested in is who he's having lunch with. You saw his reaction to learning about Stephens's murder."

"Shock that someone he worked with got murdered."

Bruce looked at her. The corners of his lips curled.

"Equally mixed with guilt," she added.

"Tell me he didn't contact whoever he leaked to first chance he got."

Together, they crossed Columbus Circle toward the Christopher Columbus Memorial Fountain.

Four body guards clad in black suits surrounded a long black limousine with smoked windows. There was a black SUV parked in front of the limousine and another behind it.

"Is the President eating in the food court now?" Jacqui asked.

Bruce took note of the license plate on the limousine: SLADE

"No, Leban Slade. I doubt if one of the world's wealthiest businessmen and philanthropists would be eating in the food court." Bruce opened one of the doors and held it for her. "Most likely, he's here to close the deal on a dirty senator."

"Bruce, I never knew you to be so cynical," she said with heavy sarcasm as she entered the white marble and gold trimmed Union Station. She paused to take in the grandeur of the historic transportation hub.

"Leban Slade owns more politicians than you have shoes. How do you think he became one of the richest men on the planet? He invests in politicians and directs them to vote his way—ways that require government contracts."

With a nod of her head, Jacqui agreed while searching the hordes of people hurrying through the station that boasted several levels of shops and restaurants. During the lunchtime hour, politicians or federal employees descended on the station to seek a quick lunch while soaking up the metropolitan atmosphere.

Jacqui searched the hundreds of tourists, travelers, and diners for the intern of a certain senator. "Slade Industries has divisions that deal in computer, cybersecurity--"

"Think about it," Bruce explained, "Leban Slade buys enough politicians to vote to increase the spending on cybersecurity. Several million more dollars go into the military's budget for cybersecurity. Not only do they need more people but they also need more …" He held out a hand in a gesture for her to finish the sentence.

"Equipment and programs, which Slade Industries designs, manufactures, and sells." Jacqui scoffed. "Is this just speculation on your part or—"

"It's a known secret in Washington," Bruce said. "Remember, I used to be the attorney general for Virginia.

I've played golf, broke bread, and socialized with all of these folks. If they weren't representing my state, they were federal politicians living in my state. Behind closed doors, they talk openly about what Slade wants and how they're going to get it for him. One of the senators in my state is practically Slade's slave boy. Slade says jump and he asks how high."

"He can't have every politician in his pocket."

Bruce's eyes narrowed. "Last year, the New York State Attorney General convicted the attorney for an influential businessman for a host of white-collar crimes—enough to earn him five years jail time. That businessman happened to be Slade's competitor for government defense contracts."

"Maybe he really was crooked. Did you ever think of that?"

Bruce chuckled. "Do you know how many laws the average businessman breaks every day?"

Jacqui's face went blank. She shook her head.

Bruce held up four fingers. "An average of four. The reason being that there are so many laws controlling businesses. Granted, people who go into business are supposed to know the laws. If not, they hire people who do. But there are so many laws controlling every facet of business that it is impossible to navigate the minefield of laws that have sprung up over the course of hundreds of years without breaking one or two." He chuckled. "I'm sure you heard the saying, 'The bigger they are, the harder they fall.'"

"Everyone has."

"Think about it. The more you traipse back and forth through a minefield, the more likely you are to step on a mine. The more successful a business owner is, the more business he is doing. The more business he does, the more laws he is likely to break. Every lawyer who knows his stuff knows that." He lowered his voice. "As a result, our country has created a judicial system where any prosecutor, district attorney, or attorney general on the local or federal level can bring down anyone they target for investigation, whether it be for ethical, political, or personal reasons. All the prosecutor has to do is dig and I guarantee, he'll find something."

"And if you are corrupt and happen to be a close ally of the prosecutor—"

"It's all a matter of whether the prosecutor picks up the shovel or not," he said. "Leban Slade has a non-profit foundation that's headquartered in New York that works on a much larger scale than his competitor. It's a fact that Slade uses the foundation for money laundering ill-gotten funds from bribes, extortion, you name it. The New York attorney general knows that. He doesn't have to do any digging to find the evidence. Instead, he took a backhoe to Slade's competitor, who had a legitimate charitable organization. They arrested his attorney and shut down his foundation for violating business laws that usually result in fines for other companies. Doesn't that seem weird to you?"

"Totally, Bruce. Politics is like carbon monoxide. As soon as politics enters anything, it drains every ounce of life and sanity from it." Jacqui walked across the station's main lobby in search of Oliver Hansen.

Not only did they have to search the main floor, but there were also three levels of cafes which looked down on the main floor. It seemed like an impossible effort for the two of them.

Jacqui took out her cell phone to suggest they split up to broaden their search when Bruce pointed at the bistro on the floor above them. "There he is. Nine o'clock."

Jacqui turned directly to her right and looked up at the top of the stairs to an Italian restaurant.

At a small table in the outdoor café seating, Oliver Hansen was making broad gestures while talking to a pretty brunette. In contrast to Oliver's apparent despair, the young woman sat back in her seat and sipped her beer.

"Something is going down." Jacqui trotted up the stairs with Bruce directly behind her.

They reached the café just in time for the brunette to drain her beer and set the mug down. "Listen, I don't have time to listen to your whining. Senator Douglas will be finished with her luncheon meeting with Mr. Slade in a couple of minutes." She rose and gathered her purse. "If you want to feel guilty about someone offing Stephens, then go ahead. My conscience is clear. Thanks for lunch." She hurried off in the direction of a hallway that led to a section of Union Station in which private conference rooms could be booked for meetings or events.

Watching her rush past Bruce and Jacqui, Oliver saw that his indiscretion had been discovered. The color drained from his face for the second time that day.

"Is there something you want to tell us, Oliver?" Jacqui took the seat that his lunch companion had abandoned.

Bruce took a chair from a nearby table and straddled the back to join them. "Who is she? She obviously works for Senator Douglas."

"Amelia Parker. She's the senator's assistant," Oliver said. "She graduated from Georgetown Law School. She's—"

"Pretty and—" Jacqui interjected.

"Ruthlessly ambitious," Bruce finished. "She used you to gather information on the senate majority leader to feed to her boss."

Oliver hung his head.

"Didn't that thought ever occur to you?" Bruce said.

"I didn't know anyone was going to get killed," Oliver said. "I assumed the letter was from some political nut job trying to throw off Cross's nomination. I mean 'treason' is a pretty strong word if you ask me."

"No one asked you," Bruce said. "Senator Keaton didn't want to send Douglas and everyone into a tailspin until he had the letter's contents investigated to see if they were serious."

"Considering that people have died, we know that the contents are deadly serious," Jacqui said. "You told Amelia—"

"Via pillow talk," Bruce said. "Who did she tell?"

"She told Senator Douglas," Oliver said.

"Did Amelia tell you what Senator Douglas did with that information?" Jacqui asked.

"Amelia said Senator Douglas was extremely grateful. As a matter of fact, she says she's expecting a very generous Christmas bonus."

"You better hope she shares it with you considering that you are now on the way to being fired," Bruce said.

"I thought it was the right thing to do," Oliver said.

"You are not in the position of doing what you think is right," Bruce said. "You get paid to follow Senator Keaton's orders and his job is to do what the men and women sent him to Washington to do. One of those things is to protect us from enemies foreign and domestic. If Daniel Cross is a traitor, as Anonymous claims, then he is one of those enemies. One of the last things you want to do is send a message to the enemy telling them that you are on to them."

"I didn't tell Daniel Cross about the letter."

"No, you told your ambitious girlfriend who tattled to Senator Douglas, Daniel Cross's biggest cheerleader."

Oliver's face hardened. "Don't you think Cross had a right to know what he was being accused of instead of being blindsided?"

"Oliver, don't you think that if Daniel Cross was capable of selling out his country to foreign governments that could harm his fellow Americans that he'd be capable of murder?" Jacqui asked. "Did your girlfriend tell you what Senator Douglas's game plan was after she found out about the letter?"

Oliver shrugged his shoulders. "She called her chief investigator to find out who'd sent it."

Bruce grinned. "See? Pillow talk goes both ways. Who is this chief investigator?"

"I'd hate to be on the wrong end of one of his investigations." Oliver shuddered. "He's huge. I mean tall—like basketball player from another planet tall. Dark eyes that scare the life out of you just to have him look at you."

"Does this tall guy have a name?" Bruce asked.

In silence, Oliver chewed his lip before answering. "Amelia calls him Lurch."

Chris felt a sense of deja vu when he turned into South Lakes, the community where he and Blair had made their home for their growing family. The quiet, tree lined neighborhood had sprouted up around Lake Audubon, a fingerling lake surrounded by condos, townhomes, and some single-family homes.

Chris felt as if he were returning home to a nightmare.

All was quiet in the gated community, which was why he and Blair had chosen to live there, until he turned the corner to find emergency vehicles lining both sides of the street. A medical examiner's van, crime scene units, two sheriff's cruisers, Ripley Vaccaro's unmarked FBI cruiser, and Francine's white Mini-Cooper made up much of the fleet.

Inside the boundary set up by crime scene tape, Ripley was talking to a short barrel-chested man in a sheriff's uniform. Chris instantly recognized the markings on his jacket designating him as Fairfax County's sheriff.

The residents of every home on the block watched the goings-on through their windows or front yards and driveways. Some were old neighbors. Others were strangers who had moved into the community after Chris had left.

Francine waved for Chris to park at the end of the line of vehicles. He ended up parking in front of his previous home, a blue house with white trim, which rested along the lakeshore. The turn onto the cul-de-sac had a sharp drop off down a steep hill to the lake.

"Matheson! Is that you?"

Chris cringed when a portly man with white hair and a pointy goatee waved to him from across the street.

"Who's that?" Elliott asked.

Even Sterling, in the back seat, stepped onto the middle console to peer at the man gesturing for Chris to acknowledge him and the collection of spectators gathered in the neighbor's front yard. In recognition of their investigation, Elliott had placed a blue cap with "FBI" stenciled on it in gold letters on Sterling's head.

"Ignore him," Chris told Elliott.

"Who is he?"

"Gordie. He's an idiot." Chris opened the door and slid from the driver's seat. Keeping his head turned to ignore Gordie, he strode around the truck and onto the sidewalk to make his way to Ripley.

"Hey, that is Matheson," Gordie shouted for all to hear. "Wonder why they called him in?"

Leaving Sterling,, Elliott climbed out and went around the back of the truck. Crossing his arms, he leaned against the rear fender and watched the scene playing out across the street.

To anyone who would listen, Gordie recounted about his years of being the Mathesons' neighbor.

"He used to live there." Gordie pointed at the blue house. "Worst neighbor in the world! One of those testosterone-packed Neanderthals. Of course, he had guns in the house. What kind of man keeps guns in the house when he's got kids? It isn't like he was a good father. He'd take off, leaving his wife and kids home alone for days on end. Plus, he had this vicious German shepherd—barked all the time. How much do you want to bet he had something to do with that dead woman? She was probably in witness protection and he got her killed."

Time for this guy to put a sock in it.

Elliott stood up to his full height and uncrossed his arms. He stared at the short white-haired neighbor until he captured Gordie's attention. That took quite a while because Gordie was so caught up in the importance that came with being connected to Chris, who appeared to be connected to the dead woman in the lake.

Elliott could see that Gordie was short, but he didn't see how short he was until he crossed the street to where he was prancing from one neighbor to another while recounting every issue he had with Chris. He started with Chris owning a German shepherd. The only acceptable dog for civilized people were dogs small enough to fit into a purse like the terrier Elliott saw peering out the window. Then there was the time Chris played his music too loud when he came home and Gordie had to shut his bedroom door. On top of it all, Chris's worst offense was working for the FBI. That made him a thug for hire.

Elliott was standing directly behind the little man before a member of his audience gestured to Gordie before making a hasty retreat to his own home a few doors down.

Elliott took his retired law enforcement identification from his pocket and flashed it quickly. "U.S. Marshal. From what I hear, you have some information about what's happened here. Would you care to go on the record?" He saw that Gordie was no taller than Helen, who was quite petite.

"Ugh—"

"'Ugh' is not an answer." Elliott made a show of taking his notepad from his pocket. "Now, what exactly do you know about the death of this woman?" He took his time digging through his pockets for a pencil to give Gordie plenty of time to think about his accusations becoming part of an official record. "Keep in mind that any false statements you make can be used against you. In other words, if they result in the wrongful arrest of a suspect, in this case Mr. Matheson, then he will be within his right to sue you for defamation of character."

Beads of sweat formed on Gordie's forehead.

"So, Mr. Gordie, what do you know about this case?" Elliott put the pencil to the notepad. "Go ahead. I'm listening."

Gordie swallowed. "I don't know anything."

"Funny, you were so talkative a moment ago." Elliott shrugged his shoulders. "Seemed to know a whole bunch."

"I was just saying …" Gordie's voice trailed off.

"Were you ever in the Matheson home?"

"No."

"Met him and his family except to complain?"

Gordie kicked at the ground.

"What were you just saying?" Elliott asked.

Gordie swallowed. "Saying?"

"That Chris Matheson was a killer—a conclusion not based on evidence but because of your narrow-minded judgment. It's a very slippery slope when you start convicting people based on nothing more than disapproval of their worldviews." Elliott returned his notepad and pencil in his pocket.

The muscular man leaned in close to Gordie, who stared up at him with wide eyes. "Take some advice," he said in a menacingly low voice. "If you don't like someone, ignore them." He winked at him. "That's what grownups do."

Elliott pointed across the road to Sterling, who was watching them from the driver's seat of the truck. Elliott pointed two fingers at the dog and then turned around to point at Gordie.

Licking his chops, Sterling focused on the little man. Between the dark sunglasses hiding his eyes and FBI cap, the German shepherd appeared quite intimidating, even without baring his teeth.

Leaving Gordie under Sterling's watchful eye, Elliott crossed the road to join Chris and the law enforcement gathered at the corner drop-off into the lake. He found Chris talking to a woman wearing a jacket emblazoned with FBI across the back and the sheriff. Chris was positioned outside the yellow crime scene tape boundary.

"Did your people get an impression of that tire mark?" Chris pointed at a clear tire mark that appeared to drive over the corner of the sidewalk and across the grass near the drop-off.

The sour expression on the sheriff's flabby face revealed that he was offended by Chris's suggestion that he had missed the evidence. "My people got it first thing."

"Sheriff, we found a phone!" One of the crime scene investigators announced from where they were searching the lake for further evidence.

"Maybe we'll get lucky and her murderer's phone number will be listed in her contacts under 'killer,'" the sheriff said.

Two men and a woman wearing crime scene garb stood in the thigh-deep water at the bottom of the steep hill. Gingerly, they positioned the basket containing a black body bag between them. The basket was attached to a pully strung up between the trees lining the lake's edge and the front of one of the sheriff's cruisers.

Upon seeing Elliott, Francine introduced him to Murphy before stepping away to answer the phone buzzing in her pocket.

"Was the medical examiner able to determine a possible cause of death?" Elliott asked them.

Hearing him, Chris shook his head and said over his shoulder, "No GSW or knife wounds. Possible drowning, but she was found in three and a half feet of water. She was a strong swimmer. The medical examiner will have to open her up."

As the crime scene technicians lifted Blair's body over the tape, Chris stepped forward to block them from loading her in the back of the wagon. "I want to see her."

"Chris," Ripley said, "I've identified her. You don't have—"

"Sorry, Vaccaro, but I allowed someone else to identify her last time."

The sheriff nodded his head to instruct the technicians to unzip the bag.

Standing up straight, Chris braced himself. As the morgue attendant parted the opening of the body bag to reveal her face, a breath involuntarily escaped his lips.

Her face was blue. A bluish green slime covered one side of her face and her hair—much shorter than she usually wore it. The tilt of her nose was identical to Katelyn's. Her features were small and delicate, much like she was.

In an instant, the day they had met replayed in Chris's mind. He had to stop by the state department to question Blair's boss about a missing person's case. The suspect refused to speak to him, so Chris waited in the reception area to intercept him when he left. Chris cooled his heels for four hours—during which he turned on his charm with the attractive blonde working in a cubicle nearby. By the time he'd left, not only did he have a confession of an affair with the missing person, but he had a date for that Saturday night.

Two weeks later, Blair moved into his condo and four months after that, she proposed that they get married. Six months after that, they were married in a huge wedding. One year after they were married, Katelyn was born.

Ten years later, Blair was moving to Switzerland.

I wish we had more time, she had said while boarding the train.

So do I. Where did we go wrong?

Conscious of many eyes watching him, Chris swallowed and blinked away the tears fighting to come to his eyes. He was aware of Elliott firmly clasping his shoulder.

"Mr. Matheson, is this your wife?" the sheriff's voice sounded like it was coming to him from the end of a tunnel.

Chris reached out to touch her cheek only to have Ripley pull his hand back. "If you've had no contact with her, then don't risk accidental transfer."

"You're right." Chris nodded to the sheriff. "Yes. That's Blair." He tugged at the zipper to note that she was dressed in a plaid outer garment. "She's wearing the same jacket she had on when I saw her at the metro."

The sheriff gestured for them to zip up the bag and take her away. "The passport we found in her bag said her name was Charlotte Nesbitt from Australia."

"That's part of our investigation." Murphy locked his eyes on Ripley's. He tossed his head toward her cruiser.

Catching onto Murphy's direction to take control of the case, Ripley said, "The FBI will be needing the victim's passport and any evidence you've collected."

"You're claiming jurisdiction on this case?" the sheriff said. "A murder investigation where the victim is your ex-partner's wife—her body dumped in his own backyard—"

"Former backyard," Ripley said. "He'd moved away over a year ago."

"Almost a year and a half," Chris said.

"How do I know you're not claiming jurisdiction on this case to cover up his involvement?" the sheriff said.

"Simple." Murphy asked the medical examiner, "Do you have an approximate TOD?" He took his cell phone from his jacket pocket.

"Based on body temperature, I'd say between midnight and one o'clock," the medical examiner said. "She was definitely dumped before four or five this morning."

"Why do you say before four and five?" Francine asked.

The medical examiner gestured at the grass leading down the steep hill. "She had grass and mud on her clothes. You can see the flattened ground where she was rolled down the hill and went over the drop off. The first officers on the scene took pictures when they arrived. The crushed grass was still covered with frost. If she had been dumped after the frost formed, then it would have come off when her body rolled over it."

"That takes the victim's husband off the suspect list," Murphy told the sheriff while tapping out a text. "We were together the entire night."

The sheriff looked the two men up and down.

Keeping one eye on his phone, Murphy muttered, "That didn't come out sounding anything like it did in my head."

"Matheson was helping Lieutenant Thornton on a very important case involving national security," Ripley said.

The sheriff peered at Chris. "If you didn't kill her, or maybe had her killed, why would they dump her body off in what used to be your backyard? Maybe to remove you from suspicion by making it look like whoever did it was trying to frame you. Meanwhile, to firm it up, you were setting up an airtight alibi."

Ripley and Murphy exchanged quick glances. Murphy pressed a button on his phone.

The sheriff hitched up his pants. "Sorry, Vaccaro. A dead woman dumped in the backyard of what used to be her home. Her husband and her living in different countries and a phony name on her passport. Something smells funny."

The phone on his hip buzzed.

"I just don't feel right handing this off to the feds." He jabbed a finger in Chris's direction while snatching the phone off his hip. "Especially when my prime suspect is a former fed." He looked Chris up and down while putting the phone to his ear. "Kind of young to be retired. Willing to bet you retired under some sort of dark cloud."

He snapped into the phone. "Hell-o!" He frowned. "Yeah, this is Sheriff Turley. Who's this?"

Chris noticed the corners of Ripley's mouth curl upward. Murphy slipped his cell phone back into his pocket.

The color drained from the sheriff's face while he listened to the caller in silence. His eyeballs darted across the street to search the windows and trees as if he were looking for someone. When he finally spoke, it was with a stutter. "Ca-case is yours, Vaccaro." He gestured to the medical examiner and county investigators. "Feds are taking this case. Everything goes to the FBI lab. It's a matter of national security."

Ripley saluted him. "Thank you for being so understanding, Sheriff."

As the sheriff hurried away to his cruiser, Chris asked Ripley, "What just happened here?"

"We got the case."

"To what end?" Chris asked as they huddled together.

"Matheson, Sheriff Turley had you and only you on his radar. He wasn't going to look anywhere else," Ripley said.

"Ripley wasn't lying when she said this was a matter of national security," Murphy said. "There have been developments in the case. Bruce and Jacqui read the letter Blair had sent to Senator Keaton. She had evidence that Daniel Cross was a traitor. That evidence was what she intended to turn over to the investigator."

"Daniel Cross has a ton of political support wanting his nomination as director of the Central Intelligence Agency to be confirmed," Francine said. "Believe me. In today's climate, just calling him a traitor or even having a witness saying it, won't be enough. We need real evidence to prove it."

"Even that won't be enough the way the media can spin stuff," Elliott said.

"The confirmation hearings start on Monday," Francine said. "That gives us two days to find out what Blair had on Cross."

"If Blair was meeting the investigator to pass on the evidence she had, then she had to have it on her when she died since the meeting never took place." Chris went to the crime scene investigator's vehicle and tapped on the window to stop the driver, who was about to leave. "We need to look in the victim's purse."

"Unless whoever killed her took it," Murphy said.

"Must be something big if they were willing to kill for it," Elliott said.

"You betcha," Francine said. "Nowadays, they could have just let the evidence come to light and then spin it to make him into a hero and half the country would have bought it."

The investigator handed the oversized brown leather shoulder purse, encased in a sealed plastic bag, to Ripley. They followed the agent to her cruiser where she placed it on top of the hood to sign the log taped to the front of it. Murphy handed her a pen knife for her to cut through the seal.

Chris reached into the back of her SUV to extract several pairs of evidence gloves and handed them out. Ripley gave the bag to him.

"Prepare yourselves." Chris squeezed the purse in his hands. Filthy cold lake water gushed from the side pocket to fill the bottom of the plastic bag. "Blair basically lived out of her handbag."

They gathered around.

"It's so slimy," Francine noted the greenish brown goo that coated the bag and its contents.

"It's the goose poop," Chris said. "The wildlife refuge is right next to us. We ended up with as many geese here as over there. Of course, they do their thing in our back yard. It makes for a nice slimy gunk at the lake bottom. That's why we'd never let the girls go swimming."

Careful to not disturb any possible evidence, Chris reached inside and extracted the first item—her wallet.

Francine examined its contents. "Most likely, she'd have it on a thumb drive or micro disc."

Chris took out a keychain, which held only three keys. One was for a domestic vehicle. Two appeared to be for doors. "No safety deposit box key."

"If she had the evidence in a safety deposit box then she'd make sure the key was someplace safe." Francine finished her search of the wallet. "I've got nothing here."

Chris was still digging items from the bag onto the hood for them to search. Small cosmetics bag. Hair brush. A pack of drenched tissues. Eyeglass case with reading glasses. Dead cell phone.

"Wait a minute," Chris said upon seeing the phone emerge from the bag. "Didn't they find a phone at the bottom of the lake?"

"It went to the lab with the rest of the evidence," Ripley said.

Chris studied the phone in his hand. Wet, it wouldn't turn on. He was more interested in the brand, model, and age of the phone. It was the same phone Blair had taken with her when she had gone to Switzerland. "Was the other one a burner?"

"I'll have to check with forensics."

"She called the investigator from a burner," Murphy said.

"This is her real phone," Chris said. "I swear this is the phone she took with her to Switzerland. That means she's kept it this whole time. She could have the evidence on this phone."

"Otherwise, why keep it?" Ripley got an evidence bag from the rear of her vehicle to place the phone into.

"But if the evidence is on the phone, how would she give it to the investigator?" Francine asked.

"Hand it to him," Murphy said. "She couldn't have been using it. If she had, it would have shown up on Chris's phone bill."

"I assumed the phone had been lost in the terrorist attack. She never went anywhere without it." Chris slipped it into the evidence bag that Ripley held out to him.

"We'll see if we can get anything useful off of this." Ripley sealed the bag and labeled it.

Their search continued.

Notepad. Several pens. Box of baby wipes. Candy in discolored wrappers. Travel box of tampons. Lip balm. Hand lotion. Metro fare card. Fast food napkins. Store receipts. Bank receipts. Notes—most of which were illegible from being in the water for hours.

The oversized bag seemed like a bottomless pit. They searched each item over and over again. Then, with a sigh, they gave up.

"If her proof is not on the phone, then they got it," Chris said in the end. "She would not have gone to the meeting without it. They got whatever it was she had, and they killed her."

"Let's pray it's on the phone," Murphy said, "because if Daniel Cross is a traitor, then he needs to be brought down. Cross has worked his way up through the CIA for over twenty years. He's come into a hell of a lot of very sensitive intelligence that our enemies would have given anything for."

"Passing on information to whom?" Ripley asked.

"The guy Francine saw Cross give a mug to this morning returned to the café to pick up another package," Murphy said. "Tristan attach a GPS tracker to the mug. It ended up at Slade Industries."

"That's an American company," Elliott said with a puzzled expression.

"An American company that's a worldwide conglomerate," Francine said. "Before I retired, I did an expose on Slade Industries. They operate in the global market like no one else with shadow companies and overseas accounts. Leban Slade has his fingers in every pie all around the globe. He's made heavy investments into foreign companies that sell weapons to our enemies. To put it bluntly, it's no accident that weapons manufactured by Slade Industries have landed in the hands of Iran and North Korea."

Murphy rubbed his chin. "Would a worldwide player like that be able to employ a team of international muscle?"

"Or death squad?" Chris asked.

"He keeps them on retainer," Francine said.

Chapter Thirteen

Helen Clarke's stomach flip-flopped while her sixteen-year-old daughter Sierra rode over the hill and out of sight with Nikki and Emma, Chris's two youngest daughters.

A horse enthusiast, ten-year-old Nikki had no problem stepping in to take her father's place for Sierra's weekly riding lesson. Sierra would have been heart-broken if Helen had cancelled the lesson, which she was tempted to do. While not likely, she feared that whoever was after Blair would track down Chris's family at his farm.

That's why Helen made sure she had both her service and back-up weapon on hand. She knew Doris would also be heavily armed under her coat, as if her entourage, Sadie and Mocha, weren't enough.

The same fears crossing her mind, Doris sent the two dogs out on the trail ride with the girls. Preferring to keep the events of the last twenty-four hours under wraps, Doris claimed the dogs needed exercise.

"They're going to be fine." Clad in a black leather coat with matching boots and gloves, Doris slipped her arm across

Helen's shoulder and gave her a hug as the riders and dogs galloped out of sight.

"If we say it enough, we'll believe it." Helen shivered in her worn winter coat. Her date weekend being a bust, she had dressed down in jeans and a comfy oversized sweater.

They went across the barnyard to the warm house.

"You should be with Chris," Doris said. "He needs you. I imagine it doesn't get any easier losing your spouse to a violent death the second time around."

"I don't want to look like I'm swooping in," Helen said. "It was only a few hours ago that I backed off because he ended up being married. Now Blair's dead *again*, and I immediately swoop in to comfort him? It'll look like I'm an opportunist."

Doris climbed onto the porch and opened the door leading into the mudroom. "It'll look like you're being there for him."

In the mudroom, they took off their coats and hung them up before going into the country kitchen.

"Chris doesn't talk that much about Blair. What was she like?"

"I try not to speak ill of the dead," Doris said.

"Blair didn't run off with another man," Helen said. "That Australian ended up being an intelligence agent trying to help her and the operative get back to the US."

In the kitchen, Doris pressed the button to brew the coffee that she had set up earlier. "I know I'm old fashioned, and I can be opinionated, but I feel it was so wrong for her to abandon her family the way she did. For what? Her career?" She put cream and extra sugar into a coffee mug. "It was Blair who wanted to get married, buy a house, and start a family. Chris gave her everything she wanted, but in the end, it wasn't good enough."

"Society keeps telling us that we're a traitor to fellow women if we don't do it all," Helen said with a grin.

"She had a career when she'd met Chris. Such that it was. She started out as a clerk and worked up to a communications officer—not making a lot of money. She was always at the bottom of the totem pole and miserable about it. So she decided to concentrate on being a wife and mother, but worked part time to get out of the house. Then—after having three lovely daughters—she changed her mind and decided to focus on her career," Doris declared with a wave of her hands.

The coffee brewed, she filled their mugs.

"Not everyone has it figured out early on about what they want to be when they grow up," Helen said. "For some of us, it's a journey."

With a frown, Doris went to the kitchen table. "Someone pointed out to me just this morning that Blair started out her marriage behind the eight ball because she wasn't you."

Helen sat across from her. "Was that Chris?"

"Elliott." Doris took a cautious sip of the hot coffee. "He was right. Maybe I didn't do it consciously, but I always compared her to you and she always came up short." She slumped. "She had to have sensed that."

"I'm sure you aren't the reason that she took off," Helen said.

"She broke my baby's heart." Doris picked up Thor, placed her into her lap, and petted her. "Don't tell me that if some man broke Sierra's heart that you wouldn't have hard feelings toward him."

"I broke Chris's heart," Helen said in a matter-of-fact tone.

It was a painful reminder.

Helen and Chris had been high school sweethearts. Theirs had been a passionate relationship. Both families had been certain the young lovers would marry. After graduating, Chris went off to boot camp and Helen went to West Virginia

University. Weeks later, he received a Dear John letter from her. Only recently had she revealed to him the reason for the break up.

"Why don't you have hard feelings for me?" Helen asked.

"Maybe because you were like the daughter I never had before you broke Chris's heart."

Helen laughed. "But *he* is your son."

"Yes, and it's because he's my son that I know what he's capable of. I'm sure you had a good reason for breaking his heart." Doris shot her a wicked grin. "He probably deserved it."

Together, the two women shared a laugh.

"No matter what you think about Blair," Helen said, "she was the mother of your grandchildren. No matter how much she hurt Chris, he did love her. She got into some serious trouble and now she's dead. Your granddaughters are going to want to know what happened. For their sake, because we love them, we need to do everything we can to find those answers."

In silence, they sipped their coffee. The only sound in the kitchen was the clicking of the anniversary clock on the mantle. As the minute hand swept to the top of the hour, the various clocks throughout the house sounded off with their individual chimes, followed by the single dong to mark one o'clock.

Accustomed to the competing musical announcements, Doris continued to sip her coffee.

Helen smiled at the racket. As the notes died away, she became aware of one lone song far off in the distance—an instrumental tune that she had to search her mind for the title. "That's a newbie," she said in a soft voice as if afraid to interrupt the song.

"What, dear?"

Helen held up her finger for her to listen. "Never heard that before."

After a long moment of listening, Doris nodded her head. "That's Emma's clock. It's a music box, too. Plays Celine Dion's 'Fly'. Blair had sent it from Switzerland for Emma's birthday." She took in a shuddering breath. "It was her fifth birthday—ten days after we'd told that she'd been killed."

"And it arrived on Emma's birthday?"

"A friend of Blair's delivered it at her party," Doris said with a nod of her head. "Oh, Emma loves that clock. It's got an angel at the top of it." She lowered her voice. "Emma thinks the angel is her mother watching over her." She glanced up the back staircase to the little girl's room, where the clock was playing the closing notes of the song. "There must be a short in it. The chimes must be setting off the music box to start playing on the hour. It's been going off all day."

"I can't see Chris marrying a dummy," Helen said. "If Blair came into some information that was a threat to national security, she'd hide it someplace safe. Someplace that those who know her would know to look for it."

"It's not here," Doris said. "Chris was living in Virginia when she died. He gave away or sold all of Blair's stuff."

"She would have made certain that it would be with something that Chris would not have sold or given away," Helen said. "Surely, he had to keep some things for the girls to remember their mother by."

"There's the stuff they shipped back from Switzerland. That he didn't even look through. He said it was too painful." Doris set Thor on the floor. "That stuff is in the storage room in the cellar."

Helen stood up. "Let's go look."

In a previous life, Chantilly, Virginia, had been home to gentlemen farmers and their families. It was close enough to feel the electricity of the Nation's Capital but removed enough for those yearning a quieter country life.

When Washington real estate burst at the seams, families scrambling for more affordable housing options migrated outside the Capital Beltway and beyond. Gated communities, along with the office parks, strip malls and convenience stores, sprouted up to replace the once lush farmland.

While Francine and Murphy returned to Georgetown to meet Bruce and Jacqui at Tristan's computer lab, Ripley and Chris went to interview the Dunleavys. Ivy and her lawyer husband lived in a luxurious French country mansion on acreage at the end of a wide cul-de-sac.

After parking her cruiser in the Dunleavys' driveway, Ripley got out to meet Chris who parked behind her. When she reached his driver's side door, she found an argument erupting inside his truck.

"Whoever drives decides on the music and I say we listen to classical!" Chris punched the icons on the radio.

Stomping his front paws on the console between the two humans, Sterling barked his argument.

"Sterling doesn't like classical music," Elliott said in the manner of a translator. "He wants to listen to Keith Urban."

"Doesn't matter anymore." Chris threw open the door, almost hitting Ripley. "We're here … Thank you, God." With a roll of his eyes, he slid out of the truck. "I should have gotten a dumb dog, who wouldn't have figured out how to work the radio." He slammed the door shut. "Then, we wouldn't have these fights."

Behind him, Chris heard the notes of a Keith Urban tune drifting through the open window from inside the truck. In the driver's seat, Sterling seemed to smirk at him from behind his dark glasses.

Elliott trotted around the front of the vehicle to join Chris and Ripley. "I let him have my phone to listen to his music while we're inside."

Stunned, Ripley stared at him. "You gave your phone to a *dog* to listen to country music?"

"He gets bored sitting in the truck with nothing to do."

Ripley dragged her gaze from Elliott to Chris, who seemed to understand the matter. Deciding it was best to get back to the reason for their visit, she said, "Considering that Ivy Dunleavy accused you of abusing Blair and hung up on you, I'm not sure you being here is a very good idea. It could make her combative."

"We can handle combative." Elliott cracked his knuckles.

"Haven't you heard the phrase, 'You can get more bees with honey than vinegar?'"

"What the hell is he doing here?" Ivy's full-throated demand sounded both outraged and cultured at the same time.

"Here we go," Ripley muttered.

Her arms folded across her small chest, Ivy stood on the front stoop. A brunette, she was dressed in gray slacks and a winter white cardigan sweater with pearls. She looked every bit of her role of country club matron, a role that Chris remembered her yearning to play ever since he had met her. The administrative assistant had set her sights on marrying a wealthy lawyer and that was exactly what she did. Ivy spent her days chairing committees, working with a personal trainer, and testing laser cosmetic treatments.

Her demeanor wavered when she caught sight of the German shepherd donning a hat and sunglasses in the front seat of Chris's truck. "You still have that damn dog?"

"Winston passed away." Chris jerked a thumb in the direction of the German shepherd rocking to Keith Urban. "This is Sterling."

"Why's he wearing a hat and sunglasses?"

"Because he's cool," Chris said. "Do you have a problem with that, Ivy?"

Failing to see the humor, Ivy scoffed.

"I'll let you take the lead with this one," Chris murmured to Ripley.

The investigator pasted a congenial expression on her face and strode up the sidewalk. Ivy glared at Chris until Ripley grabbed her attention by flashing her federal agent's badge and introducing herself. "I spoke to you on the phone. We're investigating the death of Blair Matheson."

"There's your man right there." Ivy gestured in Chris's direction. "Leaning against that truck. Chris Matheson. Blair was scared to death of him. That's why we hid her—from *him*." Tears came to her eyes.

"I'm afraid Chris Matheson has an airtight alibi for the time of her death," Ripley said. "Multiple witnesses can testify to his whereabouts."

Ivy blinked.

"We have a lot of questions, Ms. Dunleavey. Can we come in so we can sort this out? To find out what happened to Blair?"

Grudgingly, Ivy opened the door to allow them inside. "Not the dog. The maid just cleaned."

Ripley, Chris, and Elliott stepped into a two-story foyer. The winding staircase followed a curved wall to the second floor.

Stu Dunleavy was making his way down the stairs while giving instructions to a shapely brunette directly behind him. "Taking into consideration who his father is, we have to assume he's trouble. Our client pays us to make sure these issues are taken care of before they become a problem. Call Burnett and tell him to get a couple of people on it—ASAP."

Upon noticing Ripley's detective's shield, he ended the conversation. "That's all for now, Jenn. Let me know when Burnett gets the job done." As she walked out the door, Stu extended his hand to the visitors. "Good to see you, Chris."

Dressed in a green sweater, Stu was average in appearance. Average height. Average weight. Chris swore the man could walk into a room naked and no one would notice. There was nothing striking about him except his wealth.

Chris greeted him with a slight nod of his head. "Stu."

"They found Blair," Ivy said in a tear-filled voice.

"Where did you find her?" Stu asked.

"In Audubon Lake," Ripley said.

Ivy turned to Chris. "How close to your house?"

"About sixty miles. Give or take a few miles." He smirked at her. "*My* house is in West Virginia."

Ivy's eyes grew wide. Her mouth dropped open.

"I moved a year and a half ago. Guess you didn't know that, huh?"

"So whoever dumped her body there to frame Chris must not have known that he'd moved," Elliott said. "Any idea who that might be, Ms. Dunleavy?"

"Don't answer that, Ivy." Stu took his wife by the arm. "We'll talk in the sun room."

The Dunleavys led them to an enclosed patio that looked out across a swimming pool and garden. The room was so white that Chris was afraid to touch anything for fear of leaving a smudge. The only color was provided by fresh flowers delivered daily. Chris suspected they kept the room white by forbidding their young daughter from entering it.

Stu sat next to his wife on the sofa and ordered everyone to sit before asking, "How was Blair killed?"

"We'll know more after the autopsy. Right now, we're investigating the death as a homicide." Ripley took a seat on a small sofa across from them. "When did you last see her?"

"Yesterday afternoon," Ivy said. "I dropped her off at the Reston-Wiehl Metro. Blair had been living as a recluse since coming back from Europe." She shot a glance at Chris. "For good reason, from what she'd told me."

"What did Blair tell you about Chris?" Ripley asked. "Why she was so afraid of him that she felt compelled to fake her death?"

"In a nutshell," Ivy said, "he beat her."

"Seriously?" Chris jumped to his feet. Before he could move, Elliott blocked his path.

"Ripley's taking the lead." Elliott gestured for him to retake his seat. "You agreed. Remember?"

With a grumble, Chris sat.

"Did she tell you this before she'd left for Switzerland?" Ripley asked.

Ivy shook her head. "She was protecting him for the sake of the children. But then, after being away for so long, she had time to think and didn't want to go back to that situation."

"Did Blair allege that Chris hurt the children?" Elliott asked.

Stu shook his head. "Never. She said he was nice to the girls."

"Didn't that strike you as odd, Stu?" Chris asked. "You both saw me with my family. Wouldn't you think you'd see some sort of clue that I had it in me to be a monster if that were true."

"Many men have Dr. Jekyll and Mr. Hyde type tendencies," Stu said. "Crime case files are filled with examples of that. The serial killer who gave candy to kids. The church pastor whose wife kills him after he pushed his S&M games too far. We had no idea what you were like behind closed doors."

"There are symptoms of spousal abuse," Chris said. "Secluding the abused spouse, so no one finds out. Did I ever stop Blair from coming and going as she pleased? Did you ever see Blair wearing long sleeves and pants in warm weather to hide bruises?"

"She told us that being in law enforcement, you could beat her so that the bruises wouldn't show," Stu said.

"Give me a break," Chris said. "Even if I beat her so the bruises wouldn't show, she'd certainly have some marks."

"She told us that he was insanely jealous," Ivy told Ripley. "That's why she didn't want him to know she was alive. She had gone to Nice to meet another man—an Australian. She was there at the terrorist attack. By the time things were sorted out, she knew that Chris had to know that she had taken up with another man and was afraid of what he'd do." She lowered her voice. "Blair said he had told her that he could murder her and get rid of her body so that no one would ever know she was dead."

"If I was insanely jealous, I wouldn't have allowed her to go halfway around the globe without me." Chris could see by the expression on Stu's face that he realized that he had been played. He had bought Blair's lies hook, line, and sinker.

"When did you find out Blair faked her death?" Ripley asked.

"She showed up on our doorstep a few days after her funeral," Ivy said.

"Did Blair tell you how she got an Australian diplomatic passport with the name of Charlotte Nesbitt?" Ripley asked.

With a quick glance, Stu ordered Ivy to be quiet while he answered, "We have no idea. We felt the less we knew about Blair's activities overseas, the better. After all, she worked for the state department. Everything she did was classified. We had no need to know anything else so we didn't ask."

"Did she ever contact the state department or any of her old friends from there?" Ripley asked.

"Oh, no. She knew they'd tell Chris." Ivy's expression was filled with anger.

Stu shot her a chastising glance.

Ripley continued her interview. "Had Blair been in contact with any of her old friends during the three years that she'd been living with you?"

"None. She was scared to death, I tell you."

"What had she been doing for the last three years?" Chris asked.

"Taking care of our daughter. Hannah adored her." Ivy grabbed a tissue from a box on the end table and wiped her nose. "I don't know how I'm going to explain this to her."

"Our friends did not know Blair from before," Stu said. "When she came back to the States, she had cut her hair and dyed it. We introduced her to everyone as Charlotte, Hannah's nanny. Basically, that was what she did while living with us. We even paid her under the table so that she'd have some money."

"Did she go out?" Elliott asked. "Go to the gym? Socialize?"

"No, she'd been very careful. She was terrified of running into him." Ivy pointed at Chris.

"Stop it, Ivy," Stu said. "Can't you see that Blair lied to us? She was afraid of someone else. Now if you really want to help find out who killed your best friend, tell them what happened yesterday."

Ivy's mouth hung open while she gazed at her husband. For a long time, she was speechless. Finally, she licked her lips and said, "Out of the blue, Blair decided she needed a day out."

"Which was unusual," Stu said, "because Blair never went anywhere. I even asked Ivy, 'Why would Blair suddenly need a day out? She hasn't needed one for years. Why now?'"

"I told Stu, 'I guess after three years of not leaving the house, she started feeling a bit antsy.' She'd asked me for a ride to the metro. She didn't even have a driver's license because she was afraid it would be tracked back to Chris ... or I guess whoever it was she was hiding from. I drove her to the metro." Ivy dabbed her eyes. "That was the last time I saw her."

"What time was that?" Ripley asked.

"About three-thirty."

"So, Blair was basically hiding out," Ripley said. "Living here. In seclusion. And then suddenly out of the blue, she asked you to drive her to the metro and she goes into the city, which is filled to the gills with people."

"She didn't expect to run into *him*." When Stu attempted to silence her, Ivy asked, "Why would she fake her death and tell us that she was hiding from Chris if it wasn't because she was afraid of him?"

"I suspect it was to protect her family," Ripley said. "As long as they believed she was dead, then so would everyone else. If you thought she was hiding from Chris because he was abusive, then she could be certain that you'd keep her secret."

"She was terrified of someone else for another reason," Chris said forcibly. "That someone else caught up with her when she went into the city. They killed her."

"Who would want to kill Blair?" Ivy said. "She was a nobody really." When she saw Chris start, she rattled on. "I mean she didn't have any power. She wasn't aggressive. I know of at least two times when we were both working for the state department that Blair lost out on a promotion because she played by the rules." She shook her head. "I told her that some people are winners, and some are losers. The winners do what they have to do to get to the top and stay there. Don't be afraid to step on a few toes, even if those toes belong to someone you care about."

"Did Blair ever talk to you about Switzerland and what happened to her there?" Ripley asked.

"Never," Ivy said. "Everything she did overseas was classified."

His eyes were wide when Stu shook his head in response to the question.

"Ivy, you said the last time you saw Blair was when you dropped her off at the metro," Chris said. "You had to have spoken to her because when I called you, you accused me of hurting her because we saw each other in DC. The only way you would've known that was if you had spoken to her."

"She called me on my cell phone on her way back home," Ivy said.

"What time was that?" Ripley asked.

"A little after five o'clock," Ivy said. "She was frantic. Talking crazy—saying that it wasn't safe to come home now. I told her to come home and we'd talk about what to do—whatever—but just come home. She hung up on me. I drove out to the metro stop to pick her up—but she didn't show."

"What time did you go to the metro stop?"

"I was there by quarter after six," Ivy said. "The Reston-Weihl stop. The place was packed. I kept trying to call her but got no answer. I went walking around—thinking that Chris had caught up with her there." Seeing Chris's expression, she added, "What was I supposed to think? She told me that it was you!"

"How long did you wait?" Ripley asked.

"I waited until eight o'clock before I gave up and came home." Ivy sobbed. "We never saw her again."

Stu wrapped his arm around her. "You understand why we couldn't call the police to report her missing. According to official records, Blair Matheson had died three years ago."

Tristan Faraday didn't aspire to become a computer genius and build a super artificial intelligence. Actually, he had started out studying paleontology and built computers and robots for a hobby. The downside of being a paleontologist is that there aren't any dinosaurs around to study.

Not only did Tristan like working with computers, he really loved building them, and getting inside their minds to figure out how they worked. The more he studied, the more he discovered a correlation between living and artificial intelligence. One thing led to another until he ended up creating Nigel, his imaginary friend, who had managed, through technological interaction with computers and databases across the world to create an ultra-secret global network.

The super intelligent virtual "butler" named Nigel had formed many relationships with computer systems around the globe—relationships that proved to be quite beneficial to the Phantoms.

The super intelligent virtual "butler" named Nigel had formed many relationships with computer systems around the globe—relationships that proved to be quite beneficial to the Phantoms.

During his research, Tristan discovered that AIs were not unlike humans. Maybe it was because humans created them.

Computers and the networks connecting them had personalities and issues that Nigel had learned to navigate in the same manner that humans had to deal with each other. The computer network in the Capitol Building was so out of touch that it was virtually useless. Nigel, who was quickly developing a sense of humor, never went to her for anything except nonsensical quotes or anecdotes for his humor database.

Others were temperamental. According to Nigel, the Associated Press database, while chatty, was quite arrogant and had an opinion about everything. He was more interested in telling Nigel what to conclude from his data than giving it.

AIs had not yet developed human conditions like manipulation and dishonesty. However, they were only as good as the information humans put into their system. Inaccurate data fed into the system for whatever reason, whether it be lack of integrity or fact checking, produced poor data. While there was nothing Nigel couldn't find out from the Associated Press, he preferred to check elsewhere first for accurate data.

As Nigel's skills grew and he became increasingly important to Murphy's team of ultra-secret government operatives, Tristan decided, for security's sake, to move Nigel out of the guest cottage he lived in at his sister and brother-in-law's estate in Great Falls, Virginia, to a secret location in a brownstone in Georgetown.

Tristan had bought the brownstone when he was a college undergrad. He had moved in with Jessica after a water main break flooded the building. After it had been renovated, Tristan turned it into a three-story computer lab with cutting-edge technology and security.

To the few visitors permitted inside the townhome, it looked like nothing more than the average Georgetown home with hardwood floors, a living room, dining room, and kitchen that looked out onto a patio garden. Little did they know that the upper floors contained a state-of-the-art computer lab connected to satellites around the globe to feed information to Nigel.

The items from Tristan's backpack were scattered across the kitchen table. He checked the time on the clock on the microwave while taking a jar of mayonnaise out of the fridge. Spotting one last bottle of beer, he decided to take that as well.

He closed the door and turned around to see a man standing before him. He aimed a nine-millimeter Berretta at Tristan's mid-section.

"I assume you're from Slade Industries." Holding up his hands, in which he clutched the beer and mayonnaise, Tristan could feel the assassin's partner making his way down the back hallway toward him—his weapon aimed at the back of Tristan's head.

"I guess you know why we're here," the first assassin said. "Saves us having to listen to you begging to know why we're going to have to kill you."

Chapter Fourteen

"You should eat something," Elliott said to Chris who was sitting next to him in the booth at the restaurant chain before ordering two servings of cheeseburgers and fries from the server. "You didn't have any breakfast.

Flashing a smile at Sterling, who lay on the floor next to Elliott's seat, the server went to put in their orders.

"I can't believe we didn't find anything in Blair's room," Chris said.

"We agreed she took whatever evidence she had to the meeting with her." Ripley reached down to stroke the top of Sterling's head. "If her murderer didn't take it, then it has to be at the lab." She waved the straw, still in its wrapper, at him. "I'm betting on the cell phone."

"Blair wasn't stupid," Chris said. "She'd have a backup someplace." His gray eyes narrowed. "Do you know what's odd?"

"This whole case is odd," Elliott said.

"I'm talking about Blair's room," Chris said. "She was very organized—had folders for everything broken down by finance and household and recreation."

"I saw that," Ripley said with a nod of her head. "A whole folder box. We looked through each folder. She had each year rubberbanded together."

"I'm talking about what we didn't find," Chris said.

"A folder labeled, 'Evidence of Treason Against Daniel Cross'," Ripley said.

"Bank records," Chris said.

"Blair didn't have a bank account because Blair was dead," Elliott said. "Dunleavy paid her under the table."

"Then why didn't we find a cash box?" Chris asked. "She didn't go out. She wasn't a clothes horse. She certainly wasn't traveling. She had to have money. If she had money, what did she do with it? We didn't find a cash box, so she put it someplace. Yes, Blair was dead, but Charlotte Nesbitt was alive and she had a passport. With that, she could have opened a bank account."

"So Blair had a bank account under Charlotte Nesbitt's name," Ripley said. "I'm not following you."

"I'm saying someone searched that room ahead of us," Chris said. "They found Blair's bank statements and took them."

"Because ..."

"They didn't want us to know from what bank she may have been renting a safety deposit box." Chris tapped the tabletop with his index finger. "That is where she hid her backup."

"That's a pretty big jump based on the absence of bank statements," Ripley said with a shake of her head. Her face was filled with doubt. "A lot of people have gone paperless nowadays."

"If Blair was paperless, why did she have three folders dedicated to appointment calendars?"

"It'd all be easier if we knew exactly what evidence she had of what," Elliott said. "Then we'd have a better idea of where to start."

"Our team's trying to locate people who had been stationed in Switzerland with Blair," Ripley said while reading a text. "Speak of the devil. We found one. Marianne Landon. Assistant to Blair's boss."

"Are we talking about the boss who committed suicide by shooting himself in the back three times?" Elliott asked.

"Exactly," Ripley said as the phone rang in her hand. "She's retired now and living in the Outer Banks." She put the phone to her ear. "Ripley here."

"If she actually knows anything, why wouldn't she have said something before?" Elliott asked Chris, who was staring down into his glass of water.

"Because people have been dying, that's why." Chris sighed. "Maybe this is a mistake."

"What kind of mistake?"

"I have three daughters. They need me. Someone just went and killed Blair last night. They terrified her so much that she created this huge lie to make sure her friends wouldn't blow her secret—all to keep our girls safe." He lowered his voice to a whisper. "I think Blair would want me to walk away from this while I still can. She'd want me to put their safety first."

"And let them get away with whatever it is that they have been doing?" Elliott asked. "Let them just keep whacking folks?"

"Son of a—" Ripley slammed the phone down onto the tabletop so hard that she startled Elliott and Chris.

Sterling jumped to his feet and moved to position himself between Chris and the potential threat that had prompted Ripley's outburst.

Diners at the next table turned to look at them.

Aware of the audience, Chris asked, "What happened?"

Her face screwed up with anger, Ripley rubbed it with both hands. When she brought them down to reveal her eyes, they were narrowed with fury. During their many years of working together, Chris had never seen Ripley so angry. She bit off each word when she said, "They got our evidence."

"Excuse me?" Chris shook his head. "Who got … our evidence? Are you talking—"

"The sheriff's deputies took the evidence to the FBI lab. They check it into the evidence database before it is assigned to a scientist for examination. A guy walked in with a badge and ID showing that he was a scientist from the lab and said that the Matheson case had been given priority and they needed to work the evidence ASAP. So the techs itemized it while the guy waited and handed it over to him. He left. Seven minutes later, the real scientist from the lab stopped in. The clerk asked about the new guy—"

"There was no new guy," Chris said.

"He got everything," Ripley said. "Including the phone."

"There was no new guy," Chris said.

"He got everything," Ripley said. "Including the phone."

Chris covered his mouth to conceal the tremble working its way to his lips. His voice shook when he asked, "Do they at least have a description of the guy?"

"He kept his face adverted from the cameras," Ripley said. "But we do know one thing. He's extremely tall."

"And thin?" Chris asked. "Very tall? Very thin?"

"That's what they said."

"Murphy and I saw him last night. He said he was with the CIA and ordered Murphy to hand me over to him—matter of national security. Murphy didn't buy it. The guy tried to muscle Murphy, but he stood up to him. Guy backed down. I think it was only because there were too many witnesses."

"Lucky for you Murphy stood his ground," Ripley said.

Chris nodded his head as he took the vibrating phone from his pocket. He recognized the number for the incoming call as Ivy Dunleavy's. Bracing for a fight, he swiped his finger across the screen. "Hello."

"Chris, it's Ivy."

"Didn't we just talk?"

"I wanted to apologize," she said in a sweet voice. "I was rude to you. But you have to understand, for the last three years, Blair has been telling us what a monster you were. I had no reason not to believe her. It never occurred to me that she was hiding from someone else. Can you forgive me?"

Chris hesitated. He had a nagging feeling in the back of his mind that Ivy wanted something more than forgiveness. He never did trust her. Now, being aware that she had hidden Blair from him, he trusted her even less.

"Hannah misses Emma," Ivy said. "We should get the two of them together. Maybe this weekend."

"Now's not a good time," Chris said. "I'm going to need to figure out how to tell the girls about their mother."

"Are you heading back to your parents' farm now?" Ivy asked.

"Yes, we're getting some lunch and then I'll be heading back. Why?"

"You looked exhausted when you were here," she said. "You really should go home and get some sleep."

"I'll sleep after I find out who killed my wife."

Francine uttered a heavy sigh and put her Mini-Cooper into park. "This is why I hate city driving."

It was Saturday afternoon and traffic in Georgetown was at a stand-still. Both she and Murphy could see the bright lights and hear the sirens of emergency vehicles several blocks ahead.

Needing to stretch his long legs, Murphy opened the door and stepped out.

Francine shouted out to him when she saw Bruce and Jacqui making their way down the sidewalk. "There's Bruce and Jacqui! Hey, Bruce! Jacqui! We're over here. What's going on?"

Too sophisticated for shouting across the street, Jacqui trotted over. "They're saying there was a big explosion two blocks ahead. A brownstone. They think it was a gas explosion."

Explosion. The word struck Murphy in the heart as he could see the emergency crews working around a brownstone on the corner two blocks ahead.

A corner unit.

Worry overtaking him, he started walking.

Explosion. What kind of explosion?

As worry turned to fear, he picked up his pace.

Stephens. Hayes. Blair. All dead.

Fear turned to panic. Murphy sprinted as if there was something, anything that he could do to make everything go into reverse and he could go back to before he had never invited Tristan into this nasty dangerous business.

Breaking through the line of stopped vehicles, he saw that it was true—horribly true.

Tristan's brownstone was a fiery brick oven. The trucks from one fire company were battling the blaze and trying their best to protect the homes around it.

No. Not Tristan. Not Jessica's brother. It can't be. His mind focused only on trying to save Tristan, he fought to get through the human barricade pushing him back.

"Murphy, what are you trying to do?" Francine called out behind him.

"My brother-in-law," Murphy gasped to the officer. "Is he in there? Tell me he's not in there."

Before the officer could respond, Murphy overheard one of the firefighters call to another. "Looks like we got a fatality. They just found a body in the kitchen."

His legs numb, Murphy collapsed to his knees.

Chapter Fifteen

In contrast to the seemingly smooth flowing river next to the historical monuments and buildings on postcards, there is a fast moving, treacherous portion of the Potomac River called Great Falls. Sports enthusiasts in kayaks thrill at attempting to navigate the river's rocks and steep drop offs in the national park by the same name.

With its beautiful landscape made up of thick woods along the scenic river, Great Falls became one of Washington's upper-class suburbs, consisting of mansions both large and small. Residents included senators, presidential appointees, and other influential members of high society.

Lieutenant Murphy Thornton's home, called Thorny Rose Manor, was secured behind a fence and gate, tucked back in the woods next to the park.

As soon as Ripley Vaccaro had received the news that Tristan Faraday's computer lab had been blown up and a body had been found, she raced to Murphy's home to offer her support.

"You do know who Tristan Faraday is, don't you?" she asked Chris and Elliott in the restaurant parking lot on their way to their vehicles.

"Murphy's IT guy?" Elliott said.

"Faraday," Ripley said with significance. Seeing blank expressions, she added, "Murphy's brother-in-law. *Mac* Faraday's son."

"I've met Mac Faraday," Chris said. "Murphy's Jessica is Mac's daughter?"

"My point is this. If they took out Mac Faraday's son, I guarantee you that Faraday will insert himself into the center of all this and burn Washington down to the ground."

An eight-foot-tall steel fence surrounded the estate. They were forced to stop at the security gate to introduce themselves via a security camera and intercom to someone with a deep voice that reminded Elliott of Dark Vader.

"That's Nigel," Chris told him.

"With a voice like that, that's one sure way to discourage solicitors."

They made their way along a long driveway past a seven-car garage to a white mansion. They parked behind Francine's Mini Cooper and Ripley's SUV.

Chris climbed out of the truck and turned just in time for a sheltie with blue fur and eyes launch herself from the porch. She bound toward the truck.

Ripley paused at the front door that Francine had opened to invite them inside. "That's Spencer. She'll give you the safe combination in exchange for a belly rub."

Her senses picking up a new friend, the blue merle sheltie bounced next to the truck. With each hop, she yapped through the side window at Sterling, who barked back to her. He ditched his hat and sunglasses.

Finally, Chris opened the door to allow the two dogs to meet. They greeted by spinning around each other, sniffing and yapping, until Spencer broke away to run around the corner of the mansion. When the German shepherd hesitated, she ran back into sight. Stopping, she pawed the ground and barked an order for him to follow.

"I think she wants to show you around," Elliott told Sterling.

"I can't just let my dog run loose," Chris said.

"Where's he going to go?" Elliott gestured in the direction of the tall fence around the estate—as if it mattered. Sterling had taken off after the blue dog.

Assuming they could walk in since Francine had seen them, Elliott and Chris stepped into the two-story foyer that reached up to a cathedral ceiling. The foyer appeared even more grand than the Dunleavy mansion with its granite flooring. The grand curved staircase wrapped around a table and ornate chandelier. Despite the grandeur, there was a homier feel to the mansion—starting with the eight-inch-long tarantula that greeted them from the table.

Chris stopped Elliott when he reached for his weapon. "I think that's the maid."

The two men cautiously moved toward the spider. She waved her antenna at them.

"See, Elliott? She's offering to take your coat."

"Rich folks and their exotic pets," Elliott said with a grumble.

"We're not rich and we have a female rabbit named Thor who likes to wear pink ruffles and lace," Chris said while looking around to figure out where to go next.

"That's not exotic. That's just plain weird. There's a difference."

There appeared to be a choice of directions to go, including downstairs. An entranceway to the right led to a formal dining room. To the left was a long sunroom.

They heard a wail from the living room located down the hallway beyond the sun room. Chris led the way into the elegant room with a granite fireplace that took up an entire wall.

On his knees, Murphy was hugging a woman on the sofa while she sobbed. Enveloped in Murphy's arms, it was hard for Chris and Elliott to see what she looked like. What they could see, she was attractive with thick alabaster hair down to her shoulders. There was an array of medical books and a laptop on the sofa, where she had been studying when Murphy and the Geezers had arrived with the awful news of her brother's sudden death.

"I am so so sorry." Murphy's eyes were wet as he buried his face in her hair. "It was all my fault, Buttercup. I never should have let him get involved in this."

Jessica hiccupped. "But he wanted to."

"He wasn't trained for it. The people we go up against … human life has no value to them." He hugged her tighter. "I can only imagine what they did to him before they …" His voice broke.

"Oh, Murphy." She pulled away and buried her face in her hands.

"Is there anything I can do, Buttercup?"

"Isn't that what they name cows? Buttercup?" Elliott asked Chris, who responded with a sharp look. "Just saying."

"It's not polite to judge," Chris hissed.

"Murphy, can you get me a glass of water?" she blubbered.

"Anything. I'll do anything for you, my love." Murphy rose to his feet and hurried past Chris and Elliott to head for the kitchen.

Francine, Jacqui, and Ripley moved in to comfort Jessica. As they gathered around her, Jessica lifted her dry face from her hands to reveal a slim smile.

Chris spun around to follow Murphy. As he rounded the corner to enter the gourmet kitchen, he heard a male voice.

"Hey, Murphy, can you get me a beer while you're in the fridge?"

Chris ran in just in time to see Murphy put a lanky man with glasses into a headlock.

"Murph!" the young man cried out while fighting him the best he could, "I thought you'd be happy to see I'm alive!"

"I am happy!" Murphy shook him by his shirt collar. "So happy I want to hug you … until you're black and blue!"

"We need some help in here!" Chris yelled in the direction of the living room while prying the two men apart.

Bruce and Elliott each took one of the men and pulled them back. Jessica jumped between them.

"You let me think you were dead!" Murphy said while Jessica held him back.

"Gee, Murph, I didn't know you cared!" Tristan said while taking cover behind Francine.

"I don't." Murphy shook off Bruce and Jessica. "I just don't like knowing that I'm going to get killed in my sleep after your dad got the news."

"Tristan, what happened?" Ripley asked. "They found a body in your brownstone."

"They're going to find a second one, too," Tristan said while straightening his clothes.

"Who were they?" Bruce asked.

"Assassins sent by Slade Industries." Tristan waved his phone for them to see. "Recorded the whole thing. Wanna watch?" You would have thought he was inviting them to see the debut of a new movie.

They went downstairs to the family room, which included a bar and flat screen high definition television tuned to a dinosaur documentary. In contrast to the luxurious surroundings, a worn recliner rested in the prime viewing spot. A Bassett hound mix, remote tucked under his paw, occupied the recliner.

"Naw," Jessica said, "we can't watch it in here. Newman's watching *Jurassic Fight Club*."

"Newman?" Jacqui asked.

Jessica pointed to the Bassett hound who narrowed his eyes at them. They were blocking his view. Jessica eased Jacqui to the side. "He really loves his television. Whatever you do, don't touch the remote."

Tristan trotted into the hallway and opened the double doors. "We'll watch it in the home theater. You'll love it."

"Oh, yeah, I love watching people get killed," Jacqui said with sarcasm.

"They were assassins," Bruce reminded her.

In response to a scratch at the glass doors leading to the patio, Murphy opened the door to allow Spencer and Sterling to gallop inside. The two dogs made a beeline for the home theatre.

"Did we get a new dog?" Jessica asked about the German shepherd following Spencer.

"He's with me," Chris said.

"He doesn't steal, does he?"

"No, but he does cheat at cards," Bruce said.

Tristan was already offering drinks and refreshments from the minibar in the home theater, furnished in leather recliners.

Spencer nudged open the arm cover to reveal a pocket holding dog biscuits. She took one out and placed it in Sterling's seat in between his front paws. She licked his tall ears while he ate the treat.

Bruce and Jacqui were quick to accept Murphy's offer of a fine wine from the wine cellar. Since Murphy didn't drink, Jessica, who knew more about fine wines, went to fetch a worthy bottle.

"Wasn't your computer lab blown up?" Francine accepted the bottle of beer Tristan offered to her. "You don't seem upset."

"I keep everything on the cloud off-site," Tristan said. "All I lost was hardware and equipment. That's replaceable."

"But if *you* killed them, why did you blow up your own lab?" Bruce asked.

"So that Slade Industries would think they did the job," Tristan said.

"How do you know the hitmen had been sent by Slade Industries?" Bruce asked.

"They told me," Tristan said. "And they had no reason to lie, seeing as how they were about to kill me. It isn't like I was going to tell anyone."

Once everyone was seated, Tristan directed Nigel to play the security recording that had been stored to the cloud.

With the date and time noted in the bottom corner of the recording, the screen revealed the front stoop of the brownstone. People could be seen walking by the row of brownstones, many stoops decorated with colorful mums in the fall season. A black SUV parked far down the street—just within view of the camera shot. Even before the two men who climbed out came into shot, it was plain that they were interlopers. Those in the home theater recognized the bulges under their coats.

"They actually got there a little later than I expected," Tristan said.

"You were expecting them?" Francine asked.

"The tracking device I had attached to the travel mug was made by one of Slade Industries' computer tech companies," Tristan said. "As paranoid as that company is, I knew they would instantly find the device and use the lot number to track where it was sold and who to. Considering that I bought it online and used my credit card, it was only a matter of time." He gestured at the two assassins. "They stopped for lunch first. Mexican. I could smell the enchilada sauce on their clothes."

"But we still don't know exactly what it was Cross was passing to the courier," Murphy said.

"Well, considering that they wanted to kill Tristan just for tracking whatever it was to them, I'd say we can safely assume it was something he shouldn't have been sharing," Chris said.

With a sense of purpose, the two assassins made their way to the stoop where one held out his arm to stop his partner. "This is it." He gestured for him to loop around to the back of the townhome. "Keep your com on," he ordered him to stay in communication with him.

As his partner disappeared out of view, the first man cautiously made his way up the stoop to the security panel. Adjusting his earbud and mouthpiece, he lowered his body to peer through the windows to make sure he was not being watched. His face became magnified as he moved in closer to examine the camera and mike. A malevolent grin crossed his face as he fished a device out of his pocket and plugged it into the unit. He pressed several buttons on the keypad.

Beep!

Letters across the bottom of the screen read: Suspect Disabled Security System

With a chuckle, the assassin said into his mouthpiece. "Security system disabled." He pressed his phone against the door's smart lock. They could hear the application shuffle through the various number combinations before striking the code to unlock it. The whirling noise of the lock disengaging was followed by a click.

"Easy as pie." The assassin took the semiautomatic out of his holster and pushed through the door.

"He's just walking in," Jacqui said. "Did you see how easy he took out your security system?"

Tristan shrugged his shoulders.

"You set a trap for them," Bruce said with a wicked grin. "I like the way you think, Faraday. Ever think of going into law?"

"Never."

The recording shifted to a view of the back door where the other assassin picked the lock in a matter of seconds. "The system in the rear isn't even on," he told his partner through the earbud while extracting his gun. "Deadbolt isn't turned. Some people are so sloppy with their security systems that they deserve to get robbed and killed." He made his way through a rear office to the hallway.

"Wait a minute," Jacqui said, "how are you picking up their radio communications?"

"My sloppy security system hacked into it." Tristan waved his hands. "It's airwaves on my property. That makes it all legal."

The recording transitioned to the kitchen where Tristan was packing up his backpack.

"Intruders have now entered the premises," Nigel said. "Emergency services have been notified. Should I give the medical examiner a head's up?"

"That would be polite. Tell them to send fire, too. Lots and lots of fire trucks. I like fire trucks."

Tristan checked the time on the clock on the microwave while taking a jar of mayonnaise out of the fridge. He took out a bottle of beer as well. He closed the door and turned around to see the first assassin aimed a nine-millimeter Berretta at his mid-section.

"I assume you're from Slade Industries," Tristan said while holding up his hands with the beer and mayonnaise.

A split screen showed the assassin's partner making his way down the back hallway toward Tristan with his weapon aimed at the back of his head. He entered the kitchen.

The split screen showed the kitchen at a downward angle from the far corner of the kitchen. The other angle was at eye level from behind the sink.

"I guess you know why we're here," the lead assassin said. "Saves us having to listen to you begging to know why we're going to have to kill you."

"This has everything to do with me tracking stolen government secrets to Slade Industries." Tristan set the mayonnaise on the kitchen table. "Of course, your boss sent you. Is that Leban Slade himself or one of his presidents?"

Tristan waited for an answer and received none. "You have to know if Leban Slade is involved in it. His conglomerate is the government's biggest defense contractor. Wouldn't it be a kick if it turned out that he got those contracts because he had inside information about what our military and intelligence agencies needed in order to gear his bids for the contracts?" He opened the bottle of beer and took a drink of it. "Or maybe the information he's been getting is personal info that he can use to extort preferential treatment when it comes to deciding on contracts?"

"Shut up, kid."

"Whoever is behind collecting this stolen classified data has to be aware that if I figured it out, that others have figured it out as well. Maybe Slade doesn't care." Tristan took another drink from the beer. "Certainly, you don't because it means job security for you. The more people find out, the more you have to silence." He frowned. "Don't tell me I'm the first."

"Get down on your knees," the lead assassin ordered.

"Targets locked," Nigel said into Tristan's earbud. "Defense systems activated on your command, Tristan."

"I think *you* should get down on your knees," Tristan told the assassins. "Put your hands behind your heads. The police will be real impressed to find you ready to go when they arrive."

The hitmen looked at each other and laughed.

"You're funny, kid," the second one said.

"And you're stupid," Tristan said. "You broke into a smart house. You have no idea what this house is capable of."

"We broke through your system like a hot knife through butter," the head goon said. "Your house ain't very smart. As a matter of fact, it's stupid."

"I wouldn't say that if I were you," Tristan said. "Nigel is very sensitive."

Both hitmen laughed. The second one looked up at the ceiling. Seeing the security camera, he held up his middle finger. "Not only are you stupid, Nigel. You're downright retarded."

"Can I kill them now, Tristan?" Nigel asked into his ear com.

"Yes," Tristan said.

Four shots rang out from various points of the kitchen. The gunmen dropped—both with a shot through the heart and another through the head.

"Told you Nigel was sensitive." Tristan set down his beer and knelt next to the bodies. He searched their pockets for their wallets and cell phones.

"Law enforcement will arrive in ETA two minutes," Nigel said.

"Set timer to detonate in ninety seconds," Tristan said.

"Detonate explosives?"

"Detonate the lab, Nigel." Tristan placed the wallets and cell phones in the backpack with Monique on top. "Ensure everything is on the cloud. One minute and fifteen seconds." He zipped up the backpack. "I want the brownstone to go up before law enforcement arrives on the scene."

"Files already backed up, including security footage. Lab will detonate in one minute."

Tristan opened up the sliding glass door and stepped outside.

The screen filled with the numbers counting down as the sirens in the distance grew louder.

They were still in the distance when the screen went black. The noise of the explosion filled the home theater.

Chapter Sixteen

"Blair certainly liked angels," Helen said as she repacked the last of a box filled with angel figurines.

"That's where Emma gets it." Doris opened the last box, a small one that rested in the far corner of the storage room in the farmhouse's basement. "Blair liked clocks and angels."

"Then she should have these," Helen said with her hands on the lid that she was about to set on the box. "It's a shame to leave them in this dusty old box when they can be set out and admired."

"You're right. We'll give them to her when she comes back from the ride."

"We're ba-ack!" Emma sang as she raced into the room with Sadie and Mocha directly behind her. In her sock-covered feet, she was almost dancing on her toes. She launched herself into Doris's arms. Doris tickled the little girl, who squealed with delight while squirming to the floor, at which point she started wrestling with Mocha.

"Hey, Sierra! They're down here in the basement." Curiosity filling her face, Nikki stepped over Sadie, who took her post by the door. "What are you doing?"

"Going through your mother's things," Doris said. "I keep telling your father that we need to go through them. I'm sure she wanted you to have her stuff."

"Like what?" Nikki asked in a sharp tone.

Helen presented the box of angels to Emma. "Your mother had a whole collection of angels. I'm sure she wanted you to have them, Emma."

A wide smile filled Emma's face as she tore into the box. When Sierra joined them, Emma proudly showed her one angel after another. "My mommy is an angel. She watches over me every night from her home in the clock in my room. She sings to me, too."

Nikki rolled her eyes.

"I'm sure your mother would like for you to have this picture, Nikki." Doris picked up a framed photograph of Nikki, as a small girl, dressed in full cowgirl gear, sitting on top of a pony. She held a blue ribbon. "It's you at your first riding competition on your first pony."

Nikki backed away from the photograph. "I already have that picture. Dad keeps it on his dresser." She stepped over the two furry bodies lying in the doorway and ran up the stairs.

Doris and Helen exchanged sad glances.

"Nonni, do you think Dad can build me a case to put all my angels in so they don't fall and break their wings?"

"I'm sure your father would be glad to do that for you," Doris said.

Sierra offered to carry the box up to Emma's room to sort through the collection.

Doris waited for them to be well out of earshot before rolling her eyes. "You don't think Nikki has any resentment toward her mother, do you?" Her tone dripped of sarcasm.

"Children understand a whole lot more than we give them credit for. Sierra resents her father—not because of anything I've said about him cheating on me and breaking up our marriage. Her feelings are based completely on what she saw and what she heard. I'm the one who keeps trying to get her to have a relationship with him." Helen shook her head with a sigh.

"How's that working for you?"

"Not well." Helen ripped open the last box, which was filled with folders and paperwork. "To tell you the truth, she's closer to Chris than she is her own father."

"That's because they have something very much in common."

With a nod of her head, Helen agreed while leafing through the papers. "They both love riding horses. I keep saying no, but they're wearing me down. I've come to resign myself to the fact that soon, and very soon, Sierra is going to have her own horse living in one of the stalls in that barn out there." She gestured in the general direction of the barn only to have Doris grab her arm—capturing her attention from the papers in the box.

"I wasn't talking about the horses. I was talking about you. Both Christopher and Sierra love you. That's what they have in common." Doris smiled. "But you're right. They love those horses, too."

Helen's cheeks turned pink. "Bank of America." She showed a folder label to Doris. "She had an account at the Bank of America."

"So did Christopher," Doris said. "They had a joint account when she died—I mean the first time she died."

"I guess it would be too much to ask for her to have a safety deposit box."

"That would make it too easy, dear."

"Mom?" Having carried the box of angels to Emma's room, Sierra returned. Her expression was one of concern. "There's a couple of guys watching the house. Scopes and everything. We saw them up over the ridge when we were coming back."

She pointed in the general direction of the back of the farm. "In a dark blue SUV with Virginia plate. JYN-4958."

"You remembered the license plate number," Doris said. "Very good. I'm impressed."

"Sierra has a photographic memory," Helen said while putting the license number into a state police application on her phone. "It's a rental car."

"Did Nikki and Emma notice them?" Doris asked Sierra.

"Nikki did," Sierra said. "We were afraid they were a couple of pervs."

"Could be," Doris said. "Or they could be hunters who can't read our no hunting signs."

"Are you sure they were watching the house and not looking for deer?" Helen exchanged glances with Doris.

"Hunters watching the farm house with scopes?" Sierra asked. "What are you going to do? Call the police?"

"I am the police," Helen said.

"Well, I meant …"

"I'll take care of this." Doris stepped around her to go up the stairs to the main level. "You keep an eye on Nikki and Emma."

Sierra's face brightened. "Are you going to shoot them?"

Doris paused to think over her suggestion.

"Doris," Helen said, "you can't shoot them just for watching the house."

Sierra's face fell.

"But I can play with them," Doris said.

"Can I help?" Sierra tapped her fingertips together. "I love to play."

"You're too young. Helen, you come with me. If you're good, I'll let you play with my battery cables." Doris stepped into the hallway. "Oh, ladies!"

The Doberman and lab seemed to jump out of a sound sleep to sit at attention.

"Follow me."

They scurried to take their positions on either side of their master.

"It's time for you to earn your kibble."

"Right now," Bruce told the group gathered in the dining room, "all we have is a circumstantial case of unauthorize disclosure of classified information." He tossed a piece of popcorn up into the air and caught it in his mouth.

"Granted, that's a felony," Murphy said, "but killing everyone who gets close to uncovering it seems like overkill."

"We aren't even close right now because we have no idea what was in that travel mug that Daniel Cross had passed to the courier." Ripley took a handful of popcorn from a second bowl while putting her phone to her ear. "Nor do we even know if it got to Slade Industries." Tossing some popcorn into her mouth, she hurried out of the dining room to talk on the phone.

"In other words, we have nothing." Jacqui reached for the bowl of popcorn, took a handful and placed it on a napkin laid out in front of her.

"If what we have uncovered is so weak, why did they risk so much trying to kill Tristan?" Jessica asked while casting a glance in Chris Matheson's direction. He had been quiet ever since they had been introduced.

"Why did they kill Stephens and Hayes?" Murphy asked. "And tried to kill Chris just because he saw Blair at the metro station?"

"Because he killed an international assassin," Bruce said. "They assumed he did that because he was onto them."

"Conclusion. These people don't take chances," Tristan said.

"Especially now," Murphy said. "Daniel Cross's confirmation hearings are starting in two days. He's on track to become the director of the Central Intelligence Agency. If it comes out that he's been giving, selling, doing whatever with classified information—"

"And that he's been passing it onto Leban Slade to give him an inside track on government contracts," Francine said. "Think of everything that he can get his hands on if he becomes director."

"That's not all," Bruce said. "As director, Cross will get access to the agency's resources. If he's been doing everything we suspect him of doing, that means Slade can blackmail him to use those resources to do whatever he wants—beyond government contracts. We're talking about using black ops to take out Slade's enemies."

"What does any of this have to do with Blair?" Chris asked in an abruptly loud voice.

Every head turned to face where he sat at the head of the table. He had been so quiet during their energetic conversation, that some had forgotten his presence.

Chris swallowed. "Blair had never met Daniel Cross or Leban Slade."

"No," Murphy said, "but she had uncovered something very damning to Cross. My sources found out that in the days leading up to her going to France, she met with her boss about something she had discovered while archiving Lithuanian communications."

"Daniel Cross had been deputy chief of station in Lithuania when Ambassador Brown was killed in that car bomb," Francine said. "He put together the evidence that led authorities to the extremist terrorist group responsible for the bombing."

"Maybe they weren't responsible," Elliott said with an arched eyebrow.

Murphy nodded his head. "Whatever it was had to be incriminating because Blair and her boss had a meeting with the chief of station in Switzerland. According to the communications chief's assistant, Ned Schiff ordered them to bury whatever it was they had uncovered. Schiff is now deputy director of the intelligence directorate at the CIA, second to Daniel Cross. He's first in line to take Cross's place after he's confirmed."

"He covered Cross's butt," Elliott said.

"Blair implicated Daniel Cross in her letter to Senator Keaton," Bruce said.

"We have nothing," Chris said. "Lurch walked right into the FBI, took all of the physical evidence connected to Blair's murder, and walked out like he owned the place. That means even if we do figure out who killed her, we have nothing to convict them."

"We do have Blair's body." Ripley returned to the dining room. "The ME says she drowned. He found a bruise in the shape of a footprint on her back, right between her shoulder blades. Her body shows no defensive wounds, which means she didn't fight against her killer. He's thinking she was drugged. He's running a tox screen."

"Let's hope they don't steal that," Francine said.

"The fact is that they've taken *everything*." Chris gestured at Murphy. "They knew about the letter before anyone even knew who wrote it. They had a team of international assassins ready to follow us to safe houses, chiefs of station in Switzerland ordering stuff get buried and when it isn't then people shoot themselves in the back—" He held up three fingers. "Three times."

"Sounds like they have a lot of juice," Bruce said.

"They have a whole lot of juice," Chris said.

"They are also motivated by evil."

"Which is why we need to take them down," Murphy said. "They already have more than enough power."

Chris gestured at the people around the table. "And how do you expect us, a group of retirees who pretend to be a book club because our families scare the crap out of us, to take these people down?"

"The only thing necessary for the triumph of evil is for good men to do nothing," Jessica said in a soft voice.

"Edmund Burke," Chris said. "I grew up with my dad saying that all the time. That's why he went into law enforcement. But I had my mother. If anything happened to him, he knew my mother would take care of me. My daughters don't have that luxury. They lost their mother. Blair would not want me to allow them to become orphans." He rose from the table and walked out.

Elliott started to stand up, but Jessica urged him back into his seat.

"I'll talk to him. You stay here." Jessica hurried out of the room after Chris.

"But—"

"No need to worry, Elliott," Murphy said with a wink. "Jessica can be very persuasive."

"That's not what …" Elliott sat down. "He's my ride."

Abruptly, one of the cell phones resting in the center of the table rang.

Tristan rubbed his hands together. "It's about time."

"What's about time?" Jacqui asked.

Tristan pointed at the phone as it rang a second time. "One of our hitman's getting a call. Probably from the boss."

"Answer it!" Francine said as it rang a third time.

"What do I say?" Tristan's eyes grew wide. "What if they don't recognize my voice and realize—"

Murphy snatched the phone from the center of the table. He swiped his finger across the screen, pressed the button to record the call, and hit the speaker phone. "Yeah?" He had a heathy dose of annoyance in his tone.

"What did you think you were doing?" the male caller demanded. "You blew up Faraday's house?"

"Covering up evidence." Murphy uttered a wicked laugh. "If he had enough to follow the trail to Slade, then there's no telling what evidence he had stashed away in his house."

"Since when did you start thinking? I don't pay you to think. I pay you to take care of issues before they become problems. Blowing up a brownstone in the middle of Georgetown's high rent district creates problems."

"You mean like walking into the FBI and walking out with all of the evidence for a murder."

"How'd you hear about that?" he snapped.

"Word gets around. A tall man is hard not to notice."

"Listen, don't you worry about me," he said with a chuckle. "It takes more than skill for someone like me to walk into the FBI and walk out without causing problems."

"What do you need more than skill, and where do I get it?"

"Protection from all the right people."

"If the client is so protected, why would he have to send you in to remove evidence," Murphy said. "I mean, why not just make the investigation go away—if your contacts are as powerful as you say they are?"

"It was a rush job. Jenn called this afternoon. Said it was a lose end that the client thought had been taken care of years ago. I had to make sure nothing problematic ended up getting in the wrong hands." His tone became increasingly annoyed. "Why all the questions?"

"Just looking to move up to more challenging assignments," Murphy said with as casual a tone as possible. As soon as the words left his lips, he realized the caller was weighing his options.

The silence on the other end of the line stretched on forever.

Everyone held their breath.

"When's my next job?" Murphy asked.

"I'll call you."

Click.

"Jenn," Elliott said. "Who do we know named 'Jenn?'"

"Sterling!" Chris called out from the front porch in the general direction of the estate. "Come. Let's go." He listened for any sound of Sterling answering the call. He heard nothing. The last time he had seen the German shepherd, he was getting his face kissed all over by the blue merle sheltie.

"I think Spencer took him to the river to show him her favorite spot." Jessica stood on the front step looking down at where he waited for the dog with the truck's driver door open. "She seems to be quite smitten with him."

"He's got a girlfriend already," Chris said. "Her name is Thor."

"Sounds like she could kick Spencer's butt."

"Not really. Thor's a bunny."

"Ah." Jessica made her way down the steps. "Chris, I totally understand where you're coming from. Right now, we've got nothing against Daniel Cross, except a letter written by a woman who was supposed to be dead. So even if you were able to dig anything up, Cross's friends in Washington will spin Blair's allegation faster than a chocolate milkshake and smear her."

She stepped over to him and gazed up into his gray eyes. "The only thing that they value is power. Human life means nothing. Anyone who gets in the way will be squashed like a bug. They'd think nothing of making your children orphans."

"Are you trying to change my mind?" Crossing his arms, Chris leaned against the front fender of his truck. "You're not doing a very good job."

Jessica folded her arms across her chest. "My mother was murdered."

This was news to Chris. "I'm sorry to hear that."

She dropped her gaze to the pavement beneath her feet. "She was one of those women who could never be happy. She always saw what she didn't have. It was during my freshman year of college that she kicked Dad out."

"Before he inherited his fortune," Chris said.

Jessica allowed a slight smile to cross her lips. "Boy, did she regret that—especially after the man she traded him up for dumped her." She shook her head. "My point is, it's not just lip service when I say I know what your daughters will be going through. It is devastating to have someone you love ripped out of your life. The pain never goes away. You just learn to live with the hole in your heart."

"And now they'll have to go through all that again," Chris said.

"I was older than your daughters, but I still needed my dad to cling to. He made me feel safe. Mom's murder made me realize how easy it was to have someone I love taken away from me."

"You do understand why I need to walk away from this." Chris called out to Sterling who he saw round the corner of the house with Spencer. He gestured for the dog to jump into the seat, only to have Sterling stop and look longingly at Spencer, who uttered a whine.

"But I also had questions. Without the answer to those questions, I couldn't have closure." She scooped Spencer up when the little dog tried to follow Sterling into the truck. "I depended on my dad to do everything he could to get those answers for me." She rubbed her cheek in Spencer's fur while the dog cried to go with Sterling.

Chris pushed Sterling over into the passenger seat, climbed into the truck, and started the engine. "What would it have done to you if you had lost your father because he went after those answers? Then, you would have been without both parents. That's an awfully high price to pay for closure."

Chapter Seventeen

Helen didn't know whether to be impressed or frightened by the sixty-five-year-old librarian.

Within minutes of learning about the two men in the dark blue SUV, Doris had concocted a plan to capture them. She had read it in a book—though she couldn't remember the author or the title. She did recall that it had a red and black cover.

The two women put on Chris's worn work coats and rubber boots that he wore for messy farm chores and jumped into the old "farm-use" truck with Doris at the wheel. She looped around the farm to approach the two men in the rental SUV.

Then, she floored it to rear end them. Cursing, the two men, one obese and the other short and boxy, jumped out of their vehicle to check on the damage.

At the same time, Doris and Helen spilled out of the truck and went at each other—arguing about who caused the accident.

The men were equally amused and dumbfounded by the cat fight. It was when they stepped in to separate the women that Doris and Helen pulled out their stun guns and knocked both men off their feet.

After hiding their SUV in the barn, Helen hurried to the workshop.

Kirk Matheson had hand-crafted the lovely woodwork in their farmhouse in his workshop. Over the years, he had collected so many tools, that most men would consider his workshop a carpenter's heaven, which he had passed on to Chris.

In the workshop, Helen found that Doris had spread a blue tarp across the floor and had their suspects duct taped to two straight back chairs—naked. Sadie and Mocha guarded them while Doris searched their wallets and cell phones.

They looked like a human version of Mutt and Jeff. Maybe it just seemed that way because one of them was obese—mostly in his gut, which hung down to almost conceal his crotch. She was perplexed about how Doris had managed to get the three-hundred-pound man upright in a chair. Then she noticed the pully with a rope hanging from the ceiling.

"Why are they naked?" Helen asked while keeping her head adverted from the scene.

"Don't you have an AFIS app on your phone to check their fingerprints in the national database?" Doris handed a business card to Helen.

"I don't need them naked to take their fingerprints." Helen read the card.

Final Solution Agency was the name on the card.

What kind of name is that for what kind of agency?

"Oh good." Doris turned her attention to the captives who were moaning. "They're coming to. Now we can get this party started."

They looked like a human version of Mutt and Jeff. Maybe it just seemed that way because one of them was obese—mostly in his gut, which hung down to almost conceal his crotch.

Helen was perplexed about how Doris had managed to get the three-hundred-pound man upright in a chair. Then she noticed the pully with a rope hanging from the ceiling.

As soon as the larger of the two men regained consciousness to see that he was naked and duct taped, he let loose with a string of obscenities. Helen wasn't sure which made him madder—that he had gotten captured by two women or had gotten captured, stripped, and taped to a chair by two women.

"Are you through?" Doris paused to read the name on his Maryland driver's license when he stopped to catch his breath. "Ralph?"

"No, I'm not through. I have rights." Ralph struggled against Helen, who went behind the chair to scan the print from his index finger with her phone. "I want my lawyer now. I'm going to sue your asses."

Doris cocked her head and bestowed a charming smile on them. "Yes, you do have rights. I have rights, too. I have the right to protect my property and you two were on my property and I strongly suspect it was for no-good."

"We got lost," the smaller man said. "We were trying to figure out where we were when you rear-ended us."

"Now, Tony." Doris make a clicking noise with her tongue. "How can we possibly develop a mutually beneficial relationship based on trust if you're going to lie to me." With a knowing smile, she moved in closer to them. "Do I look like I was born yesterday?"

"Um—" Tony said.

"'Um' is not an answer." Doris picked up one of their phones. "There's no way you were lost. The map on Tony's phone brought you straight here to this address from Rockville, Maryland. The link to that map was texted to you from SD Associates shortly before noon. Now, I want to know who SD Associates is and why they hired you to come out here."

"To commit murder." Helen showed her phone to Doris. "They're hit men. At least Ralph seems to be."

Ralph's fingerprints had generated a hit in AFIS. His prints had been found at the scene of a cold case in the Baltimore area. The victim had been a young pregnant woman believed to have been involved with a married man. She had been killed execution style.

A salacious smile crossed Doris's face. "Oh, this is going to be such fun." She turned to them. "Who's SD Associates? What did they send you out here for?"

"I have no idea what you're talking about." Ralph stuck out his chin.

"Dinner!" Doris shouted.

On cue, Sadie and Mocha lunged from where they had been sitting docile. They bore their teeth. They actually seemed to foam at the mouth as the two men tried to pull their legs up onto the chairs out of their reach.

"Doris, you can't!" Helen said.

Doris snapped her fingers and told the dogs to stand down. Instantly, they dropped back. "Why can't I?"

Aware of the men watching them, Helen lowered her voice. "Remember what happened the last time?"

With a wave of her hand, Doris dismissed her concern. "The wise always learn from their mistakes. Believe me—" Her giggle had a touch of insanity. "I won't make that mistake again." She threw open the door. "I've checked out a new book from the library. It was written by a serial killer—of course, he couldn't use his real name. He's got this recipe that will totally dissolve their bodies in less than forty-eight hours. That reminds me—" She checked the time on her watch. "Oh, dear me! I forgot to take the roast out of the freezer to thaw for dinner. Oh, Helen, can you be a dear and gas up the wood chipper?" With that, she hurried out the door.

Both men's eyes were as big as saucers.

Helen examined the two men's phones to see if she could uncover anything about who had sent them.

"You two are crazy!" Ralph said.

"They're bluffing, Ralph," Tony said.

"They're going to run us through a wood chipper."

"Do you see her gassing it up?"

"Thanks for reminding me, Tony." Tucking their phones into her pocket, Helen picked up the five gallon can from where it was stored in the supply closet and went outside—leaving Sadie and Mocha standing guard over the two men.

Once she was outside, Helen set the gas can down and called Ray Nolan.

"Looks like the Geezer Squad has been put through its paces this weekend," Ray told her. "I've been doing a background check on Daniel Cross and it makes for very interesting reading."

"The president's nominee to lead the CIA?"

"Blair's letter to the senate judiciary committee accuses him of being a traitor and the circumstantial evidence I found on the internet kind of supports that," he said. "He was the recipient of the prestigious Slade Scholarship for undergraduate school. Got the full ride—all four years."

"Slade Industries," she said. "Leban Slade is a billionaire."

"Cross also got the full ride for graduate school thanks to Leban Slade," he said.

"Does that really prove he's a spy? He could have gotten the scholarships because he's very smart."

"If he's so smart, why'd he accept a government service job at half the salary that Slade industries, one of our country's biggest government contractors, could pay him? Answer. Because Cross could do a lot more for Slade working his way up in the CIA."

"That sounds pretty circumstantial to me," she said.

Ray grumbled. "What did you call for besides to burst my bubble?"

"SD Associates," Helen read the caller ID on Tony's phone. She read off the phone number of the last call he had received. "They texted the address and map for the Matheson farm. Who is that?"

Ray hummed while checking his information. "Stu Dunleavy, attorney at law."

"Are you kidding me?"

"Didn't Chris say last night that the Dunleavys were Blair's friends?"

"If they're such good friends, why did Stu send a couple of hitmen out here to the farm?" After disconnecting the call, Helen started up the wood chipper and turned up the power to make it as loud as possible. Then, she trotted back into the woodshop to find Tony and Ralph sitting up tall—their eyes even bigger than before.

Doris flew through the other door with a pink tool chest tucked under her arm. "Oh, Helen! You are not going to believe what I've just remembered." She dropped the tool chest on the floor and opened it up. "Kirk got me these tools for Christmas about twenty years ago." She extracted an electric drill from the case and attached a long thin drill bit to the end. "It's a little rusty, but—" She looked at Ralph. "Are you up to date on your tetanus shots?" She shrugged. "It isn't like it matters." She started up the drill and aimed it at his crotch.

Ralph tried to back away. Huge drops of sweat rolled down his flabby face.

With a shake of her head, she turned it off. "Nah, this bit is much too long. I need a shorter one." She knelt to search through the box.

"Okay, I'll talk!" Ralph said.

"Shut up, Ralph!"

"She's going drill a hole in my penis! I need my penis, Tony!" Foam was forming on Ralph's lips as he confessed. "Stu Dunleavy hired us to burn down the farm and make sure we took out Chris Matheson with it! We were waiting up on the ridge for him. She said he'd be back later on this afternoon."

"She?" Helen asked. "Isn't Stu a man?"

"His assistant. She called Tony." Ralph turned to his partner. "What'd you say her name was, Tony?"

"I'm not talking 'til I get a deal!"

"Jenn!" Ralph blurted out. "Her name is Jenn!"

"You're an idiot, Ralph!" Tony said. "So what if she drilled holes in your penis? You weren't gonna need it after she put you through the wood chipper!"

Doris agreed. "Tony does have a point, Ralph."

Chapter Eighteen

"Must be nice." As she disembarked from the private plane at the airstrip in Kitty Hawk, North Carolina, Francine turned around to take it all in.

It took one call from Jessica Faraday to secure a private plane for Jacqui and Francine to fly to Kitty Hawk and rent a car to visit Marianne Landon, Les Monroe's assistant in Switzerland.

"I must say, as down to earth as Murphy is, I had no idea he was married to money." Jacqui hurried into the small airport to pick up the keys for the rental car. Marianne's house was still forty minutes down the coast and she didn't want to be hunting for it in thc dark.

"Handsome, brave," Francine gushed. "Absolutely adorable."

"The only one more adorable than him is Christopher."

Holding the door leading into the small airport, Francine paused with her mouth hanging open. "Jacqueline, was that a sexist statement that I just heard out of your mouth about our dear Christopher Matheson?"

Jacqui uttered a deep throated laugh. "I may be demure, but I also have a healthy appreciation for a well-toned set of buns just like any other red-blooded woman."

Minutes later, Jacqui was driving their rented sedan down Route 12.

Widowed at a young age, Marianne Landon had been free to work at numerous overseas stations with the state department. After returning from Switzerland, she retired and moved into a small home on Pamlico Sound.

Marianne had sounded so hesitant when Francine had called that afternoon, that they feared she would change her mind about meeting with them. After ringing her doorbell a third time, they felt as if their fears were realized.

"Let's go." Jacqui turned to go back to the car.

"One more time." Francine pressed the doorbell.

"Coming!" They heard running feet on the other side of the door before it was yanked open. A tall slender woman with long dark hair with silver streaks stood before them. Her hair was dripping wet. She wore a bathrobe hanging open over a wet swimsuit. Clutching a bottle of beer in her hand, she looked slightly wild-eyed. "I was in the hot tub." She opened the door to invite them inside. "Can I get you a beer?"

Jacqui declined. Francine accepted. Marianne invited them to take a seat in the living area of the great room while she fetched the beers from the galley kitchen.

"Thank you so much for seeing us on such short notice," Jacqui said while moving a stack of magazines from a cushion on the sofa to make room to sit next to Francine.

"I didn't catch who you were with," Marianne said with her head in the fridge. "Did you say you were with the judiciary committee about Daniel Cross's nomination?"

"We're working with their investigators," Francine said.

Marianne returned from the kitchen with a bottle of beer in each hand. Both carried a beer glass turned upside down over its open top. "I don't see where I can be much help with that. I only met Daniel Cross once."

"When was that?" Jacqui asked.

"When I was stationed in Switzerland." Marianne took a drink from her beer. "He stopped to see Ned Schiff on his way through to ..." She shrugged her shoulders. "I don't remember. It wasn't a planned official visit by any means."

"Do you remember when that was?" Francine asked.

Marianne was silent. She took another drink. When she spoke, her voice was quiet. "Kind of hard to forget. ... It was the last day that I saw Les and Blair."

Francine and Jacqui exchanged long glances.

"Les Monroe," Jacqui said. "Your supervisor."

Marianne nodded her head. "And Blair Matheson. She was head of the project archiving communications throughout the region after we had to upgrade our satellites and systems."

Francine referred to Jacqui, who had a knack for being tactful, to ask the next question.

"Did either of them, Blair or Les, see Cross when he was passing through on that last day?"

Marianne rose her eyes from where she was staring at the coffee table between them. "That's what this is really about, isn't it? It's about time someone asked about it. But the real question is, what's anyone going to do about it?"

"Depends on what it is?" Francine asked. "If you don't tell us what it's about, then how can we do anything about it?"

"I don't have any desire to commit suicide by shooting myself in the back three times," Marianne said.

"If you knew Les didn't commit suicide, why didn't you tell anyone?" Francine asked.

"Like I said, I don't want to commit suicide." After setting her glass on the coffee table, Marianne went to the windows to close the curtains.

"Did Daniel Cross and Ned Schiff make your boss commit suicide?" Jacqui watched Marianne turn the deadbolt on the door. Not wanting to give away that Blair had not died in the terrorist attack, she asked, "Did they make Blair disappear?"

"I have no proof of anything," Marianne said. "Daniel Cross was a hero in the intelligence committee after tracking down the group responsible for killing a U.S. ambassador. Ned Schiff was his pet. I was just a little admin assistant. My suspicions meant nothing. Like anyone would listen to what I saw and suspected."

"We're listening," Francine said. "We came all the way from Washington to hear what you have to say. Would we do that if what you saw and suspected meant nothing?"

Marianne took a long drink—weighing her options.

Francine gave it one final push. "Blair Matheson had three little kids."

That did it. Marianne hung her head. She lowered herself onto the seat across from them.

"It was about a file Blair found on Lithuania's mainframe."

"What file?" Jacqui asked.

"It seemed to be an anomaly." Marianne shook her head and shrugged her shoulders at the same time. "Every communication was backed up and categorized. But Blair found this one file—I don't even know what it was. She had opened and read it. She was so upset about what was in it that she brought it to Les's attention. He took it to Schiff who said it was nothing and to delete it. Trash it. But Blair didn't want to do that. She was mad as hell about it and stuck to her guns. The fighting went on for several days. Suddenly, out of the blue, Daniel Cross shows up in our office with Schiff. All four of them were behind closed doors. The meeting went on for hours and there was a lot of yelling."

"What was being said?" Jacqui asked.

"Blair was saying that we needed to do the right thing," Marianne said. "Les agreed with her. They wanted to send this report to Washington. Then, I heard Daniel Cross laugh. He had a cruel laugh. So arrogant. He said that if Blair was to be gone tomorrow, that no one would even remember her name a month later." She swallowed. "The next day, she was gone."

"Did Daniel Cross threaten either of them?" Francine asked.

Marianne shrugged her shoulders. "Schiff told them to think about it. Give him and Cross time to cushion the blow. That's what Cross said, 'Cushion the blow in Washington.' They wanted twenty-four hours. Blair didn't want to give it to them, but Les agreed. Politics, I know. Schiff did pull rank and basically ordered him to give Cross one day." Tears filled her eyes. "Next morning, I came in and Schiff called everyone together and said Les had committed suicide."

"By shooting himself in the back three times," Francine said.

"The only reason I know that is because I saw the first autopsy report. A few weeks later, there was a second autopsy report that listed the official cause of death as suicide." Marianne fingered the collar of her robe. "I'd heard a rumor that the medical examiner who did the first autopsy had died."

"What about Blair Matheson?" Jacqui asked.

"Schiff said she had requested time off. He said it was best. She wasn't being rational and that maybe some time off would give her time to rethink her priorities." Marianne's eyes narrowed. "I think the same people who killed Les killed her and dumped her body in Nice."

"Where's that report they were fighting about now?" Jacqui asked.

Marianne sighed. "Long gone. Ned took over the communications department before Les's body was cold. He made damn sure the report was gone with no copies anywhere."

"Someone had to have printed up a copy," Francine said.

"If so, where is it now?" Jacqui asked.

"Oh dear," Doris said with a heavy sigh when she saw Chris's truck come into view on the other side of the horse pastures.

He was driving at a much slower pace than usual. Generally, Chris had a lead foot—speeding at five to ten miles per hour over the limit. Preoccupied with the news he needed to break to the girls, he took his time driving home.

Helen felt a sense of delight upon seeing Chris returning home safely and dread with having to explain the two naked men being guarded by Sadie and Mocha in the workshop. She and Doris had hoped that the police would arrive to take Ralph and Tony into custody first. It would have made explaining that afternoon's events so much easier.

Chris parked his truck in his usual spot next to the barn. He sensed something was odd by the way they blocked the workshop door. His eyes narrowed to gray slits when he slid out of the driver's seat. He held the door open for Sterling to jump out. "What's going on? Are the girls all right?"

"They're fine." Helen's tone was much more upbeat than it needed to be.

Abruptly, Doris hugged Chris and kissed him on the cheek. "You look hungry." She took his hand. "Let me fix you something to eat." She pulled him toward the house.

Chris extracted his hand from hers. In a low voice, he asked, "What have you done now?"

Doris's hands landed on her hips. "Why do you just assume I did something wrong?"

Cursing and barking exploded from inside the workshop. Chris put out his arms to part the two women. He ran through the doorway where Sterling had jumped up to turn the knob and entered. Upon discovering the intruders, the German shepherd sounded the alarm.

Helen groaned. "We are in so much trouble."

"It's about time." Doris tossed her head in the direction of the two police cruisers from the sheriff's department making their way up the lane.

Chris stumbled out of the workshop. "Why are they naked?"

"They're hitmen," Doris said. "Your friend Stu Dunleavy had sent them."

"Stu Dunleavy is not my friend."

"He certainly is not considering that he hired two goons to murder you and burn down our house." Doris hurried to meet Sheriff Grant Bassett as he climbed out of his cruiser. "Oh, Grant, I am so glad to see you. Have you lost weight?"

Chris called to her back. "Their bare butts are on my chairs!"

"Chris, did you hear your mother? Stu Dunleavy sent them to kill you. Why would he do that?"

"Did they tell you that?" Chris asked as Doris led the sheriff and two deputies into the workshop.

"After your mother threatened to hollow out their penises with a drill," Helen said.

Chris involuntarily flinched at the thought.

"I never touched them," Doris said. "All I did was show them my pink toolbox and let their imaginations go to work."

"That was enough to make Ralph sing like a canary," Helen said.

"Which one is Ralph?" Chris asked.

"The big guy."

The sheriff stepped into the doorway. "Where are their clothes?"

"Would you believe we found them like that?" Doris's face was filled with innocence. She bestowed a smile on the lawman. "Would you like a slice of pie before you go, Grant?"

"That would be really nice, Doris." The sheriff turned to his deputies. "They found them that way."

With a sigh, Helen went into the barn to collect the men's clothes, weapons, and other evidence of their planned assassination.

"According to the call log on Tony's phone—" Doris said.

"Am I correct in assuming Tony is the short goon?" Chris asked.

"Allegedly, Jenn, Stu Dunleavy's assistant called him at one-clock this morning to burn down the house with you in it. But, according to Ralph—"

"The big canary."

Doris nodded her head. "He told us it was an emergency hit that had to be carried out ASAP." She tapped his chest with a manicured fingertip. "She gave Tony the address for your old house."

"In Reston."

"By the time Tony found Ralph, rented a vehicle, and they drove all the way to Reston, Blair's body had been found and the place was hopping with police. Jenn sent texted them a link to a map with the proper address around noon."

"Stu didn't know I had moved out of the area until we interviewed him and Ivy shortly before lunch," Chris said. "Why would they want to kill me?"

"We don't know, but we'll find out," Helen said as she joined them. "I called Ripley. Since these guys are from Maryland, Dunleavy is in Virginia, and we're in West Virginia, I figured it would be best to bring her in."

"Good idea, Helen," Chris said. "There's no way Stu Dunleavy will let us near his assistant without a half-dozen warrants."

The deputies had dressed the two men and were leading them to their cruisers.

"Blair's been living with the Dunleavys for three years," Chris said. "Why would they take her in and protect her, and then suddenly out of the blue murder her and send hit men to take me out?"

"That's something we need to find out," Helen said.

Abruptly, a cloud crossed Doris's face. "Christopher, where's Elliott?"

Murphy turned his SUV off Connecticut Avenue and then right to pull into the parking lot at the Equinox Athletic Club. In the passenger seat, Elliott squinted at the clientele, all dressed for show rather than athletics, going through the canopy entrance. Bruce was meeting old friends for cocktails at a downtown lounge.

"Is Cross really going to buy this?" he asked Murphy.

"He will if you say you're my guest." Murphy slid out of the driver's seat and opened the rear compartment. He extracted two athletic bags and tossed one to Elliott. "Now remember. If Cross asks your name—"

"I know what to do, kid." Elliott slung the bag over his shoulder. "I was doing this while you were still figuring out the difference between boys and girls." He strode to the front entrance.

"We already know that he's going to deny being in Switzerland when Les Monroe was killed," Murphy said. "There's no paper trail to prove that he was ever in the country, or even left the U.S. during that time period. He didn't use his passport. The only way he could have managed to get to Switzerland, threaten Monroe and Matheson, and then kill Monroe—"

"With Schiff's help and then cover it up by making the investigators call it a suicide."

"The only way to prove Marianne Landon told Jacqui and Francine the truth is to prove he was in the country," Murphy said.

"We need to see his reaction when confronted by a witness," Elliott said.

"If you've been doing this for so long, then I'll trust you to know how much to push."

They gained entrance into the gym using a membership that Tristan had set up by hacking into their system. In a matter of minutes, Murphy was a gym member under a phony identity and Elliott was his guest.

They found Daniel Cross working out on the weight machines next to his right hand man, Ned Schiff.

Casually, Murphy and Elliott walked up to the bench press directly across from where Cross was doing chest presses while Schiff spotted for him. Four other men lingered nearby. Each one had a noticeable bulge under his jacket. As head of the CIA's intelligence directorate, Daniel Cross was entitled to a security detail.

While Murphy set up the bar for bench presses, Elliott lingered just long enough for Daniel Cross to finish his reps and sit up. It was also long enough to garnish the attention of the security detail.

"Hey," Elliott said with a friendly grin and nodded at him.

Cross offered the slightest of polite nods.

"Don't I know you?" Elliott squinted at him.

"I get that a lot." Daniel Cross shot him a crooked grin. "You probably saw me on the news. I'm—"

"Nah, I don't watch TV." Elliott snapped his fingers. "I flew you."

"Excuse me." Not unlike a teenager being forced to tolerate a nerd, Daniel Cross rolled his eyes in Ned's direction.

"I never forget a face or a flight," Elliott said. "Three years ago. July. Destination Switzerland."

The smile fell from Daniel Cross's face. Ned Schiff gave a wordless order to one of the security guards to step in.

"Sorry, old man, but we never met," Dan said.

"Did you ever get that emergency taken care of?" Elliott asked.

Ned jerked his thumb for the guards to remove Elliott. "I don't think this gentleman is a member."

Holding out his hand to the security detail, Murphy stepped forward to take Elliott by the arm. "Uncle Hank, don't bother the other members." He turned to Cross. "I'm sorry. You know how old military pilots are. My uncle can remember every flight and passenger going back forty years. But ask him what he ate for breakfast—"

"The terrorist attack," Elliot said. "I flew you out of Switzerland on the same day that terrorist killed all those people in Nice."

"You're confused, old man," Dan blurted out. "I wasn't in Switzerland. I had gone to Switzerland on business, but definitely not then. Maybe we flew, but it wouldn't have been around the Bastille Day terror attack."

"No, I'm pretty sure I flew you there before." As two members of Cross's detail ushered him and Murphy toward the door, Elliott called out over his shoulder. "I'll check my personal flight log. It's all in there."

In the parking lot, Murphy and Elliott took their time walking to their vehicle.

"Count of three," Murphy suggested a bet.

"Nah. Five. He's got a reputation to maintain." Elliott held up his hand and counted down on his fingers as they approached the rear of the SUV.

"Excuse me!"

Murphy and Elliott exchanged private grins before pasting chagrined expressions on their faces and turning to face Daniel Cross jogging across the lot. He had ordered his detail to hang back out of earshot.

"I'm sorry about what happened in there. My buddy gets a little paranoid. He's been through a lot at some overseas bases." Dan nodded at Elliott. "I'm sure, being a military pilot, you know what I mean. I bet you've seen a lot of action during your years of service."

Elliott folded his arms across his chest. "You'd be surprised."

"Listen," Cross rubbed his chin, "Uh, what did you mean in there when you said something about a private log?"

"Just that," Elliott said. "I've been keeping a private log since I started flying. Kind of like my journal. I kept track of what I flew. Who I flew, to where, and what happened. Everything."

"Now that Uncle Hank has retired, he's going to put it all in a book," Murphy said.

"I've got everything documented." Elliott tapped his temple. "Helps me to keep the facts straight. So you can bet that as soon as I get home, I'll check my log. If I'm right, and I'm sure I am, then you'll be in there—flying into Switzerland the day before and flying out the day of the terrorist attack in France."

Daniel Cross's face turned red. "You are aware that I work for the CIA."

Elliott's eyes grew wide. "You're kidding."

"That means all of my business, including my travels, are matters of national security." Dan moved in closer. "Now, whether you are right, and I am wrong about going to Switzerland is irrelevant. What matters is what you do with the information. If you go around broadcasting that I was traveling in that part of the world at that time, terrible things could happen."

"What type of terrible things?" Elliott said.

"The worst type of things," Dan said with a stern expression.

Elliott's mouth dropped open.

With a nod of his head, Dan added in a low voice. "People could die." He tapped Elliott on the chest. "So, it is very important that you do your part to protect our country and its citizens by making sure that no one knows about our little trip. Can I count on you to do that?"

Elliott stood up tall. "You most certainly can, sir."

"I knew I could make you see things my way." Cross smiled broadly at Elliott as he went around to climb into the SUV.

Before Murphy could go around to the driver's side, Cross grabbed him by the elbow and jabbed him in the kidney, sending a sharp pain up Murphy's spine. "If you care anything about your uncle and your family, you better burn that log," he hissed into his ear.

Murphy tried to turn to face him, but Cross punched him again. Cross had a tight hold on him so that no one nearby, including the security detail several feet away, could notice any type of conflict between the two men.

"You listen to me. If I ever see your face in this club again, you won't live to make it home. You got that?"

Murphy silently nodded his head.

With a hearty laugh, Daniel Cross released him. "Glad we got that sorted out!" He waved to Elliott through the vehicle's windows and backed up.

Sharp pains shooting through his kidney and back, Murphy climbed into the SUV. Dan kept a sharp eye on him through the rearview mirror as he backed up and pulled out onto the street.

"That went much smoother than I thought it would," Elliott said once they were on their way. "Don't you think?"

Pushing back against the pain in his back, Murphy slowly turned and arched an eyebrow in his direction.

"Could have been worse."

Murphy cocked his head.

"He could have put three bullets in your back."

Chapter Nineteen

After dinner and a movie in the family room, Chris started the ordeal of putting Emma to bed. It never took much to distract the seven-year-old from the end goal.

That evening, she was too excited about her angel collection. She and Sierra had spent the afternoon unwrapping and cleaning each one. Until Chris built a case for them, they had arranged the figurines on the shelves around the angel clock. When they ran out of room there, they put the remainder on the dresser.

The collection was diverse. Some angels were tall and slender with wide wings. Others were short and round with big eyes. There were angels dressed in white. Some were in gold. Some looked like regular people with wings and halos.

Emma named every angel and insisted on personally saying good-night to each one. She didn't want any of their feelings to be hurt.

"I'm glad Nonni found Mom's angels," Emma told Chris while re-arranging them on the dresser. "Now she doesn't have to be alone anymore."

"Mom never was alone." Chris pulled back the comforter on her bed.

"Now that she has other angels to keep her company, she's really happy."

"I'm sure she is." Chris urged her to get into the bed.

Emma climbed under the comforter. "She's so happy, she's been singing all day."

"Singing?" Chris remembered hearing the music box earlier in the day.

Emma pointed at the clock on the shelf. "She's been singing ever since we found her friends."

It was close to nine o'clock, Emma's bedtime. Chris heard the clocks below chiming and bonging to announce the hour.

Chris went to the shelf and peered at the angel clock. The second hand approached the minute hand at the top of the hour. The second hand swept pass the minute hand. The gears inside the clock churned. Then, the clocked chimed the hour, which was immediately followed by nine bongs.

As the final notes of the last bong died away, the music box played the melody.

"Hear her singing, Daddy?" Emma asked.

"Yes, I do, sweetheart." Narrowing his eyes, he studied the clock's face.

The melody ended. Chris waited for her to continue singing or to start again, as Emma claimed it had been doing. Instead, silence filled the room.

"She must be tired," Emma said.

"She knows it's your bedtime." Concluding that the singing angel was a figment of Emma's very active imagination, Chris went to the bed and hugged Emma tightly. He did not want to let her go. "I love you, honey."

She squeezed him back. "Love you, too, Daddy."

He kissed her good night and tucked her in.

On cue, Thor hopped into the room and pawed at Chris to lift her up onto the bed. As the rabbit snuggled with Emma, Sterling trotted in and joined them.

Chris was on his way up to the attic when he heard movement on the floor above. He eased his gun from his ankle holster and made his way up the stairs. As his head cleared the floorboards, he saw Helen on his bed, one ankle of her bare feet crossed over the other.

"If you shoot me, I am so going to dump you."

"What are you doing here?" Chris laid his gun on the dresser. "I didn't hear you come in."

"Sierra went out with her friends tonight," Helen said. "I didn't want you to have to explain to Emma and Nikki why your lady friend was coming over to see you late in the night, so I snuck in."

"How?"

"I used the same route you used to sneak out when you got grounded." Helen pointed at the huge oak tree outside the window. "Only I was sneaking in instead of sneaking out."

"Aren't we a little old to be sneaking around?" Chris plopped onto the bed next to her and kissed her on the cheek. "I'm glad you're here."

"Are you really?"

Chris looked down at his hands.

"I'm not staying the night," she said. "I just wanted to talk to you alone. I want you to know that I'm here for you."

"Even if it means scaling three floors up the side of a house and climbing through a window?"

"If that's not love, I don't know what is." She laid her head on his shoulder. "I know this is a difficult time for you."

He took her hand into both of his. "Thank you for understanding." He rubbed his cheek against the top of her head. "You know me better than I know myself."

She smiled softly at him.

Gently, he kissed her on the lips and pressed his forehead against hers. "I don't know how I'm going to tell the girls. There's so much I don't know."

"Like why Stu Dunleavy would want you dead," she said. "I have Ray digging into his background. Based on what I've learned from the detective working the cold case in Baltimore, this is not the first time Stu had hired these guys. A twenty-two-year-old college student interning at Stu Dunleavy's law firm was murdered twelve years ago. The killer had left a partial print on a window that he had climbed through to get into her apartment. Her friends claimed she was having an affair with him and got pregnant. The detective is coming out here tomorrow to question the hitman."

"Elliott says the two hitmen sent to take out Tristan Faraday had been sent by Lurch, the tall man. After I had left Murphy's place, he'd called one of the assassin's phones. Murphy pretended to be the hitman and Lurch admitted to being the one who had walked into the FBI and stolen the evidence from Blair's murder. He said someone named Jenn gave the order."

"I know Jenn is a pretty common name," Helen said, "but what do you think the odds are that the Jenn who hired Ralph and Tony isn't the same one who hired Lurch and the two assassins who tried to kill Murphy's brother-in-law?"

"Jenn is one busy lady." Chris uttered a chuckle. "I wonder how loyal she is to Stu Dunleavy. When Ripley and I walked into the Dunleavy place, I remember Stu telling her to call a guy named Burnett to take care of a situation ASAP."

"Does anyone know how tall this Burnett is?" Helen asked.

Chris dropped back onto the bed. "We have a whole lot of nothing." He stared at the ceiling fan above his head. "Jacqui told me that they interviewed the communications chief's assistant. Remember Les Monroe?"

Helen leaned over him. "The guy who committed suicide by shooting himself in the back three times?"

Chris looked up at her. "She told Jacqui and Francine that Blair had found some sort of report on the mainframe from Lithuania."

"Lithuania? Does anything happen in Lithuania?"

"Blair was archiving communications from all the different stations in the region. Lithuania was one of them," Chris said. "Whatever was in that report upset a lot of people. The chief of station, Ned Schiff ordered Blair and Monroe to delete the report and forget about it. They refused because of what was in it."

"What was in it?"

Chris shrugged of his shoulders. "Whatever it was had to be big because Daniel Cross traveled all the way to Switzerland to demand that they bury it—a trip for which Murphy says there's no paper trail. Someone had to exert a lot of authority to bury a flight from the United States to Switzerland."

"Maybe it was a flight on one of Leban Slade's private jets," Helen said. "From what we've uncovered, he has a stake in this."

"Murphy and Elliott caught up with Daniel Cross at his gym and Elliott mentioned being the pilot. Both Cross and Schiff were so upset that they had them thrown out of the gym." He shook his head. "Not the actions of innocent men." He looked at Helen. "I think Cross killed Monroe and Schiff covered it up. They even killed the medical examiner who refused to go along with the cover up. They tried to kill Blair, which was why she ran off to France. Like us, they thought she'd been killed in the terrorist attack. When she came out of hiding, they finished the job."

"What was in that report that cost so many people their lives?" she asked.

"I wish I knew." He took in a deep breath. "The problem is that these people are so powerful and have such deep connections. They don't care who they kill or whose lives they ruin—just so that they can keep their power. No one can touch them."

"No one is untouchable," Helen said.

"Thank you, Elliott Ness," Chris said. "But this time I think we're beat. They stole all of the evidence of Blair's murder. She had to have that report or whatever proof she had of what they had done in her purse. They got her purse. Her cell phone. The physical evidence from the murder. Ripley and I searched Blair's room and we found nothing. I think someone got there before us because we didn't even find bank statements."

"Maybe she didn't have a bank account," she said. "She was living off the grid."

"Something in my gut ..." His voice trailed off. "Are they corrupt? Yes, They're also murderers. But how can we possibly bring them to justice when we don't even know what their motives are?"

"I don't know, but we can't give up." Helen laid her head on his chest. "Otherwise, Blair would have spent the last three years away from her family and died for nothing."

He wrapped his arms around her and kissed her.

"Daddy!"

Emma ran across the floor. They parted just in time for the little girl to land between them. Sterling leapt onto the pillows.

"I thought you went home," Emma said to Helen while snuggling against her.

Helen gave her a warm hug. "I forgot something and came back."

"I thought you went to bed." Chris tickled the little girl.

"Mommy won't stop singing," Emma said between high-pitched giggles.

"Are you fibbing?" Chris's face screwed up with doubt. "She wasn't singing when I was down there."

"She is now."

"Let's go see." Chris took Emma's hand.

Emma took Helen's hand and the three of them, hand-in-hand, marched down the stairs with Sterling taking up the rear. They could hear the melody of the song drifting up the stairwell. The music was so loud that it drew Doris and Nikki from the family room below.

"I thought you went home," Doris said when she saw Helen descending the stairs from Chris's room.

"I forgot something," Helen said.

Doris shot her a wicked grin.

"Mommy won't stop singing." Emma trotted into the room and pointed up at the clock. "She sings to me every night, but usually it is only one song. Now she's singing all the time."

"She's been singing on the hour all day long," Doris said.

"Must be a short in the music box," Chris said.

"It's not an electric clock," Helen said. "Maybe it's a broken spring in the mechanism."

"Then it wouldn't work at all." Chris picked up the clock from the shelf. Unlike earlier in the day, the melody continued after he had picked it up. He turned it over and touched the turnkey.

The music stopped.

"There. All fixed."

When he took his fingers off the turnkey, the music continued.

Doris giggled. "I don't think so, Christopher."

Chris studied the clock. The back was secured with tiny Philips screws. Chris sent Nikki to the kitchen for a screwdriver.

"You're not going to break Mommy, are you, Dad?" Emma asked while hugging Thor.

"I would never break Mommy," Chris said. "I'm just going to convince her to sing a little less."

"Maybe she's trying to tell you something," Doris said.

"Tell me what?" Chris asked as he took the screwdriver from Nikki.

"Never give up," Helen said in a soft voice.

Chris dropped into the small chair at Emma's desk and unscrewed the six screws securing the back of the clock—handing each one to Doris. Then he turned it over and shook off the back. As the back fell loose, he peered at the gears and inner workings inside. "I don't see anything."

In search of troubleshooting instructions, he turned the back over. Instead of instructions, there was a key taped to the underside of the back panel.

"Is that an extra turnkey?" Nikki asked as Chris peeled it off the plate.

The small silver key was too big to be a music box turnkey, but too small to belong to a house or vehicle.

"Chris! I wish we had more time!" Blair yelled to him while boarding the train after he had shot Leonardo Mancini. She said it again before the doors slid shut.

"I wish we had more time," Chris murmured to himself. "She was telling me to look at the clock."

"What's it to, Dad?" Nikki asked.

"I think it's a safety deposit box key."

Emma was more interested in the clock. She picked up the silent clock and frowned at the angel on top. "Mommy's not singing anymore, Daddy."

"I think it's because Daddy finally got your Mommy's message." Helen squeezed Chris's hand.

Despite exhaustion setting in after a full day in the city, Bruce and Elliott were alert enough to notice a dark vehicle parked behind thick brush in the turnoff along the Shenandoah River. As Bruce drove his dark red SUV across the bridge crossing the Shenandoah River, both men stopped talking to sit up and take notice.

It was close to ten o'clock at night, but the moon cast enough light to reflect off the river to catch on the passenger side windows.

"Used to be a time that homeless folks would live in campers along the river." Elliott shook his head. "Never saw anyone living out of an eighty-thousand-dollar SUV before."

Bruce turned onto the road along the river to take them to the Matheson farm. "Maybe we're getting paranoid, but they seem to be parked in just the right spot to keep an eye on the farm."

They caught sight of two men dropping down low in the front compartment as they drove past.

"Just because we're paranoid doesn't mean that folks aren't out to get us," Elliott said.

Chris, Doris, and Helen sat around the kitchen table with the key, not unlike a tiny centerpiece, resting in the middle.

Emma had been disappointed that the clock had stopped playing the melody. Tears welled up in her eyes at the thought that it would never sing again. "Nonni, why did Daddy decide to kill Mommy?" she asked Doris.

Chris put the clock back together and turned the turnkey. To everyone's relief, the angel proceeded to sing. Helen was probably most relieved that she didn't have to arrest Chris for the homicide of an angel.

With the mystery of the singing angel solved, Nikki went off to her room, leaving them alone to openly discuss the key hidden in the clock that Blair had delivered to Emma.

"An educated guess would say it's a safety deposit box key." Doris got up from the table to inspect a pair of headlights that flashed in the window as Bruce's SUV rolled up to the house.

Elliott jumped out of the passenger side. "Woman, I hope you got your pistol handy." He ran up the steps onto the porch.

"Annie's right here." Doris patted her robe pocket where she had stashed a pearl-handle twenty-two-caliber handgun. She gave him a kiss. "We've had an exciting development."

"We have, too." Elliott jerked a thumb over his shoulder. "Did you know that you were under surveillance?"

"Again?" Doris squinted across the front pastures toward the river. "Or is it still?"

Bruce joined them on the porch. "I think we should stay tonight and keep watch in shifts. We know what these people are capable of."

Elliott agreed. "What developments have you made here on your end?"

Doris gave them a demure smile. "We think we found a key to a safety deposit box that Blair had rented."

It took only seconds for Bruce and Elliott to join them around the table. While Doris recounted the discovery of the key to them, everyone in the kitchen stared at it as if it had the power to stand up and confess to everything it knew.

"Okay," Bruce said, "you found it taped inside a clock that Blair had sent to Emma."

"And the clock came from Europe," Helen said.

"Does that mean the safety deposit box is in Europe?" Elliott frowned. "I don't know if Jessica Faraday would be so generous as to lease us a jet to search all of Europe for one safety deposit box."

"I don't think the box is in Europe," Chris said slowly. "The clock was not sent to Emma from Europe. Ivy Dunleavy delivered it to her." He looked across the table to Doris. "Don't you remember, Mom? Emma's fifth birthday was ten days after Blair was supposed to have died. Ivy Dunleavy showed up at the party with the clock. She told us that Blair had sent it to her earlier and had asked her to deliver it to Emma on her birthday."

"But today, the Dunleavys told us that Blair showed up right after her funeral," Elliott said. "She had to have been staying with them when Emma had her birthday."

"Exactly."

"Most likely, she smuggled it out of Europe, hid the key inside, and gave the clock to Ivy to deliver to Emma," Helen said.

"The clock was a trojan horse," Doris said.

"But what good is the key if we don't know what safety deposit box it goes to?" Elliott said. "We didn't find any paperwork in Blair's room to tell us what bank—"

"Bank of America," Helen said with a sense of excitement. "Doris and I went through Blair's things today. She had her accounts with that bank. Since she was familiar with them, she would have gone there first to get a safety deposit box."

"We had our joint accounts with them," Chris said. "I think we should start there."

"The banks won't open again until Monday," Bruce said, "about the same time that Daniel Cross's confirmation hearings begin. Unless we find some evidence of wrongdoing, the committee will just go through the motions to confirm him."

"I wish we had more time." Chris's chair scraped across the floor when he pushed back from the table and ran up the back stairs to his room.

"Yeah, I wish we had more time, too," Bruce said. "Everyone thinks Cross is God's gift to national intelligence."

"He's really a killer," Elliott said. "You should have seen the look on his face tonight when we told him we had proof he had been in Switzerland. He's a psychopath."

"Problem is proving it," Elliott said. "He's got all the right people running interference and covering for him."

Chris galloped down the back stairs and into the kitchen with a gold watch in his hand. "Ivy delivered this watch to me at the same time she gave Emma the clock. I could not understand why Blair would buy me a watch because I don't wear them. Not only that, but she had it engraved with 'Darling Chris, Fly Away with me. Your Angel, Blair.'"

"'Fly' is the name of the melody the clock plays," Doris said. "She was pointing at the clock with the watch."

Chris pointed to the engraving. "Below her name she has the date June twenty-eight, two-thousand-and-four."

"Is that your wedding date?" Elliott asked.

"No, it's not our wedding date," Chris said. "All these years, I've thought she'd gotten our wedding date wrong. Now that we have this key, I'm thinking it's the safety deposit box number. Zero. Six. Two. Eight. Zero. Four."

"What a clever woman," Bruce said with a chuckle. "She used a two-part security method. It's not an uncommon technique used in intelligence circles for the most sensitive classified information. In the military, they'll give only half of a safe combination to one intelligence officer, and then give the second half to the other one. That way, if one goes rogue, he can't access the information without the other guy."

"What if they both go rogue?" Doris asked.

"Or if one guy dies suddenly?" Elliott asked.

"We won't go there." Bruce picked up the key. "The key is the first part. If the people she was running from got their hands on the key, it would be useless without knowing where the box is or what it goes to." He picked up the watch. "She put that information on the watch and made sure you got it. If the bad guys got the watch and figured out the message on it, it would be useless without the key. The only way to access whatever it was she hid in that safety deposit box is to have both parts—" He placed the key on top of the watch. "—which she entrusted to you, Christopher." He handed them to Chris.

"Blair wasn't as dumb as I thought," Doris said.

"Not so fast," Bruce said. "Let's not get our hopes up. First thing we need to figure out is what name did Blair use to get a safety deposit box. Blair Matheson was declared dead on Bastille Day three years ago."

"That's right," Helen said. "She'd need to have some identification."

"She had an Australian passport," Chris said. "Charlotte Nesbitt. She got the box under that name."

"Even with the key, you're going to have a problem," Bruce said. "Did Charlotte Nesbitt have a husband."

"Yes, she did." Chris took the burner phone from his pocket and hit the speed dial to connect him to Murphy.

"I thought you'd quit," Murphy said without further greeting.

"I'm back," Chris said. "I need an Australian passport."

Chapter Twenty

Elliott and Doris insisted on taking the first two-hour shift of watching the vehicle surveilling the house. That left Chris and Bruce to take over at one o'clock in the morning. Chris was running on pure adrenalin. Sensing that they were nearing the truth, he doubted if he would be able to sleep if he were free to go to bed.

From his laptop, he launched the application to his home security system. After leaving the FBI, he had installed a security system on and around the farm. The entire one hundred acres was covered by hidden cameras. While his primary objective was to catch uninvited visitors with less than honorable motives, the cameras also helped to keep track of the horses when he put them out in pastures away from the barn.

Shortly after putting in the system, a newly acquired horse disappeared. Chris assumed the mare had been stolen until he checked the security recordings. The horse had jumped the fence and galloped off with a herd of deer. After a week, he was finally able to track her down to the buck with whom she had become infatuated.

From his phone application, Chris adjusted the angle of a camera perched in a tree next to the far corner of the front pasture. He zoomed in on the license plate of the SUV. It was a Virginia registration.

He recalled Helen telling him that the two hitmen claiming Stu Dunleavy had hired them, were from Baltimore, Maryland.

He texted the license plate number to Ray with the message: *Can you run a check on this plate? Staking out our farm. 2 men. Seem to be different league than 2 Mom and Helen caught. From Virginia.*

As he pressed the send button, his phone rang. He recognized the number in the caller ID.

"Good evening, Ripley."

"Your daughter and mine are putting me through the wringer."

"Let me guess," he said. "They're eating non-stop and doing a romcom marathon."

"We just got our second delivery of pizza. I have three gallons of ice cream in the freezer, and they're on their third movie."

"And you still have your sanity?"

"I wouldn't if I didn't get a break this morning to visit a crime scene," she said.

"You didn't say anything to Katelyn—"

"Of course not. They thought nothing of my going out on a call. Madison sees me get called out all the time. But today, she was horrified that I had the nerve to call Grandma to come babysit. Usually, it's no big deal. She loves it when my mom comes over. Today was different. Now, Katelyn knows the awful truth about Madison not being allowed to stay home alone."

"I'm surprised Madison didn't die from embarrassment," Chris said.

"You'll be glad to know that they have concluded that Doris is cooler than my mother."

"I'd believe it. When was the last time your mother captured and tortured two hitmen?"

"I heard about that," Ripley said. "Way to go, Doris."

"Mom threatened to drill holes in their penises."

"It isn't like they were going to need them after she put their bodies through the woodchipper," Ripley said. "Even if Doris's interrogation method was less than civilized, we got very useful information. The goons from Baltimore claimed Stu's assistant hired them to kill you. They said she used the name of Jenn. That's the same name Lurch mentioned when he told Murphy that a client had ordered a rush job to steal the evidence from the FBI lab. I don't think we'll have any problem getting a warrant to bring Stu Dunleavy's assistant in for questioning. If we're lucky, she's not in love with the guy and will flip on him."

"Jenn was at the Dunleavy home when we got there this morning," Chris said. "I'll bet they had just finished searching Blair's room and destroyed anything that could help us. They've been one step ahead of everyone throughout this whole case."

"Not necessarily," Ripley said. "They didn't get Blair's body. The medical examiner found a massive dose of flurazepam hydrochloride in her system."

"That's—"

"Sleeping pills. Four times the regular dose. The medical examiner said she had to be unconscious when she went into the lake. Then, the killer stepped on her back to hold her under the water until she drowned."

"No doubt," Chris said, "Blair was murdered."

They ended the call with Chris asking Ripley to give Katelyn a hug from him. He felt confident that his former partner would keep his oldest daughter safe and secure.

At least, he told himself that.

He heard Helen climbing the stairs to his room before he saw her. She crossed the room and draped an arm across his shoulders. From his seat, Chris lay his head back to let her kiss him on the lips.

"I should go," she said softly. "Sierra texted that she's home and I don't want to leave her alone all night."

"I don't like the idea of her being alone either."

She looked out the window. "They're not like the two we caught this afternoon. They look like they have police or military training."

"I noticed the same thing."

"I talked Doris and Elliott out of sneaking over and stuffing a potato up their tailpipe."

Chris jumped when his phone rang. The caller ID indicated that it was Ray. He put the call on speaker phone. "Talk to me, Ray."

"I guess when Stu Dunleavy realized who he was up against, he decided to call in the big dogs," Ray said.

"Big dogs?" Helen asked.

"That SUV is licensed to the Burnett Security Agency."

"Burnett," Chris said. "That's who Stu Dunleavy was telling Jenn to call to take care of a matter when we got there this morning."

"Paul Burnett," Ray said. "His company advertises itself as a security company. He's one of Washington's biggest cleanup men."

"Rent a goon?"

"More or less," Ray said. "Everyone who's anyone in Washington goes to Burnett to take care of their problems. Law enforcement on Capitol Hill knows about him. He's like Teflon because he knows where all the bodies are buried—and I'm talking literally. Anytime he starts to get into hot water, all it takes is one phone call to a judge whose troublesome wife Burnett made disappear—Well, you get the picture."

"Is Stu Dunleavy a client of his?" Helen shrugged her shoulders. "Since he hired the other two goons ..."

"Actually, it's a little weird that he had his assistant called Tony and Ralph," Ray said. "Yeah, Stu is connected to that cold case in Baltimore where Ralph's print was left, but, from my research, he's been using Burnett exclusively for the last several years. Leban Slade uses Burnett to cleanup all his messes."

"Leban Slade as in Slade Industries?" Chris asked.

"The one and only."

"Slade has been figuring prominently in this case," Chris said. "Murphy's brother-in-law Tristan tracked a courier who may or may not have been delivering classified information to Slade Industries. A couple of hours later, two men tried to kill him."

"Try this on for size," Ray said. "Leban Slade is Stu Dunleavy's biggest client. According to chatter I found across the Internet, Stu Dunleavy brags about being Leban Slade's go-to guy for fixing things when he gets into trouble—personally and professionally."

"So, if Daniel Cross, who's a hair's breadth from becoming director of the CIA, had been selling government secrets to Leban Slade," Chris said, "and someone threatened to expose it—"

"Slade would call Dunleavy as his fix-it guy, and Dunleavy would call Burnett to clean it up," Ray said.

"And killing any potential witnesses would not be off the table," Helen said.

"Is Burnett really tall?" Chris asked Ray.

"Went to college on a basketball scholarship until he got kicked out for punching the coach," Ray said. "Six foot eight inches tall."

"He's the guy who tried to get Murphy to hand me over to him last night," Chris said. "That means he's been involved in this whole thing from the very beginning."

"Leban Slade may be behind the scenes," Ray said, "but Stu Dunleavy is calling the shots to the goons on the ground."

"But why ..." Chris scratched his head. "Blair lived with them. Why did Stu hide and protect her for three years—"

"Maybe she agreed to keep quiet about it, but when Cross was nominated to run the CIA, she couldn't keep quiet any longer," Helen said.

"If Stu was Slade's fix-it guy, why did Blair go to him in the first place?" Chris asked.

"Maybe she didn't know," Ray said. "Blair's connection to the Dunleavys was through Stu's wife. How much did Blair really know about his business dealings? Maybe as much as his wife knew about your cases?"

"I think you're on to something, Ray," Chris said. "Blair told the Dunleavys that I was abusive so they wouldn't give away her secret. From what they told us, she didn't mention anything to them about what had happened in Switzerland."

"She couldn't because everything she did was classified," Ray said.

"That's true," Chris said. "I was her husband and I never knew what she was working on. I never bothered to ask because I knew she couldn't tell me."

"She didn't tell the Dunleavys who she was really running from," Helen said, "and Stu didn't tell her that he was Leban Slade's fix-it guy. It's entirely possible that he didn't know he was hiding his mega client's biggest threat right under his own roof."

"Imagine Dunleavy's reaction when she got back from Washington after almost getting killed by an international hitman he had hired," Chris said.

"At which point he killed her and dumped her in your backyard," Helen said.

"Maybe he didn't dump her body there to frame you, Chris, as much as to send a warning to stay out of it," Ray said.

"He had to know Blair would be smart enough to have a backup copy of her proof that Daniel Cross was a spy for Leban Slade," Chris said. "They searched her room before we got there. If they found anything, I guarantee it's long gone."

"Do you think they found out about the safety deposit box?" Helen asked in a soft voice.

"Hard to tell." Chris went to the window looking out on the front pastures and the bushes behind which the two men were keeping watch on them. "Dunleavy sent his cleanup team out here for a reason. It could just be to make sure I don't mess up Cross's confirmation."

Recalling Ralph's claim that they had been ordered to murder him and burn down his home, Chris narrowed his eyes while focusing on the vehicle next to the river. "What are you waiting for?" he asked the men watching him in a soft voice.

Helen stood next to him. "You know they're going to be on your tail when you go to that safety deposit box on Monday."

"Stu Dunleavy has already proven that he will do anything, including murder, to protect Leban Slade and those who work for him," Ray said.

Chris stared down at the dark vehicle in silence while Helen and Ray waited for his response. Helen wondered if he had fallen asleep on his feet.

"Do you want to sic your mother on them?" Helen asked.

Chris shook his head. At least that meant he was awake—thinking. "Let's wait. They're not going to do anything to me until they know I have Blair's backup evidence. We'll take care of them then."

Chapter Twenty-One

For the rest of the weekend, the Mathesons and Geezer Squad watched two pairs of men alternating in eight-hour shifts to surveil Chris and his family. It was all Chris could do to keep Doris from doing something awful to them. Her suggestions ranged from sticking a potato up their tailpipe to launching a full-scale paintball attack on them. He had a tough time talking her down from the paintball battle. Elliott and Francine were all for it.

Chris was more concerned with keeping his daughters from finding out. He was afraid that if they realized their father was being watched, that it would lead to a discussion about something he wasn't prepared to talk about. Luckily, the girls were so wrapped up in enjoying the brisk autumn day, that they didn't notice the big dark vehicle with two men inside.

After sending his daughters off to school, Chris plunged into Monday morning rush hour traffic to return to Chantilly, Virginia. Clad in his service dog vest and a pair of dark sunglasses, Sterling rode shotgun.

When Chris turned left out of the lane, the SUV pulled out from where it was keeping watch to follow him to Bruce's winery in Purcellville.

Sterling's ears stood erect. The dog seemed to watch the vehicle in the rearview mirror.

"I know, Sterling," Chris said. "Give them enough rope and they'll hang themselves by the time this is over."

Acting as Chris's attorney in case the bank gave him trouble, Bruce was making the trip into the city with him. Despite the volume of vehicles making their way east to Washington, Chris could spy the dark blue SUV with Virginia tags that was never far behind him.

Chris expected the team watching him to switch the surveillance off to another pair of goons after he broke from the traffic to travel the rural roads to the winery. A growl from Sterling, who was keeping an eye on them, told him that the same team continued to tail him. Chris realized why when he and Bruce stopped at a convenience store to fill up the gas tank.

The man in the passenger seat sat a head above the driver. The tall man. Paul Burnett was personally keeping an eye on Chris to ensure he didn't ruin Daniel Cross's confirmation.

Their next stop was for breakfast at a restaurant chain in Leesburg, the halfway point to Chantilly. It was a welcome break from the long drive in heavy traffic.

Upon entering the restaurant, Bruce scanned the dining room. Second booth from the far-right corner. "Over there." He led Chris, who kept Sterling on his leash, to the table. Sterling lay down next to Chris's seat.

The server arrived with a full pot of coffee as soon as they sat. Bestowing a broad smile at Chris, she struck up a conversation about the traffic and the chilly, yet sunny, day.

While Chris kept her occupied and she blocked the other patrons' view, Bruce ran his hand across the underside of the table until his fingers contacted the edges of an envelope. With a casual gesture, he detached it from where it was taped to the table. He could feel the outline of the passport Chris needed inside. He slipped the envelope into the inside breast pocket of his suitcoat and extracted his reading glasses. To anyone watching, he was simply reaching for his glasses to read the menu.

Bruce shot Chris a grin, which told him all he needed to know. Murphy had come through with the passport he needed to get into Blair's safety deposit box.

Conscious of the two men who had taken a table not far away, they kept their conversation limited to their children and sports. Bruce had a college-aged son who, to his father's horror, had decided to follow in his footsteps and study law.

"He wants to be like his daddy," Chris said.

"I'd prefer he be like his mother and study architecture," Bruce grumbled. "Shakespeare said, 'First, let's kill all the lawyers,' for a reason. As a profession, we have spent centuries carefully crafting and earning our reputation of being slime balls. Now, my son wants to be a part of it." He shook his head over his coffee. "As a parent, it is my duty to raise my son to be a beneficial member of society. Instead, he is joining the ranks of manipulative bloodsuckers. I'm sorry to say I've failed my fellow man."

Searching for some way to encourage his friend, Chris said, "It could be worse."

"How?"

"He could decide to go into politics."

Aware that Cross's confirmation hearing was scheduled to start at ten o'clock, one hour after the bank opened, they hurriedly ate their breakfast and ordered a breakfast sandwich for Sterling to go. They were back on the freeway when Bruce examined the contents of the envelope. As they had expected, it contained an Australian diplomatic passport in the name of

Ethan Nesbitt. It also held a death certificate from the medical examiner for Charlotte Nesbitt listing the cause of death as 'homicide.'

The note inside the envelope was from Tristan Faraday:

Good job! Nigel has had a long conversation with the BOA (Bank of America) database. She confirms that Charlotte Nesbitt does have a safety deposit box (#062804) at the Chantilly branch. Financial Center at 14001 Metrotech Dr, Chantilly, VA 20151. As long as you have the key, this passport and death certificate is all you should need to access it. See you soon.

Bruce shook two earbuds from the envelope, handed one to Chris, and pressed the other into his own ear.

Keeping one hand on the wheel, Chris inserted the ear com into his ear. "Testing. Can you hear me, Tristan?"

"It's about time, Chris," Murphy said. "You took your time eating breakfast. Is Bruce there with you?"

"I'm here," Bruce said.

"We're not alone." Chris glanced in the back seat to see that Sterling had finished eating his breakfast.

The dog was staring out the rear window at the SUV, which was directly behind them. Burnett was making no pretense of following them. He seemed to know where they were going and what for.

"Burnett's on your tail." It was a statement, not a question. "Don't worry. I've got him."

"Where are you?" Chris could tell by his tone that Murphy was slightly distracted—as in driving. He checked his rearview mirrors to locate him.

"Nearby."

"Listen," Chris said, "I've been thinking."

"Is that a good thing?"

"Don't be a smartass, Lieutenant," Chris said. "When we searched Blair's room, we found no paperwork for this bank or any bank for that matter. Not a statement or bank receipt. Nothing."

"Don't worry," Murphy said. "Nigel confirmed that Charlotte Nesbitt has a safety deposit box at this branch."

"I'm not arguing about that." Chris glanced at the SUV in the rearview mirror. "If Stu discovered Friday night that Blair was a major threat to his biggest client, wouldn't it make sense that he'd search her room for evidence first thing after disposing of her body?"

Sterling growled and stomped his feet. Bruce looked over his shoulder at the blue vehicle.

"You pay fees for renting safety deposit boxes," Chris said. "If she had even one bank statement in her room, Stu would have known right away that she had a safety deposit box. But I have the key."

"So he can't access it," Bruce said. "That's why they've been watching you all weekend. they're waiting for you to go check what she's put in that box."

"You're thinking Dunleavy knew Blair had a safety deposit box at this bank before you even got there Saturday morning," Murphy said. "If so, these guys may have backup waiting for you at that bank."

"If you were Dunleavy, isn't that what you'd do?"

They arrived at the Bank of America approximately five minutes after it had opened. As they turned into the parking lot, they drove past a stretch white limousine. They parked in a space as close to the entrance as possible.

"Someone has a lot of money in this bank," Chris told Bruce.

Chris attached the leash to Sterling, who uttered a low growl when the blue SUV passed them to park in the next row.

"Wait for it." Chris tightened his hold on the German shepherd's leash when a black motorcycle raced into the lot and parked in one of the smaller spaces.

Remaining in their vehicle, Burnett and his partner watched them cross the lot to the main entrance.

As they entered through the double doors, Sterling's ears stood up. With a bounce in his step, he swerved to where a woman was sitting in a wing backed chair in the waiting area. Dressed in a faux fur coat with a matching fur hat over a blue dress with a pencil skirt, she resembled a movie star from days long past. She covered her face with big rhinestone sunglasses.

Sterling wasn't as interested in the woman as the blue sheltie in the arms of the young man who appeared to be her assistant. Chris hardly recognized Tristan Faraday without his glasses. His hair was slicked back off his face.

Chris yanked Sterling back to his side. "Don't blow your cover," he muttered to the German shepherd.

With his official looking briefcase in hand, Bruce ushered Chris and Sterling to the clerk in charge of the safety deposit boxes. "Excuse me, …" He read her name from the nameplate on her desk. "Marilyn. I'm Bruce Harris, attorney-at-law. My client here is Ethan Nesbitt. I'm sorry to say that his wife has recently passed. She had, among her effects, a safety deposit box here at this bank." He took the necessary paperwork from his pocket and gestured for Chris to present the key.

As Chris reached into his jacket pocket, he turned to casually take note of who might be watching them too closely. There was Tristan and the woman in the fur coat in the waiting area.

There was a man with a red bandana wrapped around his head at the counter filing out a deposit slip. A motorcycle helmet rested on the counter. When he looked up, his eyes met Chris's. It was Murphy.

At the next counter, Chris spotted a woman with reddish blond hair in a denim jacket over an oversized dress. She was talking into her sleeve. When she saw Chris look in her direction, she turned around.

Bingo! Their inside person.

"Ethan." Bruce cleared his throat.

Startled, Chris handed the key to clerk. "Box number zero-six-two-eight-zero-four, mate," he said in his best Australian accent. It was so good that even Bruce seemed taken aback.

With a coy grin, Marilyn took the key and went to work on her computer to bring up the necessary online forms for him to sign.

While she brought up the form, Chris turned his back and whispered, "Murphy, behind you, eleven o'clock. Women in denim jacket. Talking into com. Is she one of ours?"

Murphy stepped over to a display about small business loans. "Not one of ours," he whispered back. "I'll keep an eye on her."

Chris returned to the desk and signed the online form with his finger while the clerk selected a key from a collection in a locked box. She escorted Chris and Bruce down the stairs and a corridor to the safe where the safety deposit boxes were stored.

After finding the box, Chris used his key to unlock the first mechanism. Marilyn then used her key to unlock the second. She opened the door and pulled out the box, which she handed to Chris before walking out of the room to allow them privacy to explore the contents.

"It doesn't feel very heavy," he told Bruce before placing it on the table and opening the lid.

"You got it?" Murphy asked.

The box looked empty except for a brown padded envelope. The front was labeled with black marker:

Chris
Eyes Only

"That's a government classification," Bruce said.

Chris broke the seal of the envelope and peered inside. He could feel Bruce holding his breath while waiting next to him.

"What's in it?" Murphy asked into his ear.

"Nothing." Chris frowned. "She left me an empty envelope."

"Are you kidding me?" Bruce snatched the envelope out of Chris's hands and peered inside. Seeing nothing, he turned it over and shook it.

There was a small *click.*

Sterling followed the object with his nose when the red and gray object bounced off the tabletop to the floor. It was a micro SDHC memory card— so tiny that they almost missed it.

Chris raced to pick the card up before Sterling could eat it, which he was likely to do. "It's a memory card," he said for the benefit of those who could hear through the ear com. He handed it to Bruce, who had slipped his laptop from his briefcase.

"No hardcopy?" Murphy asked.

"Too risky to smuggle out of the embassy," Chris said. "Bruce, do you have a port in yor laptop that'll read this?"

With a slim grin, Bruce inserted the disc into an adaptor and slipped it into the port on his laptop.

Tristan's voice came through the ear coms. "Bruce, be sure to turn the wi-fi off on your laptop before you open the disc. We don't want to take any chances."

"Good thinking." Bruce pressed the button to disconnect the internet connection.

Chris took a seat at the table and put his fingertips on the touchpad. He moved the curser to the file explorer to search for the drive containing the disc, which was labeled simply "Switzerland." He positioned the curser on the drive and clicked to open it.

The disc contained three files. One was a document named "Cross/Slade Industries." The other two were mp4 files. One was labeled "Les Monroe." The third was entitled, "To Chris."

He selected the one to him.

Without saying anything, Bruce left the room and closed the door behind him.

Sterling laid his head in Chris's lap.

As the movie file opened, Blair came into view. She was sitting on the edge of a bed. Her hair was dyed a dark brown, which contrasted with her fair complexion. She looked pale and sickly. Chris guessed that her fragile condition had been the result of stress.

She brought up her hand in a slight wave. A weak smile crossed her face.

"Hi, Chris." She let out a breath. "Well, you were right. I never should have gone to Switzerland." She giggled. Tears formed in her eyes and she sobbed.

Chris fought to not stop the painful video. A quick check of the time on his phone revealed that Daniel Cross's confirmation hearing would begin in less than half an hour.

As if she sensed the urgency, she took in a shuddering breath and continued.

"Since you're watching this, most likely I'm dead. I mean, I'm really dead now. For the last couple of weeks, I have been fighting for my survival. You know all those stories you've told me about cases and situations you've gotten yourself into. Well, I'm glad I listened. Yes, I did listen to you. It seems like every day I have to ask myself, 'What would Chris do?' Then I'd remember something you told me that you'd done in a situation like mine and I'd do it. It saved my life. Really. Seriously.

"A couple of weeks ago, I saw a murder. You'll learn more about that. I was hiding in the closet and they were searching the house. I had no where to go. Then, I remembered when you told me about a time when you were hiding in a closet and this gang was looking for you. You climbed through the access panel into the attic." She giggled through tears. "I looked up and there was the access panel. You saved my life, Chris. Really, you did."

Her face was filled with sadness.

"I guess the first thing you want to know is why didn't I call you. Anne Kidman, the CIA operative who saved me in Switzerland, told me not to. Anne was assigned to the embassy. I didn't even know she was CIA. She got wind that something was going down and let me know that if I needed anything to call her. Boy, am I glad I did. She got me out of Switzerland.

"These people who are trying to kill me, they'll do anything to get the report that I found on the computer mainframe from Lithuania. The director of intelligence at the CIA, Daniel Cross shot my boss in the back. Then he ordered Ned Schiff, the chief of station, to cover it up. Last I heard, they called it a suicide.

"Please, Chris, understand, I couldn't risk them coming after you and our girls to flush me out. When I found out that the state department had mistaken Anne's body for mine, I let everyone go with that.

"Ivy agreed to let me start over living with them as Hannah's nanny. I had to tell her a big lie. She'd never understand what happened to me in Switzerland. So I told her that I was hiding from you. I figured that would keep her from blabbing to anyone about me being alive."

She combed her fingers through her hair. "How do you like me as a brunette?" She frowned. "I don't like it either. I was afraid Hannah would recognize me and give me away."

She looked directly into the camera. "I wish I was more like you, Chris. I wish I was brave enough to do what I have to do with these files. I know you will. You'll know just what to do. You've always been brave enough to do what is right and still protect those you love."

She sighed. "Let me tell you about the report that is on this disc."

Her tone was direct when she said, "It's a bomb. This report was written by Samuel Goldman, the chief of station in Lithuania, back seven years ago. He had addressed the report to the director of the CIA. In it, he states that he had discovered that the deputy chief of station, Daniel Cross, had been selling government secrets to Slade Industries. I know, Leban Slade isn't a foreign government. Why would he want government secrets? Well, according to Samuel Goldman, based on his own investigation when he started to suspect what Cross was up to, he found that Leban Slade had put together a whole network of spies in the intelligence community. They'd give him all types of information. Some were classified government secrets. Other information would be personal stuff on influential people that Slade would use to extort favors. Slade would use that information to give him an advantage when submitting for government contracts or striking deals with foreign countries via one of his shadow companies. He has a huge enterprise going. Goldman also found proof that one of the major dealers selling parts to North Korea for their nuclear missiles is owned by Leban Slade. He's an American and he's making billions helping a country who wants to blow up our allies and us."

She gestured toward Chris through the camera. "You'll notice on this disc that the date on that report is the day before Samuel Goldman was killed by the car bomb. The night that Cross shot Les Monroe in the back, he admitted that he planted that car bomb. The target wasn't Ambassador Brown. It was Goldman. Then, Cross used the tragedy that he had created to make himself the hero by framing an extremist group and going after them. When he took Goldman's place as chief of station, he deleted the report and every copy of it, but he didn't know that there was still a copy on the mainframe, which I found while archiving the communications."

She fell silent. Tears rolled down her face. Slowly, she raised her eyes to the camera.

"That's what happened, Chris." She sniffed and wiped her nose on her sleeve. "I was such a fool. I love you. I love my girls. Can you tell them that for me? I've missed my girls. I think about all of you every day. Now, I'll never be able to see them again. See them grow up. I got so wrapped up in trying to have it all—a career and everything that I didn't notice that I already had it all. Now, I've lost everything."

She reached for the camera. "I've missed you. I am so very sorry for hurting you, Chris. Please forgive me." She cried. "When you think of me, and everything that has happened, remember this one thing. I love you. I really do." She blubbered. "Good-bye, Chris."

She stood up and turned off the camera.

The screen went blank.

Chris sat in silence—staring at the home screen on Bruce's laptop.

"Chris?" Murphy's voice was soft through the ear com. "Are you okay?"

Chris copied the contents of the disc to Bruce's laptop before ejecting the disc from the drive. Sensing they were on the move, Sterling stood next to him.

"It's takedown time."

Chapter Twenty-Two

Keeping Sterling at his side, Chris and Bruce climbed the stairs to the bank's main floor.

With a quick glance, Chris saw that the woman in the jean jacket was lingering near the brochure case. She turned to follow them when they proceeded across the lobby to the main exit.

Bruce switched his briefcase from one hand to the other to open the door.

At the same time, Jacqui, dressed up in a suit, briefcase and all, swept in to grab the same door handle. "Thank you very much for your time," she said over her shoulder while colliding into Bruce.

Both briefcases fell to the floor.

"Oh, I am so sorry! How clumsy of me," Jacqui said loudly. "I really need to look where I'm going."

"No problem, ma'am." Bruce picked up his briefcase and handed it to her. "Have a nice day."

Thanking them, Jacqui shot out the door. Bruce picked up the briefcase she had dropped, and they left the bank.

The woman in the jacket rushed ahead of them to see Jacqui climb into the passenger seat of a dark blue Malibu sedan. The tires squealed when Doris hit the gas pedal to speed out of the parking lot. Not far behind them, Murphy raced out of the lot on the black motorcycle. Gesturing wildly at the sedan, the woman jumped into the passenger seat of a black SUV and they took off in hot pursuit.

Burnett and his partner remained in their vehicle while watching the action.

The roar of the motorcycle was still fresh in the air when Sterling jerked his leash out of Chris's hand and galloped to where the woman in the fur coat was climbing into the back of the white limousine. An enormous man in a chauffer's suit held the door open for her and Tristan, who had Spencer on a leash.

Barking and yapping joyously, the two dogs circled each other until their leashes became entangled. Tristan fought to part the two dogs.

"Can you please control your damn dog!" the woman called to Chris, who opened the door of his truck and whistled to the German shepherd from across the lot. "Sterling! Come!"

Sterling spun around and raced toward the truck. Several feet away, he launched himself to become airborn and landed in the passenger seat.

"That is no service dog!" the woman complained loudly. "Did he soil my dear princess?" she was asking Tristan when he joined her in the back seat.

The chauffeur slipped into the driver's seat and started the engine. He turned left to head for the toll road leading to Washington.

In the truck, Chris noticed that Burnett and his partner remained in their vehicle—waiting for them to make their next move. "Looks like Burnett is sticking with us," he said into his ear com while turning on the truck.

"Tristan, tell me you got it?" Murphy asked over the roar of the motorcycle.

"Got it," Tristan said. "I'm going to upload the files to Nigel now."

"They never look at the service dog." Bruce reached into the backseat to pat Sterling on the head.

Chris focused on Burnett in the vehicle across from them. The two men's eyes seemed to meet.

"He can't let you go," Bruce said in a low voice. "You know too much."

"Fasten your seatbelt, Bruce. We're going for a ride." Chris shifted the truck into drive.

In the rear seat of the sedan, Francine shouted out directions to Doris while referring to a satellite map of the busy suburban area on her tablet. "Turn right up here."

Seeing no roads to the right, Doris spun the steering wheel to the left. Multiple horns blew at the car speeding across the crowded intersection.

"Right not left!" Jacqui tightened her seatbelt.

"You have an SUV moving in fast on your left," Ray's voice came from the speakers on the tablet.

"Which one?" Jacqui turned around to look at what seemed like a fleet of SUVs behind them. "They're all SUVs, Ray!"

The black motorcycle fighting to stay with them looked like a mouse going up against a herd of stampeding elephants.

"I don't know," Ray answered. "The one filled with bad guys. He's moving up on your left."

Without warning, Doris shifted to the right lane and turned onto a two-lane road. The car fishtailed and wiped out a collection of garbage cans on the corner. Murphy weaved around the trash and garbage cans and sped up to close in behind them.

The vehicle with the woman in the denim jacket crushed the trash cans and anything else that got in its way in its pursuit of the sedan.

"That SUV I told you about just turned right the next block down," Ray said. "He's going around the block to intercept you at the end of this road. You're going to want to turn right again."

"That will take me back to where we started," Doris said. "We need to get to Washington."

"You won't get to Washington if they catch up to you, Doris," Murphy said while checking on the vehicle closing in on his tail.

The passenger side window rolled down. Murphy saw the barrel of a gun emerge and take aim at his back. He swerved to the right as several gunshots pelted the trunk of Doris's car.

"They're shooting at us!" Jacqui spun around in her seat. "They're trying to kill us!"

"I think that's the idea," Francine said.

Tristan tried to ignore CO's eyes, hidden behind the dark glasses, staring at him from where she sat across from him in the back of the limousine. Her intimidating persona made time move at a snail's pace while he brought up the files from the disc onto his tablet. The process took less than a minute. With her drumming her fingers on the armrest, it seemed to take forever.

Laying next to her, Spencer was unintimidated. In the sheltie's world, everyone was pleased at all times and everyone got along.

If only that were so.

CO cocked her furr-capped head at him.

"I've got the secure connection," Tristan said. "All I need to do now is to transfer the files to Nigel."

"They'll be secure?"

"It'll be like locking them up in Fort Knox."

As soon as the words left Tristan's mouth, the limousine lurched forward as it was rammed in the rear. The tablet tumbled out of Tristan's hands. Spencer spilled off the seat. In the front of the limousine, Bernie cursed.

CO spun around to look out the rear window. All she could see was the grill of a tractor trailer truck pelting the bumper to plow them off the road.

"What's he doing?" Tristan asked while scrambling to recapture the tablet to upload the files.

"What do you think he's trying to do?" CO pressed a button on the console next to her. "He's trying to kill us."

Tristan finally grabbed the tablet only to have the truck ram the bumper of the limousine again. The tablet bounced off the edge of the seat and landed next to Spencer on the floor.

The back of the refreshment bar dropped to reveal an arsenal. CO grabbed the largest weapon—a Sig Sauer nine-millimeter semi-automatic rifle—and snapped a magazine into it.

With the next hit, the limousine sideswiped a van before crossing two lanes to hit a car, which swerved out of control.

Clutching the rifle, CO was knocked out of her seat. She landed on top of Tristan, who had managed to grab the tablet. He clutched it with both hands.

She pressed another button and the sunroof opened. She kicked off her stilettos. "Time to get this party started."

Instead of getting on the toll road leading into the city, Chris turned onto a four-lane freeway that snaked through the suburbs of northern Virginia.

The clandestine cloak had dropped. Burnett's SUV kept Chris's truck in sight while it maneuvered through heavy traffic. Chris did nothing to dissuade him.

The truck and SUV made their way through Lansdowne, an area that consisted of chic townhome villages and office parks connected by fast moving freeways. From there, they moved on to Herndon, an older town made up of small single-family homes with grassy lawns and two-lane roads.

They crested the top of a hill at a four-way intersection. The light turned yellow. Chris slowed down. Just as the light turned red, Chris stomped on the accelerator and raced through the intersection.

"Move it!" Burnett punched his partner in the arm and pointed to the truck disappearing out of sight. "He's making a run for it."

The SUV raced across the intersection at the same time as a construction vehicle. Horns blared. The heavy truck hit the brakes and spun around until it stopped, facing the opposite direction.

The two-lane road went down a steep hill and then up again. Gun in hand, Burnett scoured the landscape along the tree-lined road. "Do you see him?" He twisted and turned in his seat. "He has to be around here somewhere."

They kept driving through one intersection after another. Herndon turned into Vienna. As they neared the heart of town, Burnett's partner sat up in his seat. "There he is."

Burnett saw the black pick-up truck pull out of the metro parking lot. They could see Sterling's face pressed against the rear window. Burnett compared the license plate number to the one he had for Chris Matheson. West Virginia tags. The numbers were a match.

As they closed in, the truck sped up.

"Don't lose him this time. I'm through playing games with Matheson." Burnett reached behind his seat for a grenade launcher.

Doris swung the steering wheel to make a hard right into a parking lot.

Ray directed them to turn left onto the street on the other side of the lot.

The SUV in pursuit followed. Hanging out the open window, the woman in the denim jacket ejected the magazine from her gun and slapped in a fresh one just as two bullets hit her in the shoulder and back of the head. Her weapon dropped to the pavement. She slumped out of the window. The driver lunged to grab her leg before she slipped out of the moving vehicle, which swerved from one lane to the other.

With only one hand on the handlebars, Murphy looped around to the front of the SUV while firing continuously on the assailants. Three bullets found their mark. The driver dropped his grip on his partner's leg. She fell out onto the street. The rear wheels of the vehicle ran over her dead body before the SVU crashed into a power pole.

Murphy didn't wait around. He spun the motorcycle around and raced across the parking lot to find Doris.

"Okay," Ray announced from the tablet in the back seat, "we have one more team of bad guys left."

"Do they have guns?" Jacqui asked with a breathless tone.

As if to answer her, the front windshield shattered with two gunshots.

Doris hit the brakes and spun the wheel. The car swung around one-hundred-eighty degrees. Screaming, Jacqui and Francine were thrown against the side door and windows.

"I'm going to be sick!" Jacquie clutched her stomach.

"Are you serious?" Francine said. "This from a woman who made a career of cutting up dead people?"

"They never tried to kill me!"

As Doris headed in the opposite direction, Murphy came at her head-on.

"Keep on moving!" he ordered via the ear com. "Don't look back! Get to the Capitol now!" He reached under his jacket and pulled out a semi-automatic rifle slung across his shoulders.

As they raced away, they heard rapid gun fire moving further in the distance.

"The toll road is right up ahead," Ray said. "You need to get on there. Beyond that is nothing but construction for the new subway stop. You should be good now. I gotta go help Chris. I'll check back in in a few minutes."

As she approached the intersection to turn onto the toll road, Doris could see the heavy equipment lined up on the other side of the wooden barricades.

The traffic light was green.

She lifted her foot off the accelerator. The car slowed down.

"Doris," Jacqui said, "you need to speed up. We need to get to Washington. The confirmation hearing is starting, and they'll lock the doors to the chambers."

"I can't leave him." Doris hit the gas and made a U-turn.

"Murphy can take care of himself," Francine said.

"Kirk will haunt me if I leave a LEO back there to fight without back-up." Doris sped up. "Jacqui, hand me my purse."

Jacqui picked up Doris's handbag from where it had been resting at her feet. Doris reached inside and pulled out her pearl handled thirty-eight caliber Smith and Wesson revolver. Waving the gun, she let out a wicked laugh. "Time for Annie and me to kick some bad-guy ass!"

"Tristan, have you uploaded those files to the cloud yet?" Chris asked via the ear com.

Sprawled on the floor of the limousine racing to stay ahead of the truck trying to run it off the road, Tristan could barely hear him above the squealing wheels and car horns around him. Spencer had wedged herself under his arm. Tristan clung to the tablet with both hands. His fingers trembled while he tried to drag the files on the disc to Nigel's cloud where they would be secure. If anything happened to any of them, the Phantoms would be able to access the files and make sure they got into the hands of the right people.

Before any of that could happen, he needed a secure connection, which was difficult to maintain with the limousine bouncing back and forth across the freeway like a ball in some arcade game.

Barefoot, CO stood on his back and raised up through the sunroof. The wind whipped through the fur on her hat. She lifted the rifle up onto her shoulders.

The truck rammed into the back of the limousine.

Spencer whimpered and attempted to burrow under the seat. Tristan's fingers slipped from where he had grabbed the folder containing the files.

CO fell back against the edge of the sunroof and dropped down. "Damn it!"

The truck sped up and pushed the limousine down the freeway.

"I'm sending that cretin straight to hell!" She adjusted the strap on the rifle. Her face was filled with determination as she jumped onto the rear-facing seat, sprang up through the sunroof, and fired off a barrage of gunfire.

Releasing its hold on the limousine, the truck swerved to the right and then the left. It crossed three lanes of traffic before it hit the cement barricade and rolled over several times. It ended its vicious ride by bursting into flames.

Bernie regained control of the limousine and they continued on their way.

CO placed the rifle back into its case and hit the button. The drawer flipped shut. After smoothing her hat and clothes, she put on her shoes. Spencer jumped up onto the seat and snuggled next to her. The sheltie shook to smooth her ruffled fur and uttered a sigh of contentment.

"Have you gotten those files uploaded yet, Tristan?"

His knees shaking, Tristan climbed into his seat. They were transferring. "Just about."

Concealed behind the dark glasses, her eyes bore into him again. "What have you been doing?"

It was a game of chicken that Murphy could not win. There were three men in the SUV—the driver and two passengers. He was being shot at from both sides of the vehicle as it came at him on the road. Without the protection of metal barricades in an enclosed vehicle, Murphy was exposed. His only defense was speed and agility to dodge their gunfire while trying to keep them occupied so Doris could escape.

Murphy was accurate enough with his gunshots to drive the gunman in the rear seat back into the vehicle. Like a flying insect refusing to give up, Murphy managed to drive the SUV off Doris's tail and down a side street.

When one of them would get the upper hand, they would be driven back onto the defensive—each one chasing the other, intent on achieving the fatal end goal. Eventually, the SUV crashed through the heavy fence marking off the construction site for the metro.

The last straw was when two of Murphy's gunshots took out the gunman in the rear seat, who happened to be the brother of the assailant in the front.

"Kill 'em!" The gunman stepped on the driver's foot to press the accelerator to the floor.

Murphy gunned the bike over the hilly terrain—sailing up one hill and down the other while the gunman fired continuously at him—intent on revenge for the dead man in the back seat.

The course made it impossible for Murphy to steer with one hand while shooting with the other. His only hope was to kick up enough dust to conceal himself so he could outrun the gun fight.

Spotting a bulldozer nearby, Murphy spun the bike around and around until he had created a massive cloud of dirt. The driver was driving blind when he raced through the dust cloud. He had no idea what he had hit when the SUV smashed head-on into the bulldozer.

The dust cloud turned orange as the flames shot up into the sky.

With a sigh of relief, Murphy turned the bike around to head back toward the main road. He didn't hear the shot that ripped into his thigh. He fell over the handlebars. He and the bike cartwheeled down the hillside.

The motorcycle landed on top of Murphy—pinning him against a dirt mover. His leg throbbed. The bike felt heavy across his chest. He had no doubt but that he had broken several ribs.

Murphy could see the legs of the gunman making his way slowly from the top of the hill toward him. His clothes were torn and covered with soot from the explosion. Blood and ash covered his face. He carried a semi-automatic rifle in his arms.

Insane rage-filled his eyes.

Murphy fought to catch his breath. The pain from the broken ribs felt like a knife slicing through his chest. He reached under the bike for his rifle only to find it pinned under his back.

The gunman's rage-filled eyes met Murphy's. Saying nothing, he held up the rifle to take aim on him.

Murphy tried to remember if he had told Jessica that he loved her before leaving the house that morning.

He braced himself for the pain that would precede death.

He heard the shot.

It wasn't at all as loud as he had thought it would be coming from a rifle only a few feet from him. Also, he expected that the gunman would fire more than one.

He blinked and refocused.

The fury in the gunman's eyes had been replaced with confusion. His mouth hung open. Blood trickled down his chin before he dropped to his knees and keeled over.

At the top of the hill, Doris lowered Annie, her revolver. "You're welcome, Lieutenant."

Seeing Murphy injured, Jacqui scrambled down the hillside to him. "What happened to you?" She called over her shoulder, "Francine, get my bag out of the car." She took off her jacket and folded it to put under Murphy's head.

"I told you to go to Washington," he said as the three women lifted the bike off him. "Why'd you come back?"

"We Geezers have a saying," Francine said. "'No man left behind.'" She winked at him. "Especially when he's a cutie."

Burnett and his partner kept a steady distance behind Chris's truck, which merged onto Route 66, heading for Washington. Despite the seat being set back as far as it could go, the tall man's legs were cramped from hours being spent in the vehicle. His knees shook where he had the grenade launcher propped between them.

The closer they got to downtown Washington, the less chances he would have to take out Chris Matheson and his friend. His dog, too. Burnett was getting increasingly annoyed at the dog staring at him through the rear window with his tongue hanging out of his mouth.

The traffic was getting increasingly heavier—which meant more potential witnesses.

"Looks like we may have missed our chance," Burnett's partner said.

"We may have to make it a drive by." Burnett turned around in his seat to see how many cars were nearby. He turned back to see the truck take a left exit into Ballston, an older section of Arlington populated with strip malls, convenience stores, and gas stations. A slimy grin crossed his face. "Perfect."

The truck turned into a shopping center parking lot and slowed down.

"Don't lose 'em." Burnett reached into the bag and extracted a grenade.

The SUV followed.

The truck moved slowly along the row of parking spaces until it turned into a space in the far corner of the lot.

Burnett lowered his window. "Move up behind them and block them in."

As the SUV moved in crossways to block any escape for the truck, Burnett dropped the grenade into the launcher, threw it up onto his shoulder, aimed, and fired it through the back window of the vehicle.

The SUV roared out of the shopping center as the Chris's truck went up into a giant fireball.

"Bummer!" In his computer room in West Virginia, Ray buried his face in his hands when his computer lost its connection with Chris Matheson's truck and the screen on his monitor went black.

His grin filled Paul Burnett's face when his partner merged into traffic to take them into the city. With the Mathesons eliminated, all threats to Daniel Cross becoming director of the CIA were gone. Leban Slade could continue doing business as usual without inconvenience.

He anticipated a huge Christmas bonus coming his way.

Chapter Twenty-Three

The media was getting antsy. Daniel Cross's confirmation hearing had been scheduled to begin at ten o'clock. Inexplicably, the chair of the committee, Senator Graham Keaton had decided to delay the start for one hour.

That allowed Dan more time to mingle with the media and supporters in the Capitol's rotunda. Soon, he anticipated becoming an official member of the Washington elite. He was finishing his sixth on-the-spot interview with a leggy journalist when he spotted Stu Dunleavy on his cell phone.

The lawyer shot Dan a thumbs up sign and a toothy grin.

"Everything's taken care of?" Dan asked Stu in a low voice when they met at the bottom of the steps leading up to the chambers.

"Burnett just called. Matheson's husband will not be a problem."

"What about Goldman's report? All copies, including digital, deleted and wiped from any hard drives?"

"What if someone shows up with a copy?" With a scoff, Stu started up the stairs to the next level. "Samuel Goldman was a bitter jealous malcontent who saw that his deputy chief was on the fast track and would soon bypass him." An arrogant grin crossed his face. "As a matter of fact, Goldman was so disgruntled that he tried to frame you for treason."

Dan stepped back and blinked. The corners of his lips curled upward.

"That's why I'm Washington's number one fixer. I've got a team of witnesses and journalists from all major networks ready. If anyone so much as mentions Lithuania today, we'll launch a smear campaign like no one has ever seen before."

"No wonder you're Leban Slade's go-to guy."

"It's best to leave sticky situations to my people." Stu narrowed his eyes. Over the railing, he saw a group of people crossing the floor of the rotunda. "Killing the Matheson woman was sloppy. We would have had an easier time containing that situation if you had allowed my team to handle her instead of going out on your own."

Dan grabbed his arm. "Don't you try to pin Matheson's murder on me. I had nothing to do with that. After Senator Douglas told me about Anonymous' s letter, I went straight to Slade. He told me to leave everything in your hands. That's exactly what I did."

Stu was about to object when someone announced that the chamber was open. The hearing would start in five minutes.

"It's about time." Dan hurried down the corridor.

Stu couldn't take his eyes off the group making their way to the stairs.

"Surprised to see them?" Ripley Vaccaro asked.

Stu had not noticed the federal agent approaching him from behind. He wondered how long she had been there and how much of his conversation with Cross had she overheard.

Together, they watched Chris Matheson, flanked by Bruce and Elliott, climb the stairs. In his service vest, Sterling stayed at Chris's side.

"Have you ever heard of driverless cars?" the agent asked.

Stu jerked his head in her direction.

She arched an eyebrow at him. "Fantastic new technology. You might want to tell Burnett about it." She greeted Sterling with a pat on the head.

Together, they joined the spectators flowing into the committee's chamber.

Tristan Faraday had saved a row of seats for them in the back of the gallery. They filed in to take seats. Sterling at his side, Chris and Ripley opted to stand by the door.

Craning his neck to check out the spectators, Chris became concerned when he couldn't find Murphy or the ladies. He was particularly concerned about his mother. Doris could either be in the hospital or jail. He didn't know which would be worse. Both options were bad. "Where's Murphy?" he asked Tristan.

"Doris and Francine are on their way," Tristan said without taking his eyes off the screen of his cell phone. "They went with Murphy to the hospital."

"The hospital?" Chris was struck by Tristan's matter-of-fact tone.

"Yeah, he got shot." One would have thought Tristan was announcing that Murphy had stubbed his toe. "Jacquie said it went through his thigh. The bad part is that he broke a bunch of ribs when he wrecked his bike. He really loved that bike. Jessie is on her way to the hospital."

Burnett stepped into the chamber. A head above everyone else, he was very hard to miss. Upon entering, he scanned the crowd with narrowed eyes. When he located Chris, who was almost directly behind him, he focused in on him. His upper lip curled into a snarl.

Chris laid his hand on the weapon he wore on his belt. As a former federal agent with more than one contract out on his life as a result of his undercover work, he had a special concealed carry permit allowing him to carry in federal buildings.

The look on Burnett's face caused Chris to think he might be needing it.

"Let us get started!" a voice announced at the front of the chamber.

Burnett slammed his bulk into Chris's shoulder on his way out into the corridor. Elliott followed him.

"I don't think he likes you," Ripley told Chris.

The confirmation hearing opened with a speech.

For twenty-three minutes, Daniel Cross read a prepared statement about his modest childhood as the son of a school janitor, his dreams of traveling the world and serving his country, and the realization of those dreams—thanks to his nation.

A tear came to his eye, as he spoke of the price many paid for the country he loved—the self-less men and women who gave it all. They were his role models, especially the late chief of station in Lithuania.

"Samuel Goldman was my mentor," Dan said with a catch in his throat. "Not a day goes by that I don't think of the supreme sacrifice that he made in serving our country overseas. He dedicated every hour of the day to protecting our country against those intent on harming it. A humble man, he didn't do what he did for glory or riches or fame. He did it out of duty and honor to his country."

A moment of silence fell over the chamber.

Chris could see Senator Kimberly Douglas, Cross's biggest cheerleader on the committee, silently swoon.

Dan sat up tall in his seat and wiped a tear from his eye. "Since Sam Goldman's senseless murder, I strive every day to live up to his memory. I know that sometimes I fail. Many days I fail. But that goal of honor and duty is what I aim for."

Tristan looked over his shoulder at Chris.

Bruce placed his hand on Tristan's where his thumb rested on the screen of his cell phone. "Wait for it."

Thirsty after his long speech, Dan poured a glass of water.

"Thank you for giving us that insight, Mr. Cross," Senator Keaton said. "I surmise based on your comments, that you are telling this committee that you have devoted your life to protecting our country from its enemies and pursuing only what is best for it?"

"That is precisely what I am saying, sir." Dan took a long drink of water from the glass.

"Now," Chris said.

Tristan swept his thumb across the front of his cell phone.

The chamber echoed as every cell phone in the room dinged, buzzed, and vibrated. The interruption was not confined to the chamber. Cell phones all across the Capitol building, mall, city, District of Columbia and across the nation alerted their owners to an incoming text message.

The hearing paused as everyone reached for their phones to check the incoming message from the President of the United States. The message contained two attachments. One was a pdf document entitled "Cross/Slade Industries." The other was an mp4 file.

The Secret Service immediately began an investigation to find out who had hacked into the Presidential Emergency Text Message System. The White House's secure network, who had become close friends with Nigel, wasn't talking.

Daniel Cross set down his water glass and checked his phone to see what was so important that it took all attention from him. Before he could open the MP4 file, journalists were gasping. His security detail had to hold back reporters rapidly firing questions.

One of the monitors on the wall lit up to display a darkened image. As the focus sharpened, it became apparent that the recording was being filmed from inside a closet.

The voice in the recording was the same as that which had filled the chamber only moments before. This time, it was not smooth and charming.

"Monroe, do you really think that you and your lowly little girl can even touch me?" The focus zoomed in to show Daniel Cross waving his arms.

The middle-aged man on the receiving end of Cross's rage was sweating profusely. The fear in his eyes made everyone watching the recording cringe.

Dan advanced on the man while jabbing him repeatedly in the chest. "Now, Monroe, Schiff told you to delete that report. Who the hell do you think you are to defy him?"

Les Monroe tried to back away from the finger poking him. "The director needs to see this report. Goldman made some very serious claims in it and—" He paused to swallow. "The fact that he wrote it just the day before he was killed—"

No one missed Blair's gasp off-camera when Daniel Cross grabbed Les Monroe by the throat.

"Can't we all just calm down?" Ned Schiff stepped into the frame and tried to part the two men. "Dan, you said we were just going to talk."

Cross's voice was low and menacing. "If you and your com officer had any brains, you'd think about that factoid. Samuel Goldman was the chief of station. He was my boss. He tried to stop me and suddenly he died. Not only did I get away with it—but I became a damn hero. Now, I am director of the intelligence directorate at the CIA. Do you think anyone is even going to notice when you and that minion are gone?"

Les fought to force his words around where Cross was squeezing his throat. "Even if those upstairs don't have the morality to do what is right, we have to. Otherwise, Goldman's murder will have been for nothing."

"It was for something!" Cross shoved Monroe to the floor. "Don't you get it. Goldman was an idiot. That's why I killed him!"

A gasp rose up not only in the chamber but throughout the Capitol building.

In his seat before the judiciary committee, the blood drained from Daniel Cross's face.

"Like he thought he could go up against me—when I had Leban Slade and all his power and his people backing me up! He knew who I had behind me—damn it! Didn't you read the report! It's all there. And you still think you can go up against me!"

"So you admit that everything Samuel Goldman wrote in his report is true!"

Daniel Cross yanked a gun from the shoulder holster he wore under his coat.

At the front of the senate chamber, Senator Kimberly Douglas looked like she was going to cry.

Stu Dunleavy rose from his seat and hurried out of the chamber.

On the screen, Les Monroe scrambled for the door. He only made a few steps before Daniel Cross put three bullets in his back.

"What did you do?" Ned Schiff's voice went up several octaves. "You killed him!"

"No, I didn't," Cross said. "Les Monroe committed suicide."

"With three bullets in the back?"

"You're chief of station, Schiff. If you tell your security people that Monroe committed suicide, then he committed suicide." Daniel Cross waved the gun around the room.

"Search the house. We have to make sure all copies of that report are gone."

The image froze with Daniel Cross, holding the gun he had used to kill Les Monroe, filling the screen.

Daniel Cross's security detail fell back. Ripley Vaccaro and five FBI agents swam through the mob of journalists angling to get a soundbite until they surrounded him.

Senator Graham Keaton peered over his eyeglasses at Daniel Cross. "Duty. Honor. Country. Huh, Mr. Cross?"

Chapter Twenty-Four

Elliott couldn't believe he'd lost Burnett.

Paul Burnett was a busy man. Leban Slade's global corporation was so crooked, that sometimes there were just too many messes for one man to cleanup. Based on the multiple teams sent to stop the Geezer Squad from reaching Washington, it went without saying that Burnett's cleanup operation was a growing enterprise employing multiple international assassins.

As long as the Geezer Squad was in the building, Elliott wasn't going to allow Burnett out of his sight—until one of Burnett's men got in the way. He followed Burnett down the stairs to the basement level, where there were no tourists for him to blend in with. Elliott was forced to hang back and duck into doorways to keep him from seeing that he was being tailed.

After making several turns, Elliott rounded a corner to find himself face to face with a man in a security guard's uniform. "Can I help you?"

Beyond the guard, Elliott saw Burnett go through a heavy door with the sign: Security Locker Room. "I was looking for the men's room." He pressed his thighs together and did a little dance of urgency.

"That's not down this hallway." The guard pointed behind Elliott. "You need to go back to the elevator and up one floor."

"But I really need to go." Elliott pointed toward the door through which he had seen Burnett enter. "Is that a men's room? Do they have a bathroom?"

The guard him shoved in the chest. "I said to scram, old man."

Elliott paused to look the kid up and down. Former military. Most likely been kicked out due to insubordination. All brawn, no brains. "Is that any way to treat a taxpayer?"

Pleased with the opportunity to bully the old man, the guard threw back his fist in a threat, only to get jabbed with a fist in the throat. The guard staggered backwards. By the time the stars cleared from his eyes, Elliott had disarmed him of his baton and gun.

With the guard in a choke hold, Elliott dragged him into the locker room where he handcuffed him to a pipe. He searched the room, but Burnett was nowhere in sight.

"Where is he?"

The guard chuckled. "He's cleaning up."

It hit home. The guard wasn't just a cocky kid. He was one of Burnett's people acting as look out while he changed into his latest disguise. "Who's his target?"

"Whatever it takes to protect Slade. He's our first priority."

Elliott regarded the kid's uniform. Burnett had ducked into a Capitol building security locker room. Surely, that was not a coincidence. He spoke into his ear com. "Burnett is on the move. He's disguised as Capitol security."

Phone to his ear, Stu Dunleavy hurried across the rotunda for the exit at the rear of the building. "It's over, Slade. We need to cut Cross loose. … I tell you, Matheson had more than the Goldman report. She had a damn video of Cross confessing to murdering Goldman and the ambassador. Everyone in Washington and across the nation saw him shoot that communications chief in the back and order Schiff to cover it up. There's no way we can spin this. Millions of people saw him do it." He pressed his way through the double doors to the top of the stairs of the Capitol Building. "Best we can do now is eliminate Cross before he can cut a deal with the feds."

He disconnected the call and sent a text. "Stop Cross from talking."

"Do you know how many deaths are you responsible for, Dunleavy?"

Startled, Stu spun around.

"Or have you lost count?" Chris uncrossed his arms and stood from where he had been leaning against the side of the building. "I guess as long as you're removed from the event—not seeing the look in their eyes or the lives affected—ordering someone's death can be no more traumatic than sending someone a pink slip." He chuckled. "You're fired—from living."

"Chris, I think you should go home and take care of your children."

Stu turned to start down the stairs, only to find Sterling sitting before him. The dog's lips curled up in a snarl.

"Did you order Blair's death with a text or was it a phone call?"

"I did not order Blair's murder," Stu said.

"Oh, come on," Chris said. "She was hiding in your house."

"I thought she was hiding from you. I knew nothing about the communications people in Switzerland finding

Goldman's reports until last week when Slade sent Cross to me. Even then, I didn't know Blair was the one who'd discovered the report until Saturday morning when you and Vaccaro came to the house."

"You knew Blair was working for the state department in Switzerland!"

"There are a lot of state department people stationed in Switzerland," Stu said. "Call me slow, but when Cross told me that some communications officer in Switzerland had uncovered a report written up in Lithuania ten years ago, the last person I thought he was talking about was my daughter's nanny."

"Don't lie to me, Dunleavy," Chris said. "I know how you operate."

"I'm telling you the truth. I didn't put it together until you and Vaccaro started asking if Blair had ever talked about what she did overseas. *That* was when I put it together. By then, she was already dead."

"Give me a break, Dunleavy! Blair had been in your home. The medical examiner found four times the regular dose of sleeping pills in her system and the last thing she'd drank was a martini."

Stu's eyes grew wide. The expression on his face told Chris what they both realized.

"Chris!" Elliott screamed from high above them.

Chris looked up to see Elliott waving to him from the rooftop. In that same instant, Sterling hit Chris in the chest with a hundred pounds of force—knocking him off his feet. As Chris hit the ground, the bullet meant for the back of his head hit Stu Dunleavy between the eyes.

On the roof of the Capitol, Paul Burnett cursed. Chris Matheson had become a real problem. *Why can't he do me a favor and just die already?*

Now, the Capitol police were going to be on their way to the roof to capture a sniper.

Didn't matter. Burnett could dismantle the rifle, stuff it into its case, and hide it in less than twenty seconds. Then, with his uniform and police identification, he'd simply blend in with the law enforcement as they poured onto the roof and walk away.

If he hadn't become so obsessed with taking out this one man who refused to comply with the directive and die, then Burnett would have used those precious seconds. Instead, he chose to use every bit of time he had to take one more shot at the man running for cover with that damn dog who'd ruined his first shot.

Through the rifle's scope, Burnett followed Chris as he ushered Sterling out of the line of fire. He pressed his finger on the trigger. "I'm going to get you if it's the last thing I do, Matheson," he said as Elliott's shot from the other side of the roof struck him behind the ear.

Chapter Twenty-Five

The aftermath of the explosive confirmation hearing played out like a movie.

Immediately, Leban Slade left the country on one of his private jets and went into hiding while his lawyers spun things around. His American bank accounts were frozen, but that didn't matter. Leban Slade had money in banks all over the world.

News analysts were quick to point out that most likely Leban Slade would come out on top. Legally, he had only broken American laws. It was a big world and Slade had rich and powerful people from many different countries under his thumb. He could continue with his luxurious life as long as he stayed out of America's reach. Since Slade had mansions in practically every country, this would only be a small inconvenience.

Ned Schiff disappeared from his office on the fifth floor of the CIA headquarters in Langley, Virginia, before the FBI could get a warrant for accessory to murder, conspiracy to commit murder, obstruction of justice, and other crimes. The next day, he was found hanging from a beam at his beach house in Hilton Head, North Carolina. The general consensus was fifty-fifty on whether Schiff committed suicide or if Leban Slade had sent a cleanup team to make sure he didn't talk.

Daniel Cross sought to make a deal to go into witness protection in exchange for an extensive list of Leban Slade's informants throughout the intelligence community and on Capitol Hill.

Before a decision could be made, a pair of men wearing U.S. marshals' uniforms with federal IDs walked into the jail to transport Cross to a scheduled hearing. They walked out with Cross. Ten minutes later, the federal officials realized they had been duped when the real marshals arrived.

Daniel Cross was never seen or heard from again. Many rumors emerged about where his body had been hidden—including a wall in a renovated section of the intelligence wing at the CIA headquarters.

Thinking back over his life, Chris concluded that breaking the news of Blair's death to his daughters was the most difficult conversation he had ever had with anyone. It was harder than when he had told them about her supposed death years earlier. The news was especially heartbreaking with the realization that for years, their mother had been living only an hour away from them. While Chris emphasized that she had sacrificed being with them for their own safety, that did not make the feeling of abandonment any easier.

There were many tears shed that day and the days that followed.

It took no time for the media to learn the identity of the brave communications officer who had discovered the report outlining Daniel Cross's traitorous activities and revealing his murderous crimes. One could only imagine the damage he could have done if he had been confirmed for Director of Central Intelligence.

Blair Matheson was a hero who had sacrificed her life to save her nation.

The calls to interview her husband and daughters were constant.

Not wanting his daughters to become part of the circus, Chris fought to keep Blair's funeral in Harpers Ferry as private as possible. Friends of the family who happened to be off-duty or retired police officers volunteered to guard the church and cemetery to keep interlopers out.

The dreaded day of the funeral arrived much too quickly. The farmhouse was eerily quiet while the family dressed for the service. Guests were invited back to the Matheson home for a reception following the graveside service. Doris had arranged for a caterer to prepare a buffet in the formal dining room and country kitchen.

The aroma of good food floated up to the top floor while Chris got dressed in his black suit, at which time he realized Murphy had never returned his gray suit. His mouth watered at the smell of the Swedish meatballs simmering in the kitchen while he sent a text requesting the suit's return.

"Dad, are you decent?" Katelyn called to him from the bottom of the stairs.

"I'm never decent," he replied while looping a black tie around his neck and shoulders.

With a giggle, Katelyn trotted up the stairs with Sterling. She had Thor tucked under her arms. the plain black suit she reserved for funerals washed out her fair features.

"What do you think?" She held out Thor, who was dressed in a black silk dress. Katelyn had tied a black hat with lacey veil onto the bunny's head.

Sitting next to her, Sterling wore a black vest with white trim to resemble a shirt. The vest included a design resembling a black tie that was tucked into the vest. Katelyn completed the ensemble with a black hat with a wide rim.

"Well?" She prodded Chris for his reaction.

Furrowing his brow, Chris tried to think of what Sterling resembled. Unable to think of it, he said, "I'm really not the best judge for fashion."

"Nonni said Sterling looks like an Amish dog."

"She's right." Chris grinned. "That's exactly what he looks like."

Katelyn's eyes blazed.

"Not that looking like an Amish dog is bad," he said. "It's just ... Sterling isn't Amish."

She spun on her heels to leave.

Sterling dropped to the floor and pawed at the hat until he had removed it.

"But Thor looks great," Chris called down to her.

At the bottom of the stairs, Katelyn turned back to him. "Nikki says she's not going."

"She has to go."

"She says she's sick."

With a groan, Chris finished tying his tie.

Since the news of Blair's death, Nikki had been the most withdrawn of the girls. It was her way. She was not one to whine or cry or embark into drama. While Chris despised the drama that tends to be part and parcel of raising girls, he also preferred not to get blindsided by a sudden blast of emotion. He had discovered that people who keep things bottled up inside tend to explode at some point—and always at the most inconvenient times.

Chris grabbed his suitcoat and headed down the stairs.

Sterling picked up the offending hat into his mouth and shook it as if to ensure that it would not land on his head again.

The angel clock was playing its melody when Chris passed Emma's room.

Across the hall, Nikki's bedroom door was closed. Chris rapped his knuckles on it. "Nikki, are you ready to go?"

"I'm sick."

"Can I come in?" Chris turned the doorknob and waited for her reply. When he received none, he pushed the door open a few inches. "Nikki, hon, we have to leave in a few minutes."

"I don't feel good. My stomach hurts. I think I have the flu. I don't want to spread it around."

Chris opened the door the rest of the way.

Of the three girls, Nikki was the most like him. Her room was messy—the same way he had kept his room when he was a child. Her dresser was covered with clothes. Her closet door was open because it was too filled with toys to close it. He stepped on the top of a riding boot when he entered. Its mate rested across the room.

Nikki was stretched out on the bed on her stomach with her face buried in the pillows. She was dressed in her pajamas and bathrobe.

Carefully, Chris picked his way across the room to her bed. He didn't want to trip over anything. Once there, he laid his hand on her head. She felt cool. "You don't feel hot."

She rolled over. "You can be sick without having a fever."

"If you had the flu, you'd have a fever."

She glared up at him. "Where did you get your medical degree?"

"It's common knowledge." He sat on the edge of the bed. "I know you don't want to go to your mom's funeral, but you have to go."

"I already went to her funeral. Three years ago. I was there. I've got plenty of witnesses. Ask Nonni. She'll tell you. I shouldn't have to go again just because Mom faked her death and hid from us." She clamped her mouth shut into a tight line and folded her arms across her chest. "I don't want to go, and you can't make me."

Chris folded up his suitcoat and laid it on the foot of the bed. "You're right." He laid down on the bed next to her. Folding his arms across his chest, he looked up at the ceiling. "I can't make you go to Mom's funeral."

"Good." She uttered a deep sigh.

"You have every right to be angry with her," he said in a soft voice.

"Why did she leave us, Daddy?"

Chris shot a glance at the side of her head. The tough girl façade had slipped away to reveal the hurt that comes from feeling abandoned. He had shown the girls the final part of their mother's recording—admitting her mistake, apologizing for it, and declaring her love for them.

Katelyn was mature enough to accept her mother's apology.

Emma found comfort in the unwavering belief that her mother never did abandon her. She lived in the angel clock on the shelf in her room and sang to her every night.

Nikki was another story.

"She made a mistake," Chris said.

"She wanted a career more than she loved us."

"She had a choice. She made a bad decision and ended up paying for it. It broke her heart not being able to come back home to us. Being mad or holding a grudge is not going to punish her for what she'd done. She's dead. The only thing that we can do is forgive her."

Nikki sucked in a deep breath. She tightened her folded arms. Her chin stuck out in defiance. "I don't care if she is a hero like everyone is saying. She left us." She looked at him. "She left you, too. How can you forgive her, Daddy?"

"It's not easy," he said, "but I am working on it. You remember what we talked about in Sunday school?"

Her nosed wrinkled. "I know. I know." She said in a mocking tone, "You have to forgive seventy times seventy."

"If forgiveness was easy, Jesus would not have had to command it." He rolled over onto his side. "If it was easy, he'd only have to recommend it." He lowered his voice. "I'm going to tell you a secret about forgiveness."

She narrowed her eyes. Suspicion filled her face. "A secret?"

Chris looked around as if to make sure no one was listening to them. "When you forgive someone, you aren't letting them off the hook. You're actually letting yourself off the hook. You see, when you refuse to forgive someone, you're hurting yourself more than you're hurting the other person."

"I don't get it."

"Once, I got really mad at a friend of mine," he said. "He'd screwed me over really good. I was furious. I was so mad that I was trying to plot revenge against him. I just wanted to get back at him for what he'd done to me."

"What did he do?"

"I forget." Seeing that she didn't believe him, he laughed. "Seriously. At the time, I thought it was something that I could never get over, but now, I can't remember what he'd done. I guess that means it wasn't that serious."

"Mom left us, Dad. How can we ever forget that?"

"The thing is, your grandfather told me that holding on to anger is like grabbing a hot coal to throw at someone else."

Her face screwed up.

"Have you ever grabbed a lump of hot coal?"

She shook her head.

"You end up burning yourself. That's what happens when you hold onto a grudge. You end up hurting yourself more than the other person. It takes a lot of energy holding onto anger. Your stomach hurts." He sat up and looked down at her. "Your stomach hurts, doesn't it? Anger makes you sick."

"How—"

"Forgiveness doesn't happen overnight, Nikki," Chris said. "It's something that you have to work on. But over time, with a lot of prayer, it comes. The first step is going to Mom's funeral. One day, you'll look back on today, and you'll regret it if you don't go." He went to the dresser where Doris had laid out a black dress for her to wear. He held it out to her.

She refused to get off the bed. "Do you still love Mom?"

"Yes." He tossed the dress onto the bed. It landed on Nikki's head.

She pulled the dress down from where it covered her face. "You love Helen, too, don't you?"

Chris smiled. "Yes, I love Helen."

"Are you going to marry her?"

"Do you want me to marry Helen?"

She sat up. "Of course. We all took a vote."

"You all took a vote? Who all took a vote?"

"The four of us. Me, Katelyn, Emma, and Sierra. We want you to marry Helen. Katelyn said that now that Mom has died again, you can't marry Helen for another year on account of appearances. That's a bummer. If Sierra moved in with us, then she could have her own horse to ride whenever she wants."

"Well, I'm sorry your mother's murder screwed up everyone's plans."

Nikki frowned.

Chris lifted her chin to look at him. "Your mother is so very sorry for hurting us. I forgive her." He kissed her on the forehead. "And she loved you very much. Don't you ever forget that."

Nikki's face crumbled. She wiped the tears that spilled from her eyes with the back of her hands and threw her arms around him. Her tears soaked his white shirt as he held her tight.

Chris was glad to see Lieutenant Murphy Thornton, with his wife on his arm, limp into the church before the start of the service. Tristan Faraday was also on hand with Spencer tucked under his arm. They said she insisted on seeing her crush, Sterling, who had been left at the farmhouse to monitor the caterers.

Chris and Murphy greeted each other with a warm hug and pats on the back.

"Have you ever been to Prague?" Murphy asked him in a low voice. He shot him a sly grin.

"No," Chris said. "Where's my suit?"

"Would you like to go to Prague?"

"No. Where's my cell phone? It has all of my contacts."

"It's with your suit. You know there's a lot of funky stuff happening in Prague. If—"

"I'm too old for funky stuff," Chris said.

"Blue Eyes!" Francine swooped in to give Murphy a hug. "I've got some friends who are dying to meet you." She hissed into his ear, "I told them that you were my toy boy. Just go along with it. Okay?"

As she ushered him away, Murphy held his hand to the side of his head, his thumb to his ear and pinky to his mouth in the sign of a phone. "Call me," he said to Chris.

Chris was still shaking his head when Jessica greeted him with such a warm hug that one would have thought they were old friends.

"I want to thank you and your friends for saving Murphy's life," Jessica said. "I don't know what I would have done if I had lost him. I can never thank you enough."

"Hey, he helped me escape from federal custody and got me a phony ID," Chris said with a laugh.

"I just wish authorities had been able to stop Leban Slade from leaving the country," she said. "He may not have killed your wife, but he was certainly behind all of this. Murphy says some of the classified information that Slade had bought from his spies gave away the names of operatives in foreign countries. Most likely, he dealt their names in exchange for contracts. There's no telling how many people died because of him. Yet, monsters like Slade just fly away in their private jets and live on their private islands like kings."

"Maybe. Maybe not."

Jessica noted his calm demeanor. "Your children lost their mother because of Slade's greed. Don't you want justice for her?"

"There's always justice. When a case goes cold or our justice system fails, that doesn't mean the guilty party isn't going to pay. The guilty always pays, because God is just."

"We want to see Slade in an orange pantsuit," Jessica said.

"Seeing Slade in handcuffs confirms that sense of justice," he said. "We have to see him suffering for his crimes to prove that there is justice in this world. Doesn't that indicate a lack of faith?"

Jessica cocked her head at him. "What does faith have to do with it?"

"If you truly believe that God is just, then you know there will be justice." Chris tapped his chest. "You know it here. I don't need to see Slade in an orange jumpsuit or handcuffs, because I have faith that God will take care of it. No matter how far Leban Slade flies in his private jet, he won't be able to escape God's judgment."

"But they still haven't arrested Blair's killer," she said. "It would be nice if you could give your daughters that closure."

Chris saw Ivy Dunleavy making her way through the church's double doors. "They'll have closure soon."

Unsure of how Spencer would react to Thor, Nikki ran into the house ahead of everyone to lock the bunny in Emma's room. Sensing Sterling keeping company with another animal besides her, the rabbit thumped the floor with her hind paws and grunted her protest.

The buffet set up in the country kitchen offered a lovely view of the backyard blanketed with fallen leaves. As guests arrived at the farm, many would stop to admire the view of the river and the horses grazing in the pasture.

Bruce manned the bar, which included a wide selection of wines from his winery. Between serving guests tastes of vino, he played blackjack with Sterling and lost miserably, much to Tristan's amusement.

"You do know he's counting the cards?" Tristan asked while trying unsuccessfully to pull Spencer's tongue out of the German shepherd's ear. The sheltie knew nothing about playing it cool.

His eyes blazing, Bruce turned to Jacqui, who covered her mouth to conceal her giggle. "Didn't I tell you? The dog is a cheat!"

In the living room, the younger guests took great delight in hearing Ray's account about how he had led two killers in a car chase via remote access from the comfort of his computer room.

Chris was still trying to explain to his insurance company how his truck had gotten blown up. Instead of the truth, he told them that some unknown suspects had stolen it while he was traveling on the metro.

Murphy was the center of attention for a collection of female guests, both young and old. Sitting in a wing-backed chair to rest his injured leg, he was waited on by no less than five women—Francine among them.

While Doris admired Murphy's good looks, she was more smitten with Elliott, who had saved her son's life from Burnett.

They were making plans for a beach getaway in the spring for her to finish the portrait she had started.

Mourning the death of her best friend and her husband, Ivy Dunleavy arrived in her red Mercedes. While Chris and Helen gave her a tour of the hundred-and-fifty-year-old farmhouse, Ivy remained strong until they were alone in the study.

Breaking down, she apologized for her husband's role in Blair's murder. "I never dreamed," she sobbed. "Stu always kept his business dealings to himself."

Helen offered her a drink to ease her nerves and asked what she would like to drink.

"Do you know how to make a martini?" Ivy asked.

With a pleasant grin, Helen went to the kitchen to ask Bruce to make the drink.

Chris sat across from Ivy. "As world famous as Leban Slade is, you had to know that he was Stu's biggest client."

"I knew he'd met him, and that his firm had done some work for him, but I never knew—" She gazed up at Chris with tear-filled eyes.

He said nothing.

She cocked her head at him. "Don't you believe me?"

Doris arrived with the martini. "How's this, Ivy?"

Helen and Ripley slipped into the room while Ivy tested the drink.

After taking a healthy sip, Ivy sat back in the chair and uttered a sigh.

"Do you still drink your five-o'clock martini?" Chris turned to Doris and Helen. "Ivy has to have a martini every day at five o'clock."

"Five o'clock cocktail hour," Doris said with a nod of her head. "I remember when I had to have my five o'clock cocktail. I gave that up when I discovered yoga."

"You have no idea how hard it is running a household and maintaining appearances," Ivy said. "Yes, if you must know,

I knew Stu did some horribly immoral things to keep Slade happy. You've seen the news. It's coming out about what Slade was capable of if you dared to say no to him." She took another sip of her drink. "Stu was only trying to protect our family."

"I imagine knowing what was going on must have made things stressful for you," Helen said.

Nodding her head, Ivy took another sip of her drink.

"Do you still have trouble sleeping at night?" Chris asked.

Ivy stared at him with a blank expression.

"Blair told me that you often, as in every night, took sleeping pills," Chris said. "You had a prescription, didn't you?"

"Flurazepam hydrochloride," Ripley said from the corner in which she had positioned herself to watch their conversation.

"What does that have to do with anything?" Ivy asked.

"The medical examiner found flurazepam hydrochloride in Blair's system," Chris said. "Four times the normal dose."

"That and a martini." Doris arched an eyebrow in Ivy's direction.

"Martinis were not Blair's drink of choice," Chris said. "She would only drink martinis when she was with you, and you have a prescription for flurazepam hydrochloride."

"You don't know that," Ivy said.

"Yes, we do," Ripley said. "We got a search warrant for your home. Our investigators found your prescription in your medicine cabinet. You got your latest thirty-day prescription filled at the beginning of the month. One pill a day. You should have fourteen pills left. But you only have ten. Where did the other pills go, Ivy?"

"You slipped them into Blair's martini," Chris said.

"I didn't," Ivy said. "Stu did that."

"Blair called you after that hitman tried to kill her," Chris said. "She was scared. She trusted you. Why wouldn't she? You were her best friend. You'd been hiding her for years."

"You had to see how upset she was when you picked her up from the metro," Helen said. "Being her friend, you must have asked her about what had happened."

"At which point she told you everything," Chris said. "That was when you discovered that you had been helping the woman with the power to bring down your husband's most powerful client. If she did that, then your big house, luxury cars, country clubs, big vacations—powerful friends—it would all go up in smoke. So you took her home and gave her a martini mixed with sleeping pills. Then, after she got nice and drowsy, you put her in the car, drove her to where we used to live, and pushed her down the hill into the lake."

"Then you stepped into the lake and stood on her back to hold her under the water until she drowned," Ripley said.

"No." Ivy shook her head. "It had to have been Stu."

"Stu had no idea that Blair had been a threat until the next morning," Chris said. "As long as he didn't consider her a threat, he had no motive to want her dead."

"With everything that has come out about Stu's business dealings," Ivy said with a scoff, "why would you not assume he'd killed Blair?"

"Because Stu didn't get where he was by not thinking things through," Chris said. "If he had murdered Blair, he never would have left her purse behind, and he wouldn't have had to have hired Burnett to go into the FBI to steal her belongings."

"It was essential for Stu to locate and destroy every copy of Goldman's report about Cross selling classified information to Slade," Ripley said.

"I guess it was Daniel Cross then," Ivy said. "He caught up with her."

"Before he disappeared, Daniel Cross told us that your husband had accused him of killing Blair," Ripley said. "Stu thought he had been covering up for a murder that Cross had committed."

"Whoever killed Blair did it more out of emotion than business," Chris said, "and they didn't think it through."

"You can't prove Stu or one of Burnett's people didn't kill her." Ivy held up her martini glass, which was almost empty. "Stu knew I drank martinis. He also knew I took sleeping pills. He probably framed me. Or maybe it was his so-called assistant Jenn."

"Oh, yeah, Jenn," Chris said. "Your husband spent a lot of time with her."

"Don't you know it."

"Lucky for us, she's turned into a government witness," Chris said.

"Singing like a canary," Doris said.

"We checked Stu's cell phone records," Ripley said. "He made quite a few calls, all bouncing off the cell phone tower in downtown DC next to where Jenn lives. Also, she lives in a secured building. We have video of him going into the building with her at five o'clock the evening of the murder and leaving the next morning at around four."

"The call made to the hitmen in Baltimore?" Doris said. "That call was traced to a cell tower in Chantilly while Stu was with his—" She cleared her throat. "Assistant."

"Jenn has stated that Stu never had any business dealings with those hitmen in Baltimore," Chris said.

"And you believe her?"

"Yes," Chris said. "SD Associates was the name of your husband's original law firm, which was located in Baltimore. He stopped using that name over a decade ago when he moved his practice to Washington."

"He kept his business license in that name," Helen said, "but he closed up his office there and moved everything to

Washington. Jenn told us that he doesn't use any contractors in Baltimore."

"You pretended to be Stu's assistant and hired those hitmen to take care of matters that threatened your affluent lifestyle," Chris said.

"Like the intern Stu had gotten pregnant twelve years ago," Helen said. "The police thought Stu had arranged it, when really it was you because she and her unborn child threatened your livelihood."

"I called those hitmen, huh?" Ivy's lip curled up into a snarl. "Even if the call bounced off the tower in Chantilly, it didn't come from my phone. Therefore, you can't prove I hired them."

"No, it was made from Blair's phone," Chris said. "I'm sure you've gotten rid of it. Senator Keaton's investigator received a call from the same burner phone used to hire Tony the hitman. That means, whoever murdered Blair took her phone and used it to contract a hit on me."

"We found two phones at the murder scene," Ripley said. "One was the phone that Blair purchased under the name of Charlotte Nesbitt after coming back from the States. The second was the one she had taken to Switzerland."

"Most likely the one she had used to record Monroe's murder," Chris said. "We believe there was a third phone that she purchased with cash when she decided to come forward with what she knew about Daniel Cross."

"You know Christopher," Doris said. "You must have realized as soon as you killed Blair that you had unleashed the wrath of hell. He wasn't going to stop until he hunted you down. So you hired those goons to take him out first."

Ivy's eyes were wide with anger. "You can't prove—"

"You called Tony in the middle of the night," Chris said. "I think you were in such a panic—thinking of all the things that you had to lose—that you just hastily put together this plan to get rid of Blair and frame me for it. But then, when you got home, after dumping Blair's body and throwing her purse in the lake, that was when you thought things through." He shook a finger at her. "You realized Blair had been in possession of evidence that could bring Leban Slade down."

"And you knew that if anyone could find it, it would be her husband," Ripley said.

"That was when you called your old friends the hitmen in Baltimore," Chris said. "You used Blair's phone, which maybe she had dropped it in your car. I don't know. You used Jenn's name so that if things went sideways, she'd get blamed."

"After all," Ripley said, "contracting assassinations was in Jenn's job description."

"Was it you who searched her room or Jenn?" Chris asked.

Saying nothing, Ivy regarded him with a frosty glare.

"I think it was you," Chris said. "Because Stu told me that he didn't realize Blair was Anonymous until we questioned him after Blair's murder. At that point, her room had already been searched. You found bank statements showing that Blair had a safety deposit box. After we left, you told Stu about the safety deposit box and that was when he ordered Burnett to keep an eye on me."

"Meanwhile," Helen said, "you sent your hitmen a corrected address of where to find Chris."

"I have to admit I was a little perplexed when you called me after we had left your place," Chris said. "You told me that it was to apologize, but I didn't buy it. Later, when I replayed our conversation, I remember you urging me to go home and get some sleep. The real purpose of that call was to find out when I would be going home so that you could let Tony and Ralph know."

"We had one pair of hitmen waiting to kill Christopher and burn down the house," Doris said, "and another waiting to confiscate whatever Blair had in her safety deposit box."

"I admit that was confusing," Chris said. "But then, when I realized Ralph and Tony had not been hired by the same perpetrators, it made sense."

"You can't prove any of this," Ivy said with a laugh. "I never saw Blair that night. I waited at the metro and she never came out."

"Ah yes," Chris said, "you never saw Blair."

Ivy shook her head.

"We had to do a lot of hunting on that."

"I suppose you searched all of the metro security cameras and cams on the freeway," Ivy said. "Did you find any pictures of me and Blair in my Mercedes coming back from the metro?"

"No," Chris said.

Ivy set her glass on the desk and stood up. "Then I'll be going."

"But we did find goose poop," Ripley said.

Ivy jerked her head in the agent's direction.

"One of the big problems I had when living on Lake Audubon was goose poop," Chris said. "You see, we lived close to the wildlife refuge. While our backyard was not a refuge, those animals spilled into it. It felt I spent half of my time scraping goose poop off my shoes and hosing it off the tires on my vehicle." He cocked his head at her. "I didn't see any geese hanging out in your neighborhood when we were there." He turned to Ripley. "Did you?"

His former partner shook her head. "This time of the year, the leaves have fallen from the trees around the lake. Geese are getting ready to fly south. Based on all of the wildlife evidence left at the crime scene, forensics will have no problem placing you in that section of the lake," Ripley said. "Of course, you're smart enough to have cleaned your car. But, according to our forensics people, you didn't quite get all of the goose poop and algae out of the crevices of your Alexander Wang boots. Not only will that prove you were in the area, but we can also place you in the water."

Chris pointed at Ivy's foot. "Also, the size of the boot and the shape of the sole will place your foot on Blair's back when you held her under the water after she had passed out from the sleeping pills."

"I know they were expensive," Doris said, "but you should have thrown the boots away."

Tears returned to Ivy's eyes. "She had no idea. She lived with us for three years, but she had no idea that Leban Slade was Stu's biggest client. If it wasn't for Slade, we'd never have been able to put Hannah in that private school, live in our house, or go to Europe every summer. Blair was going to take everything we had, everything we worked for, away. I had to do what had to be done to protect us. I had to protect my family." She raised her eyes to Chris's. "You understand that, don't you, Chris? I did love Blair."

He shook his head. "But you loved your stuff more."

Epilogue

Leban Slade's private jet sliced through the skies over the Philippine Sea heading for his private island. After several days of rallying his allies, the billionaire had decided to take a break.

Slade told no one where he was going. He planned to disappear for several weeks while the lawyer he had hired to replace Stu Dunleavy ironed things out.

"The truth is irrelevant," Slade told his attorney after he expressed trouble keeping the billionaire's influential friends united in his defense.

Blair Matheson's recording of Daniel Cross confessing to spying for Slade before shooting Les Monroe in the back had been seen by most of the population in the United States. How do you tell people that what they saw is not what they had seen?

"You tell those cowards that I own them!" Slade shouted into the phone when he learned that most of the lawmakers in Washington were running from him like rats jumping a sinking ship.

"These politicians, the police, and the FBI are getting intense public pressure for justice. They want to see you arrested and convicted for espionage," the lawyer said.

Leban Slade's laughter could be heard in the cockpit of his private jet. "None of you get it yet, do you?" His bloated face turned red. He screamed into the phone, "I'm untouchable!"

He slammed the phone onto the table. It bounced and landed on the floor at his feet.

"Arrest me?" Chewing on the end of his cigar, he laid his head back and closed his eyes. "Justice? Justice is for the little people."

The phone on the floor rang.

Slade's bushy eyebrows arched. He peered down at the vibrating and ringing instrument. There was no caller ID listed on the brilliant purple screen. He had never seen it that color before.

"Shut up," he muttered an order for the phone to stop ringing.

It disobeyed.

He scooped up the phone and put it to his ear. "Who the hell is this?"

"I'm your maker, Leban."

He laughed.

"I know we haven't talked in a while. Even so, I decided to give you a heads up about our upcoming meeting. We have so much to go over, it seems only right to give you time to prepare."

"Meeting? I've got—"

"Tell me, Leban, are you still an atheist?"

Leban sputtered. "Who the hell is this?"

"Looking at your portfolio, I have to tell you that I've been very disappointed—"

"I have the world's best portfolio—" He jumped out of his seat.

"Not when it comes to the business of humanity. You have made some seriously disastrous decisions."

"Like what?"

"For example, it's never a good idea to give weapons of mass destruction to a mad man."

"I deny that I have anything to do with anyone selling weapons to the North Koreans."

"Lying to me does no good, Leban. No matter how hard you spin it, I know the truth. Where was I?"

"You said I was selling weapons of mass destructions to North Korea, which I wasn't," Leban snarled.

"If that's the story you want to stick to, Leban, go ahead. We'll be talking about breaking that commandment in our meeting as well. Anyway, it turns out that some of the parts you sold to them were faulty. As a result, there's been a glitch in the missile that they launched one minute ago, and they've lost control of it."

Leban's mouth felt dry. "What are you telling me?"

"Well, to go back to my original question, Leban, are you still an atheist? You've got eighteen seconds to reassess your position on that matter."

Leban heard a high-pitched wail outside the jet. He looked out the window and saw the nose of the missile closing in on him.

"Be thankful that you've packed for warm weather."

Helen arrived at the Matheson farm at the usual time after Sierra finished her weekly riding lesson. She had backed off from Chris after Blair's funeral. It was best to let him take the lead in their relationship.

After not hearing from him for three days, Helen suspected that Chris was in need of serious time to heal his wounds. As gruesome as it was, she was thankful for a double homicide case to keep her mind occupied. She did not want to be one of those women waiting by the phone.

At least, she concluded, they did love each other enough to be friends. They had agreed that no matter what happened between them, Sierra would continue her riding lessons. When they arrived for the lesson, Chris greeted Sierra with a hug and gave Helen a polite kiss on the lips and a nervous grin.

Hours later, after capturing the prime suspect in the double homicide, Helen practically held her breath as she drove up the Matheson driveway. Her first clue that something was amiss was the horse trailer parked next to the paddock instead of in its usual spot next to the barn.

A horse that Helen had never seen before was in the paddock. Her face glowing with excitement, Sierra was exercising the mare on a lead.

Chris's father had rescued race horses—horses who were in need of lots of space and tender loving care in which to spend their retirement. It had been Helen's experience that most of those horses were too high spirited for her daughter, whose horseback riding experience had been limited until she started taking lessons.

As far as Helen was concerned, Sierra was no way, no how, going to get a race horse of her very own.

Now here Sierra was in a paddock with a new horse.

With her entourage at her side, Doris confirmed Helen's suspicions. "I had nothing to do with it. It was all Christopher's idea. And Nikki's. And Sierra. I think Sterling had a hand in it as well, but I'm not sure. He's been looking guilty, but that could be because he cheated on Thor."

Bouncing with excitement, Sierra handed the lead to Nikki and climbed over the fence. "She's not a race horse, Mom! She's a quarter horse and she's really gentle. Can I keep her, Mom? Please?"

With Emma's arms wrapped around his waist, Chris didn't move from where he chewed on a bit of straw while leaning against the paddock fence. Sitting on the ground, Katelyn petted Sterling who was watching the mare as if trying to decide if she was friend or foe.

"Where did she come from?" Helen asked.

"She's a 4-H horse," he said. "Her previous owner went off to college and didn't have any time for her. She hasn't been ridden in more than a year."

"The owner's mother is a patron at the library," Doris said. "She knew Christopher would take good care of her."

"Totally healthy," Chris said. "Good temperament."

"And she's *beautiful*." Sierra pressed her hands together in a prayer. "Please."

"She'll be here even if you don't agree to take her," Chris said.

"Can she be mine, Mom? I won't ask for anything else. Please. Please. Please."

Helen felt six pairs of eyes on her. Nine counting Sterling's, Mocha's, and Sadie's. The only one missing was Thor, who was still giving Sterling the silent treatment since he had spent time with that blue sheltie.

Helen looked at Chris, who peered back at her from over his shoulder. "I need to talk to Chris."

"Let's step into my office. Ms. Clarke." He tossed his head in the direction of the barn.

"Oh, boy, your daddy's in *trouble*," Helen heard Doris say as she stepped inside the barn.

Chris closed the door. "I did not buy that horse for Sierra."

"Oh, yes, you did!"

He went to the stall where he kept Traveler, his gray gelding. "I bought her because she needed to be ridden. I knew that if I brought her here that she'd get the attention and love she's used to."

Rushing to his side, Helen gestured with her arms at the horse outside. "What did you expect bringing in a horse that's perfect for her?"

"I expected Sierra to ride her." Traveler hung his head over the gate, and Chris stroked him.

"You expected me to let Sierra keep her."

"I didn't *expect* that. I hoped for that."

"Why didn't you ask me?"

"Because I knew you'd say no. You always say no."

"I don't always say no!"

"When it comes to horses, yes, you always say no."

"Because I don't want her to have a horse."

"Well, she wants a horse."

"Well, we can't always get what we want."

"Don't I know it and so do my girls!" He gestured toward the door, on the other side of which were his daughters. "They want their mother and that's never going to happen!"

Helen covered her mouth with a gasp. "I'm so sorry."

"I didn't set out to …" His voice trailed off. He pressed his forehead against Traveler's neck. Traveler rubbed against him. The horse seemed to give him comfort. Even as teenagers, Chris sought comfort with the horses rather than people. Maybe because the animals never failed him the way humans did. "I was bringing her here anyway. She's very gentle. Sierra's really taken a shine to her."

Helen swallowed. "And what about us?"

"I'm not sure. I think she's taken a shine to us, too. I mean, she keeps coming out every weekend. Could be she likes the horses more than she does me. I don't know."

"I meant you … and me … us."

He squinted at her. "What about us?"

She struggled to come up with the right words. No matter how she said it, she sounded like an insecure teenager. "You haven't called me in the last three days."

"You know my number. If you want—" He cleared his throat. "*You* haven't called *me*."

"I've been busy chasing after the suspect in a double homicide," she said. "Why didn't you call me?"

Chris swept his arm in the direction of the paddock. "I've been sneaking around trading horses."

She covered her mouth with her hand. "Then we're okay?"

"I didn't know we weren't okay." He cocked his head at her. "Were we having problems?"

Helen felt her cheeks flush. She shook her head.

Chris wrapped an arm around her waist and pulled her in close. "Are you going to let Sierra keep the horse?"

"Depends." She lifted her face to his. "Kiss me."

He looked up to the rafters. "Ah, the things I do for you." He kissed her softly on the lips.

With a sigh, she rested her head on his shoulder. "Sierra can have the horse."

There was a shriek of joy from the other side of the barn doors. "She's mine! Mom just said I can keep her!" A chorus of high-pitched screams of joy mixed liberally with barking dogs filled the air.

Clasping her hand, Chris picked up the tack box and went to the door.

"Listen, I just want to say something." She pulled him back. "I can't begin to understand what the last two weeks have been like for you and the girls. I mean, I can only imagine. You were moving on from losing Blair and then to lose her again."

He said nothing as his eyes held hers.

"I know that this is hard for all of you. I backed off this week because I didn't want to push you into something that you weren't ready for—at least—ready for now. But I'm always going to be here for you. No matter what. Because I love you, Chris Matheson." She waited for his response.

In silence, he reached into the tack box and picked up a brush. He held it out to her. "Now that you own a horse, you need to learn how to take care of her. We'll start with learning how to brush her."

Her fingers brushed over his when she took it.

"No need to be nervous, Helen Clarke." He gave her a soft kiss on the lips. "I'll be gentle."

The End

About the Author

Lauren Carr

Lauren Carr is the international best-selling author of the Thorny Rose, Lovers in Crime, Mac Faraday, and Chris Matheson Cold Case Mysteries—over twenty titles across four fast-paced mystery series filled with twists and turns!

Book reviewers and readers alike rave about how Lauren Carr seamlessly crosses genres to include mystery, suspense, crime fiction, police procedurals, romance, and humor.

Lauren is a popular speaker who has made appearances at schools, youth groups, and on author panels at conventions. She lives with her husband and two German Shepherds, including the real Sterling, on a mountain in Harpers Ferry, WV.

Visit Lauren Carr's website at www.mysterylady.net to learn more about Lauren and her upcoming mysteries.

Check Out Lauren Carr's Mysteries!

All of Lauren Carr's books are stand alone. However for those readers wanting to start at the beginning, here is the list of Lauren Carr's mysteries. The number next to the book title is the actual order in which the book was released.

Joshua Thornton Mysteries

Fans of the *Lovers in Crime Mysteries* may wish to read these two books which feature Joshua Thornton years before meeting Detective Cameron Gates. Also in these mysteries, readers will meet Joshua Thornton's five children before they had flown the nest.

1) A Small Case of Murder
2) A Reunion to Die For

Mac Faraday Mysteries

3) It's Murder, My Son
4) Old Loves Die Hard
5) Shades of Murder
(introduces the Lovers in Crime: Joshua Thornton & Cameron Gates)
7) Blast from the Past
8) The Murders at Astaire Castle
9) The Lady Who Cried Murder
(The Lovers in Crime make a guest appearance in this Mac Faraday Mystery)
10) Twelve to Murder
12) A Wedding and a Killing
13) Three Days to Forever

15) Open Season for Murder
16) Cancelled Vows
17) Candidate for Murder
(featuring Thorny Rose Mystery detectives Murphy Thornton & Jessica Faraday)
23) Crimes Past

Lovers in Crime Mysteries

6) Dead on Ice
11) Real Murder
18) Killer in the Band
25) The Root of Murder (2019)

Thorny Rose Mysteries

14) Kill and Run
(featuring the Lovers in Crime in Lauren Carr's latest series)
19) A Fine Year for Murder
22) Murder by Perfection

Chris Matheson Cold Case Mysteries

21) ICE
24) Winter Frost
(featuring Thorny Rose Mystery detectives)

A Lauren Carr Novel

20) Twofer Murder

Attention Book Club-bers!

Want to add some excitement to your next book club meeting? Are you curious about this mystery author's theme regarding cold cases? Do you wonder where she picks up her inspiration for such interesting characters? What does she have planned next for the Geezer Squad? Well, now is your chance to ask this international best-selling mystery writer, in person, you and your book club.

That's right. Lauren Carr is available to personally meet with your book club to discuss *Winter Frost* or any of her best-selling mystery novels.

Don't worry if your club is meeting on the other side of the continent. Lauren can pop in to answer your questions via webcam. But, if your club is close enough, Lauren would love to personally meet with your group. Who knows! She may even bring her muse Sterling along!

To invite Lauren Carr to your next book club meeting, visit www.mysterylady.net and fill out a request form with your club's details.

THE ROOT OF MURDER

A Lovers in Crime Mystery

Homicide Detective Cameron Gates learned long ago that there is not such thing as a typical murder case. Each mystery is special in its own right—especially for the family of the victim.

The murder of a successful executive, husband and father seems open and shut when the murder weapon is found in his estranged son-in-law's possession. When J.J. Thornton agrees to act as the defendant's public defender, he assumes his first murder case will be a loss.

Only the report of a missing husband proves that this open-and-shut case is not so simple. Strap on your seatbelts for a wild ride in this mystery that all started with a simple DNA test from a geneology website.

Coming Early 2019!

8-6-21

Made in the USA
Middletown, DE
07 February 2019